Stolen Moments

Stolen Moments

Clifford "Spud" Johnson

www.urbanbooks.net

Urban Books, LLC
300 Farmingdale Road, N.Y.-Route 109
Farmingdale, NY 11735

Stolen Moments

ISBN 13: 978-1-64556-207-8
ISBN 10: 1-64556-207-7

First Trade Paperback Printing July 2021
Printed in the United States of America

10 9 8 7 6 5 4 3 2 1

Distributed by Kensington Publishing Corp.
Submit Orders to:
Customer Service
400 Hahn Road
Westminster, MD 21157-4627
Phone: 1-800-733-3000
Fax: 1-800-659-2436

Prologue

Petty Officer Third Class Razier Coleman sat outside of the captain's office on board the USS *Enterprise* awaiting his fate. He was a nervous wreck, not only because he knew that his brief two-year stint in the United States Navy was about to end abruptly, but also because he feared the wrath of his mother when he told her he had been kicked out of the navy, all because of his "tender dick."

Sadly, he shook his head as he thought back to the very first day he set eyes on the drop-dead gorgeous Senior Chief Carmi Felton. He was a fresh recruit at the Naval Academy Boot Camp in Orlando, Florida. He just finished his rigorous routine and was headed back to the barracks to shower and take a much-needed nap when Senior Chief Felton walked by him, looking incredibly sexy in her starched white naval uniform. *As she passed him, he couldn't help but admire the firm ass she was packing and how good it looked in that snug uniform.* Damn, she is one badass woman, a senior chief at that. Boy, would I love to get balls deep in that right there, *he thought as he continued to stare at the officer, not paying any attention to her returning his stare over her shoulder. When she suddenly came to a stop and turned around, he knew he was busted.* Uh-oh, *he thought.*

"Do you have a problem with those reckless eyeballs, Petty Officer?" asked the senior chief.

"Uh, no, ma'am. Please excuse me. I meant no disrespect. It's just that where I'm from, I was taught to give praise where praise is due."

She smiled at him and laughed. "So by staring at my ass, you were giving me, or should I say, my ass, praise?"

Figuring he couldn't get into any more trouble than he already would be in, he decided to see if he could flirt his way out of this jam. He smiled and said, "Both. You are a beautiful woman, and your body is mesmerizing, ma'am. Please accept my most sincere apologies if you feel offended."

"You do know that I'm a senior officer, and I could have you brought up on formal charges for such actions? You do understand that, Petty Officer?"

"Yes, ma'am, I do."

"I'm also a woman, and all women love to receive compliments, especially from handsome young men in the armed forces. So I'll let this little mishap slide by me this time. Don't let it happen again. Am I understood?"

"Yes, ma'am," he said and gave the senior chief a salute.

She returned his salute, turned, and started walking away. She had taken no more than ten steps when she stopped, turned around, and caught Petty Officer Coleman still staring at her ass. She laughed and shook her head as she turned and continued on her way.

With a smile on his face, Petty Officer Coleman turned and went to the barracks, thinking that if he ever had the opportunity, he would have the senior chief bent over and serving her some of his good dick. That thought made him laugh aloud as he entered the barracks. That had been more than two years ago, and now as he sat outside of the captain's office waiting for his captain's mast hearing, he knew that that day had come back to haunt him big time. All because of his tender-dick issue.

His mother always told him that his lack of dick control would be the end of him. Mothers know best.

The day Petty Officer Coleman was assigned to the USS *Enterprise* was one of the proudest days of his life. He made it through the naval boot camp with ease and felt he was on the fast track for advancement as long as he continued to become the best seaman he could be. He felt his good fortune had only gotten better when he came aboard the battleship and saw none other than Senior Chief Felton talking to the captain while greeting all the new seamen as they came aboard the ship.

"Well, well, lookie here. Ooh ooh ooh," he said to himself as he stared at the beautiful senior chief. A bronze complexion, almond-shaped light brown eyes, and a body that men would kill for had him just as mesmerized as when he first laid his eyes on her in Florida. "And to think, I'm going to be out at sea with this wonderful woman. Thank you, God. Thank you so much. I know this is you giving me a blessing, and I intend to take full advantage of it," he said to himself as he approached the senior chief and the captain.

After introducing himself to them, he was uncertain if she even remembered him. She told him where to go and report, and she showed no signs of recognizing him, which was somewhat deflating to his ego. Somewhat. He grabbed his bags and went deeper into the ship to find his way to his living quarters.

"Excuse me, Petty Officer Coleman."

He stopped in his tracks with a smile on his face when he heard Senior Chief Felton call his name. He put a serious expression on his face and turned around. "Yes, ma'am?"

"Don't tell me you don't remember me. Should I turn around? Maybe that will help you out?" she asked as she did just that without waiting for an answer to her question.

He laughed and said, "There is no way I would ever forget a face or a backside like yours, ma'am."

"I will tell you that it will be my pleasure to deal with you in any which way you care to be dealt with." She stared at him and openly admired his six-foot-two muscular frame, then smiled.

His deep dimples were her downfall because she always had a thing for men with dimples. To her, they made grown men seem so vulnerable and innocent looking. She shook her head to get focused and said in a stern voice, "We will always remain professional. This is the United States Navy, and we are never to forget that. Am I clear, Petty Officer?"

"Yes, ma'am."

"Maintain your military bearing at all times, and everything will be just fine."

"Yes, ma'am."

"Good. Do you have any questions?"

"One, ma'am."

"Ask away, Petty Officer."

"What about R&R? Will I have to maintain my military bearing then?"

"If the time is right, and it presents itself, then we'll cross that bridge when we get to it," she smiled and winked at him. After that, she turned and rejoined the captain to finish greeting the rest of the seamen as they came aboard the USS Enterprise.

Again, Razier thanked God for His blessing as he went to find his living quarters. His blessings continued for the entire two years he was assigned to the Enterprise. He made love to the lovely senior chief every chance they had. It got to the point where neither of them could keep their hands off each other. R&R was too far in between for them, so they started taking more and more risks. Razier would sneak and meet with her on differ-

ent parts of the ship where they would have quickies. He loved bending her over and taking her from behind. He loved the way her ass was so firm and soft as he hit it deeply from the back.

Carmi was equally enticed with him, and her feelings for him were getting deeper and deeper every time they got together. She knew the risks she was taking by being with him, but she couldn't help herself. Razier had her hooked as if she were on drugs. She had to have him as much as possible. She would actually ache whenever he wasn't inside of her. All that risk taking finally caught up with them when they were caught having sex in the galley. The most embarrassing moment in her life was when she heard her superior officer, Captain Lewis L. Starks, scream, "What the hell do you two damn fools think you're doing?"

Razier was so caught up with sexing Carmi that he didn't realize the captain had busted them until his orgasm had subsided. When he finally focused, all he could think to say was, "Oh, shit."

That had been two weeks ago, and now, here he was, awaiting his fate. Carmi was inside with the captain and the rest of the senior officers having her captain's mast hearing, and he prayed that she wouldn't get kicked out of the navy because of him. He felt 100 percent responsible for this situation, and he didn't want her to suffer because of him and his damn tender dick. He wanted to go in first so that he could take the brunt of the blame for their actions, hoping she would get off lighter than him. She had been in the navy for almost ten years and had hoped to be a career navy woman. She was 28 years old and had a bright future. He would never forgive himself if she were kicked out of the navy and her career ended.

He sat there with sweaty palms for another twenty minutes when the door to the captain's office finally opened, and Carmi came out with her head held high. Her bottom lip was quivering, and that was the telltale sign that it was all bad—the worst had happened. He started to say something to her, but she raised her hand to stop him and gave him a look with hate and disgust in her eyes.

"Don't," was all she said as she marched right past him and out of his life for good.

The captain's aide came to the door and motioned for him to enter the captain's office so he could receive his punishment for being a tender-dick asshole. Carmi had been inside of the captain's office for over forty-five minutes. Razier wasn't inside longer than ten. The captain told him that his actions were insubordinate and disrespectful to the United States Navy. He, along with Senior Chief Felton, was being dishonorably discharged from the navy. As soon as the *Enterprise* arrived at the Port of San Diego, California, they were to be off his ship, and both of their careers were over. All Razier could think about was what he would tell his mother when he went back to Oklahoma City.

He returned to his quarters with none of his fellow seamen having the courage to ask him what they already knew was the answer. He got on his bunk and sighed loudly. *Damn, moms always told me my looks, combined with my tender dick, would be the death of me. Mothers know best. Damn.*

Chapter One

It had been one year since his dishonorable discharge from the navy for conduct unbecoming of an officer and six months since he moved out of his mother's home. She had been so angry with him when he returned home that he honestly thought she was going to try to spank him as if he were still a little kid. Razier smiled at that thought as he got out of his bed to start his day. He had a busy schedule and didn't have any time to waste. He hoped that his mother cooked breakfast because he was starving. Since his first yard to service was in the neighborhood he grew up in, he figured he'd slide on by his mother's home and snatch a quick bite to eat. Though she had been disappointed in him, his mother would forever be his most loyal supporter. She proved that by loaning him the money to start his lawn service. In one year, he paid her half of the $60,000 she loaned him. Now that he paid off his debt, he was ready to start up his next business—a pool cleaning service.

When Razier returned home, he was determined to do what he needed to do to make an honest living. First on his list was to start the lawn service. Then he would begin the pool cleaning service with the money earned through the spring and summer months. He had another plan for the winter, and it was already set in motion. He was going to cater parties for the grown and sexy. He wanted to cater to adults who were serious about having the "right" type of parties. No way would he do anything for anyone under the age of 30 unless he was positive they were on a mature level. The kids nowadays were so off the charts that he didn't want to have anything to with that type of atmosphere. He was in a serious grind mode, and he intended to get the money and had no problems working his ass off to get it.

Razier slowly built up the lawn service by outbidding every other lawn service in the city. He had the lowest prices with quality work that spoke for itself. He went from three yards a week to six, and before he realized it, he was doing ten yards a week, and the money started rolling in. To see him working so hard made his mother proud of him, even though she had been devastated by his dishonorable discharge.

When Razier told her of his plans to open the pool cleaning service, she felt he was adding too much to his plate too soon. But he assured her that this was what he needed to do, and he was determined to handle everything he put in front of him. Failure wasn't an option. He stuck to a strict system, and so far, he'd been able to handle everything, and his bank account showed his hard work was paying off.

He'd gotten a loan for the preowned truck he would use for the pool cleaning supplies, and he already built up several clients, most of whom he did weekly yard work for. Razier had a plan, and it would fit right into his weekly schedule without interrupting his daily program. He would schedule pool cleanings around the areas where he would do the lawns. So after he did a lawn, he would come back in the evening when it was cooler and clean pools. He calculated with the extra income from the pool cleaning, he would be in a prime position for when the winter months arrived.

Razier had cards made online for all his businesses, and every time he did a yard, he made sure he left a card to let his clients know that he was a man wearing many hats. Lawn service with the best prices weekly, a pool cleaning service with two pool cleanings a month at a superlow price, and last, his catering service that served everything from seafood to soul food . . . He was serious about his grind, and he was winning, and it felt really good.

The one thing that bothered him on a daily was the fact that he hadn't been able to locate Carmi. Razier thought about her every single day, and every single day he felt ashamed of ruining her stellar career as a senior naval chief. Carmi was the reason why he had chosen to work so hard. He used his work to replace sex. He didn't think he would be able to do it, but he chose to remain celibate because he had to get control of his tender-dick issues. Razier smiled while he was showering as he thought back to when he told his mother about his decision to abstain. *She laughed and said, "That will be the day, boy. You need to quit that storytelling."* Her words stung but gave him more motivation to stick to the script he planned. And so far, he'd been back home for eighteen months, and he hadn't had sex once. There were plenty of nights that he made love to his right hand while watching pornstar.com on his laptop, though. He admitted to himself that it was hard, but no matter what, he would make it.

Razier kept busy and worked hard every day so that when he came home, the only thing on his mind was sleeping. Every night he closed his eyes, he saw the beautiful face of Carmi, and his heart ached. He missed her, and what was even crazier to him was that he realized that it had been way more than just sex with them. He loved her. Damn.

When Razier pulled into his mother's driveway, he saw that the widow who stayed next door to his mother was outside watering her grass while wearing a pair of shorts and a tiny T-shirt showing plenty of cleavage. He laughed because Mrs. Hopkins was every bit of 60-plus. Even still, she looked good, and she knew it, so she made sure she came out every morning and gave the males in the neighborhood an eyeful, pissing off plenty of wives on the block. He jumped out of his truck and admired Mrs. Hopkins for a moment, then said, "Good morning, Mrs. Hopkins. How are you?"

She waved and said, "Hiya, Razi. I'm fine. How you today?"

"Good. Getting ready to work hard all day long in this heat. I'll be sure to do your yard Saturday unless you want me to squeeze you in this afternoon?"

"No rush, baby. Saturday is fine with me."

"Okay, see ya later."

"Mm-hmm, you sure will."

He laughed as he went inside his mother's house to the aroma of some bacon and eggs. "Yes," he said to himself as he stepped into the kitchen and saw his mother standing in front of the stove.

"Hi, Mama."

"Hey, Razi. Now, how did I know your butt would be here this morning to eat up all my food?"

"Because you know your son works like a dog and barely has time to cook something to eat. I'm sure glad you made something I want because I'm starved."

"Something you want? Humph, boy, you need to quit that. I haven't seen a meal you would turn down. And you know my rule."

Laughing, he said, "Yes, I know your rule, Mama. There are only two choices on your menu: take it or leave it."

She smiled lovingly at her only child and said, "That's right. Ever since I heard the great comedian Buddy Hackett use that quip when your father took me to see him back in the day, I took it and stuck with it, and, boy, did that make your daddy mad sometimes."

"You're something else, you know that?"

"That, I am. Now sit your tail down and eat. I know you have to hurry up and start your day."

Once he was seated at the dining room table, Mrs. Coleman came and set a plate full of bacon and eggs before him and then asked him whether he wanted milk or juice. Before he could answer, she came and poured him a glass of milk. "I knew you would say juice, and that's why you get milk. Does the body good."

"If you knew I wanted juice, why give me milk, Mama?"

"Mothers knows best, Razi, and don't you ever forget that."

With a mouthful of eggs, he mumbled, "How can I ever forget that when you make sure you tell me that at least three times a week?"

She wore a smile on her face as she popped him on the back of his head. "Eat, smart mouth. Now tell me what that heifer, Mrs. Hopkins, was saying to you when you pulled up. I know she's still not trying to get you in her bed, is she? Dang shame she done went and lost her mind since her husband passed. She's trying her best to get every man in the neighborhood. Can't believe she went and actually got that boob job. What woman her age does something like that?"

Razier almost choked on a piece of bacon and asked, "Boob job? Are you *serious?* Mrs. Hopkins has always had big boobs, Mama."

"True. But do you notice how they stand up nice and firm now? She had a lift or something because those bad boys have suddenly defied gravity. Dang shame."

"Sounds like you're hating a little bit, Mama."

"Hating isn't in my DNA, son. Trust me. If your mother wanted, she would outshine Mrs. Hopkins any day of the week, and I'm five years older than her."

Razier knew his mother spoke the truth because she was stunning, even at the age of 67. His mom, rocking her mature, short pixie cut combined with her flawless complexion and slim frame, was on point for sure. With pride in his voice, he said, "I know that's right, Mama. Can you tell me, since you know you still got it going on like you did back in the day, why don't you date?"

She smiled at him with a hint of mischief in her eyes and said, "Just because you don't see men around me doesn't mean I don't do me, Razi. My business is not everyone else's business, ya dig?"

He rolled his eyes as he finished the last of his food and downed his large glass of milk. "You know I hate it when you still try to talk like you hip with it."

"Look who's hating now. Gimme those dishes so that you can go on and get out there and get that cake."

"Mama!"

Laughing, she took the dishes to the sink and stepped back in front of him. She kissed him on the cheek and said, "You have a good day, Razi. You do know I'm proud of you and all you've achieved thus far, right?"

He smiled because he loved his mother with all his heart, and she knew it. "I know, Mama. I ain't done yet either. We about to get our clown on real big in a minute."

She rolled her eyes at him and said, "Mm-hmm. What, you gon' cop me something foreign soon? You know, like a Benz or a fly new Beamer? You know I'll look way too fly hopping out of that new 750."

"Mama, stop. You're killing me with the lingo. Act your age, *please*."

Laughing, she popped him on the back of the head again and said, "Get! Make sure you drink plenty of water outside in that heat all day. I don't need to receive a call that you've been taken to the ER for falling out from dehydration."

"I got my big twenty-gallon jug filled with ice water, Mama, I'll be fine."

"Good. Oh, Tracy Briggs called me last night."

"Was it collect?"

"You know, if it were, I would have still accepted. No, he called me on a dang cell phone. You know, I asked him how in the heck did he get a cell phone while in prison."

"What he say?"

"He laughed and told me that he would always have the best no matter where he was, so I just left it alone."

"What was he talking about?"

"He wanted your number. He didn't know that you moved out. I gave it to him, and he said he would give you a call today or the evening because he can only call at certain times. I guess because of those guards roaming around him or something."

"Okay, that's cool. Did he say when he was getting out, 'cause I know you asked?"

"Are you implying that I'm a nosy woman, Razi?" Before he could answer her question, she said, "Yes, I asked, and he told me soon. I asked how soon, and he laughed and said real soon. You know that irritated the heck out of me, so I told him bye and hung up on his tail."

"I was hoping he would be home soon. It should be close. I want to try to get him to help me with the stuff I'm doing. I think if I can get him to work with me, we can really make some money together."

"You know how lazy that boy is? I don't know about that one, Razi."

He shrugged and said, "We'll see. Okay, Mama, let me go. Love you," he said and kissed her.

"Love you too, Razi," his mom said as she watched him leave the house.

Just as Razier was climbing inside of his truck, Mrs. Hopkins came to her front door with her hands on her hips, smiling at him. When she winked at him, he smiled and shook his head. *She knows she needs to stop that,* he thought as he started his truck. As he was pulling out of his mother's driveway, he shot another glance toward Mrs. Hopkins, and he couldn't help it when he felt a little stirring in his groin. "Damn, I must be really horny if I can let an old broad like Mrs. Hopkins get me fired up. Jeez, looks like it's going to be a pornstar.com night tonight for sure," he said to himself as he pressed the pedal to the metal. It was time to get to work.

Chapter Two

The harder Razier worked, the faster his day seemed to go by. He was so thankful for his navy training and proud of himself for keeping his well toned body in tip-top shape by maintaining a healthy diet. He wished he could work out, but his schedule didn't allow him that luxury, so he relied on his daily yard work in the sun to keep him fit. After finishing his last yard for the day, he was exhausted. All he wanted to do was grab a bite to eat from Subway, go home, shower, and hit the bed.

While he was loading his equipment on the back of his truck, his client came out to pay him, and it took all his self-control not to stare at the voluptuous older woman as she came toward him. Ms. Tolliver was somewhere in the late forties or early fifties, but her body made one think she was in her thirties. Tight and extra nice. She wasn't all that pretty but was still sexy as all out. With her brown skin with slanted eyes that gave her a foreign, exotic look, she turned him on, causing Razier to ignore her somewhat large nose. "Calm down, boy," he told himself as he closed the bed of his truck and turned to face Ms. Tolliver.

"Once again, I'd like to thank you, Razier, for adding me to your client list. I really like the work you do. I swear, those Mexicans I had used just rushed and left bags full of grass on my front lawn, and that irritated me to no end. When Wanda told me about your lawn service, I hoped and prayed you would be able to fit me in. I know you're extremely busy."

"No problem at all, Ms. Tolliver. Your yard is relatively small, so it was an easy fit. Glad you like my work. I hope you give me a good word to your friends who may need my services."

She smiled at him, and her pearly, white-capped teeth seemed to be extra bright as she stared at him for a moment before speaking. "Oh, I'm sure I can find some friends who would love your services, Razier. As a matter of fact, I think I have a few in mind. Tell me, are you done for the day?"

"Yes, you were my last yard for the day."

"How many yards did you do today?"

"Twelve."

"Have you eaten anything?"

"I had a good breakfast. Other than that, just a couple of PowerBars and water."

"You must be starving. Why don't you let me have the honor of taking you for a bite to eat? We can go to the Flint located at the bottom of the historic Colcord Hotel. It has a great view of Myriad Gardens on one side and sits in the shadows of the beautiful Devon Tower. You know, that tall building downtown?"

"I'm really kinda tired, Ms. Tolliver."

Shaking her head no, she said, "First, you call me Olivia. You make me feel like a grandma with that 'Ms. Tolliver' crap."

He smiled. "Okay, Olivia."

"Second, I'm not taking no for an answer, Razier. You are an extremely handsome young man, and I'd love to take you to the Flint for a nice meal and some conversation in hopes of getting to know you better. So, you go home, get showered, and give me a call. Then I'll come and get you, and we'll go out and hopefully have a very good evening. I know you're a very hardworking young man, so I won't keep you out too long."

"I guess since you insist, I have no other choice but to accept."

"That's correct, Razier, you don't. Here's my number," she said as she gave him a card with her name and number on it. She also handed him his money for the month and said, "No need to get dressed up. Some casual clothing will suffice."

"Okay. It'll take me a couple of hours to get home and get my equipment cleaned up for my jobs tomorrow. After I handle that, I'll get showered and give you a call."

"No problem. I'll be waiting for your call," Olivia said as she turned in her flip-flops and walked back inside of her home.

Razier stared at the slim goody frame she had and moaned, "It's going to be really hard to maintain this celibacy crap," he said as he got inside of his truck and headed home, thinking at least he'd get a good meal tonight.

It took Razier longer than he expected because he had to fix a gas leak in one of his lawn mowers. When he had that task taken care of, he went inside his apartment, took a quick shower, and started getting dressed. The shower refreshed him, but he was still tired and almost called Olivia to cancel their date, but something told him he'd better not. He didn't want to make a client feel rejected was his excuse as he grabbed her card and gave her a call to give her directions to his apartment located on the North Side of town not too far from her home on the Northwest Side.

After he hung up the phone with Olivia, he sat down on his couch and thought about the fourteen yards he had to do the next day. Friday was his busiest day, and he knew he would need all his strength to handle them. He had some pretty big yards to tackle in Edmond and Midwest City. As those thoughts crossed his mind, he was also thinking about his best friend, Tracy Briggs. He hoped he came home soon because he needed his help in a major way. If he could talk Tracy into coming into business with him as a partner, they could handle his workload easier, and that would open up the room he would need to start the pool cleaning service. He would then be one more step closer to getting that food truck he wanted so he could join the H&8th Food Truck chain, and then the money would really start rolling in. He was determined to get that truck along with his catering service in the winter. Accomplishing that, he would be able to get that brownstone condo he had his eyes on. He heard Russell Westbrook just purchased one for a little over $2 million. He wouldn't get that fly with it, but he would definitely be nice staying in one of the two to three hundred thousand-dollar ones located close to downtown.

He sat there daydreaming about that condo and didn't even realize that he'd dozed off until he heard the doorbell ring. He opened his eyes, jumped up from the couch, and straightened his clothing as he walked to the door. When he opened the door, Olivia was looking stunning in a sundress with some sandals on her small, pretty feet. She smiled at him and said, "You ready to take an old lady to dinner, Razier?"

Though he was dead tired, staring at her firm C-cups with cleavage pouring out of her dress, Razier smiled and said, "Definitely. You're looking beautiful this evening, Olivia. Age is nothing but a number, and you're living proof."

She laughed and said, "Flattery will get you in trouble, Razier, so be nice, or I'll be naughty."

Laughing, he said, "I thought I *was* being nice."

She grabbed his hand. "You were. I just want an excuse to be naughty." She saw the look on his face and laughed. "Don't be scared. I won't bite you . . . not too hard at least." They both laughed as she led him out of his apartment toward her BMW 5 Series. Once they were on their way, she asked him a few questions about this and that, making the conversation flow nice and easy. He knew she was flirting, and he was flattered, but he just wasn't interested. He was sticking to his guns, even though his man piece was screaming at him, telling him he needed to get deep inside of some women's flesh.

By the time they made it to the restaurant, he knew that tonight might just be the night he loses his eighteen months of celibacy. He felt a twinge of guilt because he thought about Carmi. Life had to keep rolling, and he couldn't keep torturing himself for a past wrong. He didn't mean to get Carmi kicked out of the navy. He knew that, but he still felt guilty about it.

After enjoying a nice meal of baked chicken breast, salad, and string beans, Razier and Olivia enjoyed the view of the Myriad Gardens and chatted about the state of their beloved Oklahoma City Thunder and the upcoming season.

"We need to make a move for another big man, and I think we'll be ready to make a serious run at the championship next season. I love me some Ibaka. Big Perkins does his job defensively, but he gives us nothing on the offensive end. We need a low post presence so that it can open things up for Westbrook to knock down those jump shots," Razier said as he sipped some water.

"I agree. I think this is the year that Scott Brooks makes it all gel the right way. K. D. loves his partner in crime, but he has to get Westbrook to be more of a true point guard at times. To me, that will only happen if Scott Brooks puts his foot down. Westbrook is great, don't get me wrong, but we need him to learn to facilitate more. We're still in for a big fight with those Spurs. The Western Conference is deadly deep. Not only do we have to worry about the Spurs, but those Clippers are also dangerous as well. We almost got beat by them, and that would have broken my heart. I hate everything about Los Angeles. Thank God in heaven those Lakers suck. I can't stand Kobe. I was so happy when none of the top free agents went to the Lakers this year."

"Wow, that's some serious hate right there. Don't get me wrong. It's the Thunder or nothing, but growing up, I was a die-hard Laker fan. I loved how Shaq and Kobe did their thing. It's kinda sad that he's got no help out there with him now. Boozer is nothing. Nash is old and needs to hang it up. The young talent the Lakers have can help, but they won't make any noise in the West. As you said, the West is loaded. Golden State, Portland, Houston, and Dallas can all be legitimate threats."

"True, but those dang Spurs are the ones we have to worry about. Coach Pop has them running like a well-oiled machine," she said as she took a sip of her Chardonnay and stared at Razier. "You look tired. I'd better get your butt home so you can get some rest."

"Yeah, I am pretty beat, but I can hang a little longer if you want to." *There it is. Let's see if this slim goody is with it or not,* he thought.

She smiled. "I most definitely want to hang but not a little longer, Razier. I want you to last a long time. Can you last a long time, handsome?" she asked, staring directly into his brown eyes.

"I know no other way, Olivia."

"Good." She signaled for the waiter so she could pay for their meal. When Razier tried to stop her so that he could pay for their food, she shook her head and said, "No way, Razier. This date was on me. I love that you're a perfect gentleman, though. That's sweet. Please understand that I'm a hungry woman right now, and I need you to leave your sweetness right here in this restaurant. I don't want sweet when we make it back to your place. I want to be fucked. I want to be fucked long and hard. I want you to talk dirty to me as you fill me up. I like pain, and I can take all that you can give me. You just make sure you give it to me good. You hear me?"

"Loud and clear."

"Great. Let's get going. We got some serious work to put in."

As soon as they entered his apartment, Olivia pulled the straps of her sundress off her shoulders and let it slide to the floor, showing Razier that she had chosen not to wear any underwear. He laughed and said, "Why do I feel like you planned this entire evening to a tee?"

"Because you're not only handsome and sexy as fuck, but also you're perceptive and a smart young man. I've been planning to fuck you silly ever since I laid my eyes on your fine self. I'll let you in on a little secret too. I'm not the only client you have that wants to fuck your brains out. You have a pretty nice fan club around the city, Razier."

"Huh?"

"Don't be shocked. You must know that some of the ladies' mouths water every time you come to their homes to mow their lawns."

"Most of the women whose yards I cut are married."

Laughing, she said, "And what does that mean? You have to understand that when a woman, especially an older woman, sees a fine young man like yourself, all they're thinking about is how good that dick could be. They get to thinking about how good their husbands *used* to give them the dick because, odds are, they aren't getting fucked good at home any longer. Trust me. After tonight, if you impress me, as I'm confident you will, you will be the talk of the ladies even more."

"So you're going to kiss and tell, huh?"

"Fuck me silly, Razier, and you're damn right. I'm telling every last one of them. Then watch how your stock will rise even higher. I want them to eat their hearts out when they hear that I was able to get your sexy self first."

"Damn, like that?"

"*Exactly* like that. Now, enough with the talk. Let's fuck. Show me my instincts are correct about you. Show me that you can handle an experienced woman."

He stepped toward her, pulled her into his arms, and started biting her neck. She moaned loudly as he scooped her into his arms and carried her into his bedroom, where he proceeded to fuck her silly—*exactly* as she expected him to.

Chapter Three

Tracy "Mad Dog" Briggs woke up at five a.m. with a smile on his face. It was his last few hours in prison, and he was ready to get to the real world so that he could put his plans in motion. He was about to get paid with one of the most solid hustles he'd ever come up with. He laid the groundwork for the last two years of the four years he served in Boley State Prison. One of the main hustles inside of the prison was illegal cell phones. A cheap, prepaid flip phone ran for $150, whereas a smartphone went for as much as $1,500. The correctional officers who brought them inside to the inmates were killing the game, and Tracy was determined to get a piece of that easy money.

Tracy knew he couldn't mess with any of the guards who were getting their money that way, so he set out to lock in a female guard who he knew was feeling his get down. With everything set, he was about to change the game on the prison cell phone hustle. He would have his female CO friend bring in phones for a slightly lower price and deal with about fifty solid inmates that he personally vetted to make sure that they would remain solid and keep their mouths shut if they got caught. Everything would be good, and the money they would make every ninety days or so would be too damn sweet.

He laughed when he thought about how he would have his female CO friend let each inmate with phones she brought them know just before their unit was about to be raided so they would dump their phones without getting caught with them. It was a sweet setup because the raids would be real because she would drop a line to the SIS officers, letting them know that there were cell phones on specific units, and they would raid those units. Once the prisoners dumped their cell phones, she would let them know she would bring more as long as they had the funds to pay for them.

The prisoners she would be dealing with are the main hustlers inside the prison that had the means to keep purchasing the phones no matter the cost, which was the sweetest thing about the entire setup. They looked to gain close to seventy-five thousand every ninety days. *Sweet.* Tracy was ready to get out so he could make everything right, and that would happen once he was able to make love to the not-so-attractive female CO. She wasn't all that easy on the eyes, but she had a firm, fit body, so it was all good to him, especially after four years on lock. She was already in love with him, so everything else was a mere technicality. By his calculations, he would be well over five hundred thousand within a year or so. Then he could make some other moves with his best friend, Razier.

Razier was out there working his ass off, and he wanted to make sure that he helped his one and only true friend get that paper up with his small business. *Yeah, everything is about to be right for both of us really quick,* he thought as he brushed his teeth and got ready for the call for him to be led to R&D to start the long process of releasing him back to society.

He heard his name called over the prison's PA system and smiled when his cell gate was automatically opened. He turned and shook hands with his cell mate and said farewell. When he stepped out of his cell, he saw a few haters gritting on him because it was his time to shine.

He smiled brightly as he strolled confidently toward the Receiving and Discharge Building. When he came out of his unit, he saw Lavonda, his female CO friend, and smiled as he stepped toward her.

"Hi, babe. You ready to be a free man?" she asked as she fell in step with Tracy, walking by his side toward R&D.

"You better say it. The question is, are *you* ready for me to get balls deep in that good pussy?"

She blushed and said, "You so damn bad. You already know the answer to that question, babe. What time are you going to call me?"

"After I get with my moms and pops and spend some time with the family, I'll hit you up. Start heading to the city just as soon as you get off work. Stick to the script and get a suite at the Skirvin. Then get asshole naked and wait for the Mad Dog to come and get deep in them guts because we freaking all night long. You did let your superiors know you won't be coming in tomorrow, right?"

"Mm-hmm. I took two days off, babe, just like you told me to. I want to be able to spend as much time with you as possible. I'll take you to see your parole officer. After that, we can go shopping so I can get you some clothes and stuff."

He smiled. "*That's* what's up. We also have to set up that PO Box for the money drops when it's time to get that popping. By you living way out here in Boley, it will fit just right, so you won't be linked to the get down just in case some shit goes left. My main concern next to getting all that fucking money is making damn sure we keep you safe. That's a must."

She smiled and said, "That's the only reason why I let you talk me into doing this scam. I feel you're sincere in protecting me as well as helping me make some money. More important, I can't wait until we reach our goal so that I can quit this dead-end job and live happily with you in the city. You promised me we'll be together, Mad Dog. Please don't break that promise to me, babe."

"You've held me down the last two years of this bid. You've proven your loyalty to me, baby. There's no way in the world I would ever betray you. Don't doubt me. I got you. You belong to me now and always, ya dig?"

"Yes, babe, I dig. You just be ready to do some *very serious* digging later on," she said and giggled.

"No doubt," he said as he stopped in front of the door of R&D.

Lavonda reached out her hand and shook his hand to keep things looking kosher in case any of her peers or superiors were paying any attention to them from the many prison cameras and watchtowers located all around the prison yard. She let her hand linger a little longer and smiled. "Damn, I can't wait to have you inside of me, babe."

"Don't trip, baby. When I see your pretty face again, I'll be a free man, and all of this dick you've only been able to grab on for the last two years will be yours. Now, let me make it. It's time for us to start a new journey together. See ya later," he said as he turned and knocked on the door to the Receiving and Discharge Building.

Lavonda stood there and watched as he entered the building. Then she went and started her regular workday routine. The quicker she got to work, the faster the day would be over, and the sooner she would be able to be with her Mad Dog. That thought alone made her pussy get really wet. She moaned as she stepped into the loud prison unit.

When Razier woke up a few minutes after six a.m., he noticed that Olivia wasn't in bed with him any longer. He got out of bed and went into the bedroom to relieve himself. When he finished, he brushed his teeth and jumped into the shower. While showering, he thought about how good the sex had been with Olivia. For an older woman, she was a damn tiger, and her aggressiveness threw him for a minute, but he regrouped quickly and rocked her world until they passed out, sated completely. Now that he had ended his bit of being celibate, he was ready to get his groove going all the way back right. One thing he was going to make sure of, though, he would not let sex interfere with any of his business moves. No more tender dick or bad decisions behind some pussy. As long as he stuck to that rule, he felt everything would be just fine.

After he finished with his shower, he went back into the bedroom and cut on the light so he could get dressed. When he turned toward the bed, he saw an envelope on top of the pillow that Olivia slept on. Curious, he grabbed the envelope and opened it. He was shocked to see ten one hundred-dollar bills inside of the envelope along with a folded piece of paper. It was a note from Olivia.

> *Razier,*
> *I enjoyed the sex you put on me last night, and I want to make sure that we do it again and again and again. LOL. Seriously, it's important to me that you understand that what we shared was special. It was also a business opportunity for you that I think you're perfect for. I don't want to get too deep with it right now, so meet me at eight p.m. at the Park House back down at the Myriad Gardens. They have some of the best burgers in the city. We can chill out and have some drinks, eat, and chat more about what I have planned for you. I'll see you at eight sharp. Have a great day, you supersexy handsome man, you. Oh, and, yes, you handled*

this pussy like a champ. Hope I'll be able to have an encore tonight. Smile.

One last thing, I want you to pay close attention to the last part of this note. These are rules that you must stick to in order to benefit from the plans I have for you. See you later, sexy Razier. Kisses. Olivia.

1. Never fuck when you don't want to. Remain in control at all times.

2. Always use protection no matter what you're told. Always.

3. Pay close attention and always listen more than you talk.

4. Never fuck for free. Never.

5. And last, make sure you find a way to enjoy your "Stolen Moments." It's for business as well as pleasure for all *parties involved.*

Razier sat there, stunned, with the piece of paper in his hand, wondering what the hell did Olivia have going on. One thing was for sure . . . He was going to make damn sure he was on time for their date because if she thought he was about to get caught up in some illegal shit, she was out of her damn mind.

He stared at the thousand dollars she left him, and he couldn't help but think what if . . . What if this was something good? What if she was willing to help him come up? *This could be a blessing for real,* he thought as he continued to stare at the note and the money left by Olivia. He shook his head, stood, and got dressed, thinking about what Olivia said in the message. He was so distracted he forgot to go and have some breakfast at his mom's.

He went straight to his first yard for the day on the South Side of town. It was after seven in the morning, and the sun was already burning up the city. He drank some bottled water and got to work. He finished the yard in under forty-five minutes and was on his way to his next yard. He loaded his truck and headed toward Midwest City, where one of his bigger yards was located so he could tackle that and get it out of the way because the rest of his yards were on the North Side of town and Edmond.

During the drive to Midwest City, his mind was all over the place. Damn, what if Olivia could help him get the money needed for his food truck? Or even better, what if she could help him get the cash to purchase the condo he wanted? He was smiling, but then the smile faded from his face as he thought about his mother and one of her many sayings. *Anything that comes easy comes with a steep price, so you must ask yourself, Razi, is easy money worth losing your soul?* He sighed and came back to earth with his extra thoughts. There was no way he would ever risk his freedom. Life was too short for him to waste any of his behind somebody's prison walls. Nope. No. Way.

Thinking about prison made him think about his best friend. He needed the Mad Dog to be with his plans so they can make it out here together like they always said they would when they were kids. Their lives went in separate directions because Tracy was with the easy-money route. He wasn't lazy like his mom thought he was. He was a go-getter, but he would never let an opportunity slip away from him when he saw a chance to get some easy loot. And that's why he ended up in prison. Razier was determined to make sure that his best friend would be with him and live right so that they could enjoy life together doing what they swore they would do when they were kids—get rich.

When Razier pulled into the driveway of the home of his next client, he was surprised to see that Mrs. Willow was home. Usually, whenever he came over to do their yard, she and her husband would be already gone to work. He hopped out of his truck and started unloading his equipment so that he could get to work. Their front yard was one hell of a task because they wanted him to trim and groom the large bushes to perfection. The backyard was just as tough as the front. He sighed and went and grabbed his twenty-gallon jug of water and set it down close to where he would begin work and got started. He was working for close to twenty minutes when Mrs. Willow came outside and called out to him. He shut down the lawn mower and went to the front to see what she wanted.

Mrs. Willow was a slim, big-breasted blonde with cat-green eyes that were mesmerizing. She was in her mid- to late fifties and was really easy on the eyes. Her bright smile was always sincere, and she seemed like a nice woman. Plus, she tipped him well when it came time for him to collect his monthly fee for doing their yards twice a month.

"How are you doing today, Mrs. Willow?"

"I'm fine, Razier. Actually, I'm great. I decided to have a cheat day today, so I took the day off. I'm going to have a massage and get a mani and a pedi. I need to pamper myself since my old fuddy-duddy husband won't pamper me," she said and pouted.

Laughing, Razier said, "Don't be so mean to Mr. Willow. I'm sure he doesn't mean not to pamper you. You might need to talk to him and tell him what you need. Sometimes, we men tend not to pay enough attention to the lady in our lives, but that doesn't mean we don't care."

"You may be right there, Razier. I'll think about that when I'm spending his money pampering myself today."

"That's cold, Mrs. Willow."

"If you say so. I know he'll pay attention when he gets that credit card bill from my day today." She laughed, and her robe opened slightly, which gave Razier an eyeful of her big, firm, double-D cup breasts. She saw Razier's eyes grow wide and smiled. "What's wrong, Razier? You act as if you've never seen a woman's chest before."

"Uh, um, yes, ma'am. I've seen my share. It's-it's just, well, that kinda caught me off guard, is all."

"Do you like them?"

"Huh?"

"You heard what I said. Do you like them? Do you think they look nice?" she asked as she opened her robe wider for him to get a better look at her tits.

"Yes, they're perfect," he whispered as he turned and looked behind him to make sure no one could see this mature white woman flashing her tits at him. Lord knows he didn't need to get accused of some bullshit.

"Good. Maybe you'll get to give them some special 'attention' one day. Have a good day, Razier. I know I will. I'm so looking forward to having a stolen moment with you. Byeeee," she said as she closed her robe and went back inside of her home, leaving him speechless as he turned and went back to work thinking, *What the fuck? A stolen moment?* That phrase was bouncing around in his head for the rest of the time he worked on Mrs. Willow's yard.

Mmmmm.

Chapter Four

Razier was totally perplexed. The females of the homes on every yard he did on the North Side and in Edmond seemed to flirt with him without any shame. This was a first, and all he could think about was Olivia and that damn phrase, "A Stolen Moment." *What the hell is going on?* he thought as he loaded his equipment and headed to the last yard he had for the day.

Though he was tired, he was hyped because he had a feeling that something special was on the horizon. The thousand dollars Olivia gave him had dollar signs swirling around inside of his head. He didn't know what was going on, but he knew one thing for sure. He was going to be all ears during his dinner date at the Park House with Olivia in a few hours. "A stolen moment," he said to himself. Was it possible that a stolen moment meant having sex with the six women who flirted with him today? Each of the ladies was married. Each one was sexy in her own right. Each seemed to be financially stable whether they were stay-at-home housewives or career-working women. The age didn't matter one bit to him, even though they were all kind of close to his mother's age. The oldest was Mrs. Beckman, who, at 59, was so damn fine that he could care less how old she was. She was by far the sexiest of them all.

Hold up, tender dick. Here you go, starting that shit already, and you don't even know what the business is, for real. Cool it, he scolded himself as he climbed inside of his truck and drove toward the last yard he had to do for the day. He was smiling as he drove toward the Wilkinses' home, located behind Quail Springs Mall on the Far North Side. He hoped Mrs. Wilkins would be as flirtatious with him as some of his other clients had been today. Her supersexy fine ass could definitely have as many stolen moments as she wanted. He laughed aloud at that thought because he knew he was being silly. Even though he was clowning with those thoughts, he still hoped it would happen.

Mrs. Wilkins was an exotic-looking woman with long, flowing hair that he once had the pleasure of seeing loosely hanging almost to her waist. She usually kept it piled high on her head, but, boy, was she a head-turner. She too was in her mid- to late fifties but looked as if she were in her forties. Her body was slim yet thick in all the right places. He never had the nerve to ask her the mix of her heritage, but she was definitely mixed with something foreign, which was one of his main weaknesses. He loved him a sister. Nothing was sweeter than a natural chocolate Black woman. But he had some kind of fetish when it came to women who were mixed or from another country like the D. R. or Jamaica.

He shook his head to get focused because Mrs. Wilkins's husband was really picky when it came to his yard, and this yard was *huge*. The last yard of the day would take him at least ninety minutes, so he had to put on his game face so that he could handle his business. He hoped that Mr. Wilkins would be there so he could pitch his pool cleaning service to him. They had an Olympic-size pool in their enormous backyard, and he was hopeful that they would let him clean their pool for a cheaper price than they were already paying. That was his best sales pitch, giving a lower price, and then let his work impress them so they would spread the word. Word of mouth was always the best commercial as far as he was concerned. So far, it had worked perfectly for him with his lawn service, so he didn't see why it shouldn't work with his pool cleaning service. Grinding it out was what it was all about, and Razier was prepared to work hard for his money.

When Razier pulled into the driveway of the Wilkinses' home, he saw Mr. Wilkins as he was leaving the house headed toward his Bentley Azure. Mr. Wilkins waited for Razier to get out of his truck and then approached him with a friendly smile on his face. After shaking hands, Mr. Wilkins said, "Good to see you, Razier. Right on time, as usual. I was hoping I wouldn't miss you today."

"You know I try to be on time every other week, sir. It's been a heavy day for me, but all is well."

"Good. I need you to make sure you trim the bushes in the back down a little more than usual. They seem to be growing extremely fast. I'm thinking about having you cut them down, but I wanted to get your opinion first."

"I think they're a key part to your backyard landscape, sir, and would make the yard seem as if there was too much space if they were gone. Trimming them down a little more than normal should do the trick and give you the look you want."

Nodding his head in agreement, Mr. Wilkins said, "I agree. Okay, I'll let you get right to it. I left your fee with the missus. I got to run. Late for a business meeting. See you soon, Razier," Mr. Wilkins said as he jumped into his expensive car and eased out of the driveway.

Razier checked the time and saw that it was almost five p.m., so he put a pep in his step and got to work. He cut the front yard and trimmed the hedges, setting the pace while humming to himself. He was smiling as he worked because, again, he saw flashes of Mrs. Willow's ample-size breasts. He groaned when he thought about how good Mrs. Bin looked when she came out to pay him wearing a pair of Capri pants that hugged her thickness that made him feel as if he could see the pussy print between her legs.

As he was hard at work, he continued to think about the older women who flirted with him. The slim Mrs. Salley was a blonde bombshell for real. Though he didn't do white women too often, he would definitely enjoy getting balls deep in that sexy, white lady. Those eyes of hers made him think of the beautiful Mrs. Willow. That's one deadly combo right there . . . a white woman with some sexy eyes. Wow, that could be the death of him, he thought and smiled.

He then switched his thoughts to Mrs. Collins and Mrs. Simmons. Ump ump ump. Two older sisters that kept themselves together. Sure, they had a few spiderwebs around their eyes, but they were still some fine women. He tried to imagine how good they looked when they were younger. *Boy, I bet they were some showstoppers for sure,* he thought. Nevertheless, even in their fifties, they still could get it. He laughed aloud at that thought and couldn't believe that he let his imagination run rampant behind some innocent flirting from some well-off older women. He shook his head and continued with his work.

When he finished the front yard, he went to his truck to gas up the lawn mower so he could go to the back and tackle the most challenging task of the Wilkinses' place. He stopped in his tracks when he saw Mrs. Wilkins standing at the end of their deck, staring out toward the pool, crying softly. He stood there and watched her for a few seconds because he was mesmerized with all that ass she was packing in the bikini she wore, covered by a sheer black wrap. He knew he couldn't keep standing there staring at her, but at the same time, he didn't want to intrude on this private moment she was having; plus, he had work to do. He set the gas can down rather loudly so she would hear him.

She turned, wiped her eyes quickly, and said, "Hi, Razier. I didn't know you were here. Let me get out of your way. I'll come back when you're finished and give you your check."

"No problem, Mrs. Wilkins. I should be done within an hour or so."

She stared at him for a moment as if she were apprais-ing him and said, "Mmm . . . Okay, Razier. Maybe we can have a chat before you leave, that is, if you have the time."

"A chat? Come on, are you serious? Okay, now it's time to see if I've been fooling myself all damn day," he said to himself. He boldly told the beautiful, older woman, "I have no problem chatting with you, Mrs. Wilkins. Especially if the topic is about a stolen moment." He stared at her to see what type of reaction he would get.

Mrs. Wilkins wore a grin on her lovely face and said, "Aah, so you've caught on to the stolen moments phrase, I see. Good, really good. You need to be careful, though, Razier. A stolen moment may not be all that you think it is. It may be more demanding than you think," she said with a twinkle in her light brown eyes. For some reason, she reminded him of Carmi . . . maybe because of the similar bronze skin complexion.

"Would you care to break that phrase down to me, ma'am? I mean, I kinda got the feeling I know what's up, but then again, I'm like lost here. It's like I'm the brunt of an inside joke."

"No joking, Razier. You're being taken extremely seri-ously, trust me on that one. On second thought, I don't think it's necessary for us to have that chat."

Disappointment clouded his handsome features when he asked, "Why not, Mrs. Wilkins?"

She smiled and said, "Don't worry, Razier. Everything is going to be A-okay. Trust me on that. There's no need for us to have that chat because I'm sure we will have plenty of time to chat during our stolen moments. Until then, I'll let Olivia explain everything to you this evening during your dinner date at the Park House." She laughed when she saw the shocked expression on his face, turned, and entered her home.

"Okay, this is getting Twilight Zone weird here," he said as he shook his head and got back to work.

By the time he finished with the Wilkinses' yard, he was dead tired. All he was thinking about was going home, showering, and hurrying his ass up to get to the Park House so he could find out what the hell was going on with all these old, flirty broads. Mrs. Wilkins came out front and met him at his truck and was all businesslike with him when she gave him the check for his services. She smiled sweetly at him when she turned to go back into her house, and he could have sworn the lady had an extra wiggle in her hips as she walked away.

Olivia, your ass got a lot of explaining to do, he thought as he got into his truck. As he was pulling out of the driveway, he received a call from his mother. He prayed before he answered the phone that she wouldn't want him to stop by her house. He was too tired for that, and he didn't want to be late for his now very important dinner date with Olivia.

"What's up, Mama? How was your day?"

"Just fine, and it just got a little better. I know Friday's your busiest day, Razi, but I need you to come over before you go home. It's crucial, so no will not be accepted."

He sighed, then said, "I'm on my way, Mama, but I can't stay long because I have a date at eight, and I need to hurry and get home so I can shower and get fresh."

"A date? Who is the lucky woman? I see your hormones have finally won out, huh?"

He regretted telling his mother his business because he knew she would get goofy with him and get her clown on. She swore his tender dick would be the death of him, and he should have known better than saying he had a date. He figured he had to so she wouldn't make him late. "It's more of a business meeting with a client who wants to throw some more business my way, Mama."

"Yeah, right. If it's a woman you're meeting in the evening time, that's called a date, son. Anyway, you need to hurry up and get here. Then you can be on your way on your date—excuse me, I meant *business meeting,*" she teased.

"I'll be there in the next fifteen minutes, Mama," he said and ended the call.

Fifteen minutes later, he pulled into his mother's driveway. He got out of the truck and was walking toward the front door when it opened, and to his surprise, the one man in the entire world he considered his best friend and brother was standing in the doorway with a grin on his face. Tracy Mad Dog Briggs stepped to Razier and said, "Body up, clown. The Mad Dog is back."

Razier smiled and opened his arms wide and let Tracy punch him two times in the chest. When he finished, Tracy opened his arms and let Razier punch him two times in his chest. Razier's mother stood at the door, watching the two best friends' exchange, shaking her head.

"Will you two fools get in the house? I can't believe you are still doing that 'body up' stuff after all these years. You're not kids any longer."

Both men laughed as they gave each other a manly hug.

"Welcome home, Mad Dog. Man, am I glad you're home," Razier said sincerely.

"Glad to be back, dog. You ready to get rich?"

Razier smiled at his best friend and said, "Definitely. We got a lot of talking to do. I have some major plans for us."

With a bright smile on his face, Tracy Mad Dog Briggs said, "So do I, Razi. So do I."

Chapter Five

Razier and Tracy went inside the house and started catching up on things with each other. Razier couldn't believe how fast the four years Tracy did had gone by. He told Tracy all about his naval experience and how he screwed that up and decided to remain celibate since he came home. He conveniently left out that he ended his celibacy the previous night.

"So you're telling me you not getting none? You must be outta your dang mind," Tracy yelled, knowing better than using any curse words inside of Mrs. Coleman's home.

She smiled at them and said, "I'll go on in the bedroom so you two can talk freely."

Razier checked the time on his watch and said, "That won't be necessary, Mama. I got something to do. We're going to have to get together tomorrow, Mad Dog, and talk some serious business. I want you in on my businesses all the way . . . full partners just like we planned when we were kids. I'm about to start up the pool service thing 'cause the lawn money is good, and I think I'm ready to take the next step. With you here to help me, I know we can make it work out just fine."

Nodding his head in agreement, Tracy said, "I'm with that. Plus, I need a job, so my parole officer won't be all on my back. I got to give them two years on paper before I can discharge off that stuff."

"OK, it's settled. Monday, we'll get at your parole officer and let him know the business. Then we'll get right on it."

"Bet. We still need to chop it up, though, ya hear me? I got some things to bring to the table too."

"Cool." Razier checked his watch again and said, "All right, do you need me to take you somewhere because I got to get to the pad and change for this meeting I have at eight."

Mrs. Coleman snorted loudly and said, "Meeting, my tail, boy. You need to quit that. Why don't you admit you're going out on a date and trying to get your swerve on?" she laughed.

Tracy laughed too and said, "Now, where did you pick that 'swerve on' stuff from, Mrs. C.? You done got hip on me since I've been gone?"

"Say what you want, Tracy Briggs, but I've *always* been hip. You two have been too dang slow to realize it is all."

Razier rolled his mother's false swag and said, "Please, Mama, you're killing me here."

"Whatever, hater."

"Anyway, you need a lift, Mad Dog?"

Shaking his head, Tracy pulled out his new cell phone and called Lavonda, who was getting her nails done at a nearby Walmart. "My girl should be almost finished getting her nails done, dog. I'm good. She'll come back and pick me up. Then we're going to go get something to eat and chill for the rest of the night."

"All right. Hit me up in the a.m. We can do some breakfast before I get to work. Saturdays are my late days. I don't get started until after ten in the morning, so we can get together then."

"That's cool. I got a suite at the Skirvin so you can come there, and we can order some room service and holla like that."

"The Skirvin? So you come right home and ball out like that, huh, Tracy? You know you need to let me hold something then," Mrs. Coleman said as both men rolled their eyes at her and frowned. She laughed, shook her head, and said, "Haters," as she turned and left the room.

"For real, though, you got it like that to get a suite at the Skirvin, Mad Dog? You don't need any money?"

"Razi, ya boy is good. I got a friend that's holding me down. You'll see her in the morning when we hook up to eat. I'll text you the suite number so you won't need to call me when you get up. You can bounce right on over. It's all good, so don't even think I'm on any shady shit. My mack game is still holding me down."

"You always was a suave one when it came to getting the females to do whatever you wanted them to."

"True. But you were the one who always got the prettier broads with your pretty ass."

"You know that's a violation. If I wasn't so damn tired, I'd make you body up, fool. Right now, I got to go. I didn't want Moms to know, but I killed that celibacy shit last night with this female I'm about to go meet now."

Laughing, Tracy said, "I knew damn well you couldn't be with no goofy shit like that for too damn long."

"Whatever. It's some serious stuff going down with this female I'm meeting, and I think I may be entering into something crazy."

With concern in his voice, Tracy asked, "Something crazy like what, Razi? Do you need me to roll with you to this meeting?"

Shaking his head, Razier said, "Nah, man, nothing like that. I'll tell you all about it in the morning because then, I'll have a better idea about what is what."

"Okay. You be safe, dog, and make sure you get at me. Here's my number." After Tracy gave him his cell number, he walked Razier outside to his truck. "You've been on the grind real serious like, Razi. That's what's up. You know me, dog. I'm not really with all that hard work. But I got your back, and I will pull my weight with this stuff."

Razier smiled and said, "I know you will, Mad Dog. Trust me, though; we're about to get bread for real."

Tracy smiled and said, "I hear you. I'll see you in the a.m., Razi."

"For sure," Razier said as he climbed into his truck and sped to his apartment so he could shower and get dressed for his important date with the sexy Olivia.

Razier made it to the Park House with five minutes to spare, so when he entered the restaurant and saw Olivia sitting at the bar where they decided to meet, he smiled and stepped her way. He gave her a peck on the cheek and said, "Good evening, Olivia. You're looking quite edible this evening."

"Comments like that will make me skip this dinner stuff and take you back to your place and let you devour me like you did last night, darling. Be nice so that we can enjoy our dinner, 'K?"

A couple sat a few stools down from where they were seated, who showed their disgust at Olivia's bold statement. Razier saw that their disdain didn't bother Olivia one bit, so he added to her bold and flirtatious banter with some of his own.

"I agree, babe. Honestly, though, I can't wait to take you back and devour you. I mean, eat you up *totally*."

Knowing that he was having fun at the nosy couple's expense, she smiled and said, "I sure hope you spank me like you did last night, daddy."

With a loud huff, the couple hopped off their stools and stormed away from the bar to the bartender's dismay. He shook his head at them and started laughing. "Okay, you two have to tip me really well for running off my customers."

Razier laughed and said, "No prob, my man. I got you." He turned toward Olivia with a serious look on his face and said, "We need to get our table so we can talk."

The seriousness in his tone told her that it was time to handle the business. Fun time was over. She nodded, stood from the bar, and waited for him to lead her to the front of the restaurant so they could be seated at the table reserved for them. After they sat and ordered their food, she sat back in her seat and asked Razier, "How was your day? Did you work hard?"

"I always work hard, Olivia. You know that. Stop with the stalling and come on with the real. What's going on? I've been doing this yard thing for over eighteen months now, and not one of my female clients have ever flirted with me—not a one. Then today, the day after I've had some incredible sex with you, I go to work, and Mrs. Willow, Mrs. Collins, Mrs. Salley, Mrs. Beckman, Mrs. Bin, Mrs. Simmons, and Mrs. Wilkins all decide that they want to flirt with me like crazy. Not only flirt but damn near tell me that we're about to get it poppin' real soon by using the same phrase you used in that note with the five rules you left at my place. What's up this, Olivia? I need you to serve me the real, ma, for real. Talk to me."

She smiled at him for a moment as she sipped some of her Chardonnay. She liked Razier, and she knew that all the ladies were attracted to him, which made everything easy for them. Their small, closed clique wanted more these days. They wanted to have some fun and feel desired again. Though they loved their husbands, they were tired of the "normal" routine they were caught in. They wanted more—*needed* more. They wanted a few stolen moments, and Razier's fine self was the perfect male specimen that could give them *exactly* what they needed—what they *craved*. The thing was, would he be able to handle servicing all of them? She smiled at that question because, in her mind, she had absolutely no doubt that he could handle all their needs. The way he performed with her, she knew he was stud enough to satisfy and take each of them to heights that they hadn't experienced in years. His sex game was definitely up to par. She could also tell that he was an honest young man, and that gave her pause. She had to be cautious. She didn't want to offend him with the offer that they came up with. So treading lightly was the best course of action until she figured out whether he would be willing to play their game by their rules. She set her wineglass on the table and continued to smile.

"The real is this, Razier . . . You're a handsome young man, and I enjoyed you so much last night that I told my friends about the pleasurable experience we shared. I'm speaking about the same women who recommended you to me. They all fancy you, and I might add, think that you're extremely hot."

"Hot? Me? All of them? Come on."

"I'm serious. *Very* serious," she said with a look on her face that told him she wasn't playing a game. "So serious, in fact, that I've been given their approval to ne-gotiate a . . . um, deal of sorts."

"A deal? What kind of deal?"

"Before I answer your question, I need you to answer some for me."

He shrugged and said, "I don't have a problem with that. Ask away."

"Are you attracted to any of the women you mentioned?"

He laughed. "Are you kidding me? In one way or another, I'm attracted to every one of them. *They're* the ones who're hot."

"Good. Very good. So it's safe to say that you wouldn't have a problem being with any of them sexually if that opportunity presented itself?"

"Very safe to say."

"Would you have a problem doing certain things to their liking?"

He had to think about that for a moment because there was no way he would do anything that would humiliate him or degrade him in any way. And he definitely wasn't into anything gay. He took a deep breath and answered her honestly.

"I'd be willing to do what it took to please them just as long as it doesn't involve any form of homosexuality. I'm not gay. I don't get down like that at all. Nor do I do any form of penetration other than me being the one who is doing the penetrating."

"I don't think any of the ladies will have an issue with that. They each like different things but nothing too extreme. I don't know their exact preferences, but I will make sure to inform them all that you will not indulge in anything that can be deemed as homosexual activity."

"Cool."

"Do you remember the rules I left you?"

"Yes, I do. I've been thinking about them all day long."

"Good because they're critical. I'm going to set this up for you, Razier, and you're going to not only be able to make love to these women but me as well whenever you like. Would you like that?"

"Hell yeah."

"Do you want to have us whenever you like, plus get paid for your services?"

"Stop playing. You mean to tell me that you're going to set it up so that they *pay* me to fuck them?"

She frowned at his use of foul language and said, "Crudely put, but yes. You will be paid to give us what we like to call a 'stolen moment.' A time away from our mundane lives. A time of pure pleasure given to us by a younger man. A man whose body is firm. A man who can please us like our men no longer can or care to. A man that will make us feel special as our husbands once did. A man that can give us a stolen moment we can relive whenever we want. Can *you* be that man, Razier? Can you handle *all* of us? We won't interfere with your work. On the contrary, we'll add to it. We'll help you in any way that we can. Do you think you can handle that?"

Again he answered with, "Hell yeah."

She smiled at his enthusiasm and said, "Great. Tell me the first rule I left on that note."

He sipped some water, sat back in his seat, then said, "Never fuck when I don't want to and remain in control at all times."

"Very good."

With a puzzled look on his face, he asked, "If you and the ladies are going to pay me for my . . . um, services, shouldn't you all be in control of things when we get down?"

She shook her head and said, "No. This is about you being the man. You being the one who controls everything. You will have to be creative. You will have to be exciting. You must be daring, or should I say, risqué. And most importantly, you must always remain in control. You are the one who will be running the show. You set the time, when, and where. You make the rules of engagement for every stolen moment. No matter what you're asked or told, you must always stand firm and remain in control of the situation that presents itself. If you show weakness in any way, it will end abruptly, and that will be that. Do you understand?"

"Yes."

"Good."

"I have a question."

"Yes?"

"How much money will I be paid?"

"The price will vary for every stolen moment. You will never receive anything less than what I gave you last night. Does that sound fair?"

Again he answered with, "Hell yeah."

She laughed at his excitement. *Yes, this is going to work out fine,* she thought. "You will be reimbursed with any money you spent while setting up the stolen moments, so don't worry about that. Now, tell me rule number two of the five rules I gave you."

He didn't have to think about that rule for a second. "Always use protection no matter what I'm told."

"Never—I mean never for any reason—break that rule, Razier. Protect yourself as well as all of us. Trust me, some of the ladies will try their best to persuade you to have sex with them unprotected. Never go for that—not for more money, more favors, or anything. Just don't do it. Do you understand me?"

"Yes."

She smiled and said, "Good. Now, I have one more question for you, and we can finish enjoying our meal before we go back to your place for the rest of the night."

"Yes?"

Her smile seemed to turn from pleasant to a more wicked one when she asked him, "When do you want to begin giving us our stolen moments?"

He stared at her for a few seconds, still trying to comprehend all of what she told him, then smiled. "Please inform the ladies that I will accept this honor and will do my absolute best to make sure every stolen moment they receive will be pleasurable and memorable—guaranteed. They have my number as I have theirs, and I will set up some discreet times to let them know when I'm ready to give them their stolen moments."

Olivia now smiled shyly and said, "Oh yeah, daddy, you got that take-charge tone that has made me wet this very instant. You're going to do us all just right."

With a proud smile on his face, he simply said, "Yes, I am."

Chapter Six

Olivia had been so excited by Razier's acceptance to service her and the other ladies that as soon as they made it to his place, she practically ripped off his clothes and began to ravish his body. The sex was animalistic-like . . . rough, no passion whatsoever, and she loved every heart-racing minute of it. By the time she came for the third time, Razier was so tired he crawled away from her. When he made it to the bathroom, he stared at himself in the mirror and wondered if he would be able to take what the women who wanted the stolen moments had to give him. He smiled and shook his head. *What a hell of a worry to have,* he thought as he got into the shower and let the hot water soothe his weary body. The combination of work during the day with the exertion from the crazy sex he'd just finished having with Olivia had just about done him in. All he wanted to do was finish his shower, climb in bed, and sleep soundly.

Luckily, when he came out of the bathroom, Olivia was passed out on the floor at the foot of the bed where he had left her. He smiled as he went to her, scooped her up in his arms, and gently laid her onto his bed. He then slipped on a pair of boxer briefs and a wife beater and joined her and quickly fell into a deep sleep . . . exactly what he desperately needed.

When Razier woke up the next morning, the first thing he did was turn toward the pillow on his left because he was hoping to see Olivia gone and another envelope would be waiting for him. He smiled when he saw the envelope. This was her MO, and he didn't have a problem with it one bit, he thought as he grabbed the envelope and opened it. Inside was exactly what he hoped for . . . another thousand dollars. Yes! The note she left him this time was brief.

> *Call the ladies, all of them, and talk to them. Get to know them. That way, you'll figure out how to make sure our stolen moments with you will be more memorable. Remember, you're the boss.*
> *Olivia*

He let his head rest on his pillow as he let the words he just finished reading sink in. *Damn, this is really about to go down. If this goes the way it seems it will, I'll be able to get that food truck, my condo, and that brand-new foreign sooner than I ever imagined. Jeez, is this a dream, or is this the beginning of a damn nightmare?* he wondered as he hopped out of bed and went into the bathroom to brush his teeth. Then he dressed and headed to the Skirvin. It was a must that he broke everything down to Tracy because there was no way he would handle this business with his clients without his best friend's advice. The Mad Dog was built for this type of craziness. He wasn't, he thought, as he sped toward downtown.

He entered the hotel that was most known for housing the visiting NBA teams who came to play the OKC Thunder. He pulled out his phone and gave Tracy a call to let him know he was at the hotel.

"What up, Mad Dog? You up?"

Tracy smiled as he stared at Lavonda between his legs giving his early morning hard-on one of the best blow jobs he ever had in his life. She may not be all that easy on the eyes, but her head game was so over the top, who cared what she looked like? "Yeah, Razi, I'm up. I mean that in more ways than one. Where you at?"

"I'm downstairs in the lobby. What's your room number?"

"I'm on the sixth floor, suite 659."

"On my way up now. Go on and order up some grub 'cause I'm hungry as I don't know what, and, man, we got some serious stuff to talk about."

Tracy felt the first tingles in his groin indicating he was about to come, so he said, "Will do," and quickly pressed the end button on his phone and grabbed the back of Lavonda's head, holding her firmly in place while she continued to suck him off. He came like gangbusters, and like the champ she is, Lavonda swallowed every single drop of his seed.

"Damn, baby, is it going to be like that every time you suck the dick?"

Licking her big lips, she smiled and said, "Yep. I love how you taste, baby, and every chance I get, I'm swallowing all that good old nut. I love it more when you're deep inside of me, baby. It feels so right. I know your friend is on his way up, but can you give me a quickie, babe?"

He shook his head and was about to say no but stopped when he watched as she grabbed a condom off the nightstand, unwrapped it, and put it inside of her mouth. She then proceeded to suck his dick again, this time sucking him hard while applying the condom at the same time.

"Damn, baby, you got plenty of tricks up your sleeve, I see."

Once he was nice and hard, and the condom was secured firmly, she removed her mouth from him and smiled proudly. "You ain't seen nothing yet, babe. There's plenty more I got to show you that I'm sure you're going to love. But right now, lie there and enjoy this ride I'm about to take you on," she said as she climbed on top of him and guided his erection inside of her. She turned so her back was to him and was kneeling forward with her hands on the side of the bed while bouncing up and down on his dick at a pace that she knew would get him off much faster than normal. She was enjoying how deep his dick was hitting her insides and moaned loudly as she continued to bounce on it.

Tracy was mesmerized as he watched as his dick slid in and out of Lavonda's pretty pink pussy. He seemed to get harder when he heard her yell that she was coming. He watched as his dick went in and out of her slowly and saw her milky cream coat the condom as her juices poured out of her. That was so fucking hot that it triggered his orgasm, and he exploded and filled the condom as he reached and pulled her down hard on his dick and held her there until he finished coming. Meanwhile, Razi was knocking on the door, and it took Tracy two minutes before he had the focus needed to speak.

"Hold up for a minute, Razi." He watched Lavonda climb off him and stood at the end of the bed. She smiled as she dipped two fingers inside of her pussy, put the same two fingers inside of her mouth, and sucked her cum from each of them. He moaned. She smiled and went into the bathroom to shower.

He shook his head and said, "Damn, that broad is a freaky one. Love it." He was laughing as he got off the bed and went to open the door for Razier.

"What took you so long, clown?" Razier said as he entered the suite. When he saw Tracy in his boxers, sweating profusely, his question was answered, and he started laughing. "Oh snap, you getting it in, son? My bad. You should have told me. I would have given you some more time with your breezy."

"Man, that's all we been doing all night. After I came back from seeing Moms and Pops, we went to eat, came back here, and been fucking off and on all damn night. This girl is a freaky one who never gets tired."

"After four years in the Zoe, you should be loving, so what you complaining for?"

"It's not what you think, Razi. I mean, when you down, all you think about is pussy, pussy, and more pussy. But once you touch and get some, it's like, OK, done that. You get some more, and you good. It's like all those thoughts of pussy, pussy, pussy fades. It's really overrated, for real. Don't get me wrong, though. I loves me the pussy, but this broad is a beast. Shit, I don't think I can handle her, and you know that's really rare for the Mad Dog." He shrugged his slim shoulders and said, "It is what it is, though." He stared at the bathroom door in the other room to make sure it was closed, then said, "This shit with her is more business than anything else, Razi. You'll peep it when you see her."

With a curious expression, Razier asked, "What? She a duck or something? What you mean by 'business'? Don't tell me you're right out of the damn Zoe getting ready to get back on some other shit, Mad Dog."

"You know me, and you already know I refuse to live without having the best of everything. No matter how, I gotta trust that. What I got lined up is basically foolproof with a real low-risk factor for me to get into some shit. I mean, so low, you won't believe it."

"Is that right?"

"Yep."

"Okay, let's chop it up, eat, and see what this master plan you got going on is working with. When you done, I'll put you up on my moves and what I got going on for us. Hopefully, together, we can make things work out good all the way around."

"You know that's how it has to be . . . Me and you till the wheels fall off, Razi."

Razier smiled and said, "That's right."

Tracy stepped back into the bedroom and told Lavonda through the door since he no longer heard the shower running that he wanted her to order them some breakfast from room service. "I need you to stay in the room while I chop it up with Razi."

"'K," she said from the bathroom.

Tracy returned to the living room and sat down on the couch next to Razier and told him all about Lavonda Price, the prison guard he cracked while doing his time in Boley State Prison. He started from the beginning on how she flirted with him in conversations until he could get her in a position to cop a few feels here and there. He was even lucky enough to get a hand job a few times. Once that happened, he knew he had her locked in. So his time was relatively easy because she would look out any way she could. When she brought him a cell phone so that they would be able to have phone sex while doing Facetime, he devised the plan that would get them some serious money really quick. He broke it down to her and explained how he would start getting at the real convicts inside the prison and get things right so when he touched, she would be able to get at them and make it happen. Cell phones inside of prisons were a gold mine. All you needed was a CO willing to get down, and the rest was a wrap. Tracy finished with a smile on his face by saying, "And you're about to meet my CO who's willing to do whatever I tell her to."

"I have to give it to you, Mad Dog, this is one of your smarter schemes. I'll give you credit for that. I thought it would be some dope-boy scheme or something wilder. This, though, seems real low risk, at least for you, that is. Your CO gets knocked, and she wouldn't even be able to tell on you to get you twisted."

Tracy smiled and said, "Exactly. It's even better than you think, Razi. I'm going to make it so she gets the units raided every ninety days so the dudes will have to get rid of their phones. Then a week or so later, when the heat seems to have cooled off, here comes CO Lavonda getting them more phones for the low. The low in prison is the fucking roof out here in the real world. Most COs who get down charge like a hundred bucks for the cheap li'l fifteen to twenty buck prepaid flip phones. That's a neat twist in itself. You still make like eighty bucks for each of those.

"The smartphones get the money. Niggas be wanting to be on the internet, you know, Facebook, Twitter, and all that shit. The COs are getting them joints off for like two Gs, some a li'l less. I'm going to have Lavonda drop them for 1,500 bucks a smartphone. She has a list of fifty solid convicts who would rather get the death penalty than snitch. These are the heavy hitters inside that's getting that fucking money, so there won't ever be a problem with that part of the business. She gets the money sent to a PO Box here in the city. When I get the ends, I get the phones and take them to her in Boley. Spend the night serving her the dick, maybe do a movie and a dinner, then I'm out. She takes the phones inside, and we wait ninety days. After that, we do it all over again. We not doing the flip phone shit. It's a smartphone or nothing, so she gets the bread like we want it. Now do the math. Fifty convicts get smartphones for 1,500 apiece."

Razier quickly did the calculations in his head and whistled. "Wow, that's seventy-five racks."

"Exactly. Seventy-five racks every ninety days, Razi."

Razier did the math again, and again, whistled. "That's 300 racks a year."

"Yep. We'll be able to do everything you want to do businesswise. So you won't have to be breaking your back out there like you been doing since your ass got kicked out of the navy," Tracy said and laughed.

"Not funny, Mad Dog; not funny at all."

"Oh no, you're wrong there, buddy. That shit is hilarious. It's so fucking funny that every time I think about that shit, I tear up. Only Razier Coleman could find a way to get caught fucking his superior officer. Not only did you get caught balls deep in the broad, you got knocked by the damn captain of the ship. That right there, dog, is hilarious, believe that."

"Fuck you."

Before Tracy could respond, someone knocked on the door. He got up and let the waiter from room service bring in their food. After he tipped the waiter and closed the door, he called out for Lavonda to come and join them so they could all eat. When Lavonda went into the living room, Tracy made the introductions.

"Lavonda, this is Razier. I call him Razi. He's the only man in this wicked world I consider my friend, my very best friend."

Lavonda shook Razier's hand and said, "It's a pleasure to meet you, Razier, or should I call you Razi?"

"Whatever you prefer to call me is fine."

"'K. I've heard a lot about you. Tracy speaks highly of you all the time."

"He should. I'm the only man in this world who can deal with him and all his foolishness. Seriously, it's nice to meet you too. I hope you'll be able to keep the Mad Dog calm. Lord knows he's more than a handful."

"I know that's the truth. I'll do my best, though."

"Cool."

"All right. You two got that out of the way, so now, let's get our grub on," Tracy said and proceeded to open up the lids and see what Lavonda ordered for them. He smiled as he scooped some eggs onto his plate and prepared the rest of his food. "Looks like we're going to have to stay here more often, baby. This is a cool spot."

"I don't care where we stay, babe. As long as we're together, I'm good," she said as she bit into a sausage link while staring directly at Tracy.

Razier watched the interaction between the couple and smiled. Lavonda was definitely not the type of female Tracy was known to rock with, but she wasn't as bad as he thought she would be. She was an OK-looking, brown-skinned sister. From what he could tell, she was thick as Free was back in the day before she got fat. That joke made him smile as he made himself a plate. When they finished eating, Lavonda excused herself so Tracy and Razier could finish talking.

"Okay, you now know what the business is on my side of things, so what's this master plan you got for us on the legal business tip?" asked Tracy as he sat back on the couch, relaxed and full from the big breakfast they had just consumed.

Razier was just as full as Tracy, but he became animated as he began to tell him of his plans for the pool service and how he would be able to get the money he needed to buy the food truck so he could join the moneymakers with the food trucks out there on Harvey and Eighth Street. When he finished, he could see that Tracy wasn't impressed with anything he had just told him.

"You looking like you not feeling anything I've just said, Mad Dog. What's up?"

"I'm feeling you. I know that's how you rock, Razi, and I ain't mad at you at all. We need that legal move right there because it will be easy to clean up the ends from the cell phone moves. It's just . . . Damn, I don't know. You working yourself like that makes me feel funny, is all. I mean, I don't have a problem getting out there with you doing the yards or pool thing. Fuck, I'll even rock with

you in the food truck shit. Money is money. But where
the fun at? Where's the traveling and living life at in
these grand plans of yours? We can't be all about work
and no play, Razi. Life too damn short for that shit. I've
wasted four in the Zoe, and I got no more time to waste."

"We're going to do all that *and* some, Mad Dog. We got
to get the money right, and things will come from there.
When we get the yard and pool service rolling the way I
want it, everything will come into play. Trust me. There's
something I haven't told you, though, and I need your
attention and your boss game mack status on full alert
for this because what I'm about to hit you with will most
likely be the game changer for both of our plans."

"Game changer?"

"Like E-40 says, 'Yep.'"

"Speak then, fool. I need to hear this shit."

Razier spoke, and when he finished, Tracy Mad Dog
Briggs was so floored with what he had just heard that all
he could think to say was, "Damn."

Chapter Seven

Razier left his best friend in a state of shock. The look on Tracy's face was priceless. Razier was laughing as he got inside of his truck. Before he could start the engine, it started raining so hard, and that brought a smile to his face as he sat back in his seat and pulled out his cell. He pulled up the weather report and saw that it was an 80 percent chance of thunderstorms. He sighed with relief—a day off work. *God is good,* he thought. Usually, he checked the weather report for the next day on his phone before he went to bed, but last night, his mind hadn't been on any damn weather. It was focused only on pleasing the sexy Olivia, the woman who was about to put some serious money in his pockets. Not in the mood to drive back to his place, Razier climbed out of his truck and went back inside the hotel and called Tracy as he stepped into the elevator.

"It's raining cats and dogs out there, Mad Dog. I'm on my way back to your suite. Cool?"

"You already know it's cool. Plus, we need to chop it up some more 'cause I'm still stuck on this shit you told me."

"All right. I'm on your floor now. Let me in," Razier said as he stepped toward the suite to be met by Tracy with the door opened. "I can't believe my luck, man. I needed this day off, for real."

"You've been grinding like this for almost two years now. What's wrong? It's finally getting to your ass? Thought the navy whipped you into fighting shape."

"It's not that. I'm in the best shape of my life, clown. Last night, I was with one of the ladies I told you about, and, man, when I tell you this old jazzy broad is a tiger, let me tell you . . . she's a *freaking* tiger. She worked me out real swell, and I was so deep in it that I forgot to check the weather report before falling asleep, and that's something I never forget to do."

"I hear you. So, you telling me you've already started fucking those old birds and getting bread for it?"

"Kinda sorta."

Tracy stared at his friend like he was stupid and said, "If you don't get to talking, you gon' have to body up, fool. Spit it out."

"Whatever. Olivia is the one who approached me about the stolen moment thing. Before she got at me with it, she came on to me real strong, and we got our freak on. The morning after, she left me a note with some rules that she told me I would have to follow, along with a rack."

"Wait. You fucked this old bird, and she gave you a thousand bucks the next morning?"

"Yep. It gets better because now, the women who are my clients on Fridays all want to get at me."

"How many old birds are there?"

"Seven . . . no, eight counting Olivia."

"So, you got eight old broads willing to pay you to fuck them?"

"Yes and no."

Tracy gave him the "the stupid look" again and frowned.

"Olivia told me that there might be times when I don't have to fuck them. Some may want to be consoled, held, or have some good conversation, so I must always be prepared to be a good listener for them."

"I can dig that. How much will you get for services rendered?"

Razier shrugged and said, "I don't know for certain, but I do know it won't be anything less than a rack."

"*What?* You trying to tell me that no matter what you do with these old birds, the minimum you gon' get is a rack?"

In his best imitation of E-40, he said, "Yep."

Tracy started laughing. "You are still one lucky sum-bitch. I can't believe this crazy-ass shit."

"Neither can I. The more I think about this stuff, I feel as if this may be the blessing I need to get ahead of the game. Like I said, this could be the game changer, Mad Dog."

"Could be? Are you fucking *kidding* me? This is the easiest come-up any man in his right mind could ever dream of. All you gotta do is please some old birds with the dick or good conversation and get paid for it. Nigga, do you know you're about to be bringing in some serious bread?"

"Yeah, I know. What has me puzzled is, why me, though? What made them even think I'd be with that type of stuff?"

Shaking his head, Tracy said, "Why *not* you? You know damn well the ladies have always swooned over your ass. That's why you've always had the tender dick-itis. It's only right you've stumbled into this shit. You're perfect for this move. I mean, man, look at it. That's a minimal of eight racks every time you get with all those old birds. More if they are satisfied with your servicing, and that, my man, is one thing we're going to make damn sure you are ready to do at *all* times."

"What you mean by that, fool? I'm not taking any drugs to stay hard. I can handle my own in that department."

"No, you won't. You will in the beginning, but sooner or later, your piece will conk out on you. I got something for you that this old head put me up on when I was in the Zoe.

It's called Horny Goat Weed. It's not a drug. It's a natural aphrodisiac that you can buy at any GNC store. Trust me. You need to get some of that shit in your system now, so when it comes time for you to put this demo down with these old birds, you'll be ready for any and every freaky moment they want."

"It's called a 'stolen moment.'"

"Whatever. So, when does this shit with the others start?"

Before Razier could answer, his phone started ringing. He checked the caller ID and saw that it was Olivia. He smiled. "I don't know when, but I have an idea I'm about to find out. Hold up a sec. This is Olivia now," Razier said as he answered his phone. "Hello, Olivia. How you this morning?"

"I'm great, Razier. Really great. I have some good news for you. Looks like the ladies are excited about sharing stolen moments with you, and they're eagerly waiting to get started."

"Okay, I'm with that. How you want to kick this off?"

There was a brief pause, then Olivia said, "No, Razier, it's not about how *we* want to get this started. It's about how *you* want to run things. Remember, *you're* in total control. You have the ladies' telephone numbers. You need to set up everything. The ball is in your court, Razier. One bit of advice, though. Make sure you're creative. Trust, you don't want to bore us, baby."

"I'm feeling that, but how will I know what you all are into? You got me flying blind here, Olivia. Not feeling that."

"You may be right. I guess we're so anxious to get our hands on you collectively that we didn't give that any thought. We did think of everything else, though. The finances for the stolen moments that we handle. Look under your tray of colognes on your dresser. You'll see another white envelope. Inside is a Visa Debit Card with $5,000 on it. That will cover your stolen moment expenses. When you go through that, we'll add more funds to your card. You will not spend a dime of your money on this venture."

"That's cool. Okay, I got this, Olivia. Sit tight. You'll be hearing from me in a few minutes. I need to put some things together really quick. Matter of fact, I want you to get the ladies and let them know they will be receiving a call from me within the hour, and I need them to be able to speak freely. So if their husbands are around, they need to go somewhere so they can answer some questions I need answered."

"I'm all over it, baby. Can you call me first?"

"No. I want you off balance, just like the rest of them. Make the calls," Razier said in a stern voice that shocked not only himself but also Olivia and Tracy as well.

"Damn, Razi, what got into you? You sounded like one of those old-school pimps that used to rock it hard in the city back in the day. Ronnie Slim and Keith Prince would be proud of your ass."

Razier smiled at Tracy and said, "As I was listening to Olivia tell me how the ladies want me to take control of this thing, I figured I'd better toughen up really quick before I blow this opportunity. Trust me, Mad Dog, there's no way I'm blowing this move."

"That's what I'm talking about. How you gon' play it, though?"

Razier stood, went over to the desk, grabbed the complimentary stationary pen and pad, then came back and sat down next to Tracy. "I'm about to call each of the ladies and conduct an interview of sorts. Olivia told me the ladies expect me to come up with the ideas for the stolen moments, so for me to come up with the right stuff, I'm

going to ask each of them what they like, dislike, and figure out how to roll from there."

Rubbing his hands together anxiously, Tracy said,
"You're fucking right on the money with that there move,
Razi. Let me help you come up with some questions for
those freaky old birds."

Lavonda came into the doorway of the bedroom before
Razier could answer Tracy and said, "Since it's raining
out, are we going to stay in all day, babe? You know we
still need to go get you some more clothes and stuff."

"Yeah, I know. Right now, me and Razi is taking care
of some serious business, though. When we done, we can
go hit up the mall and get my gear right."

"'K. Is there anything I can help you guys with?"

"Nah, baby, we got this here."

"Wait. Yes, come join us, Lavonda. Your input may be
what we need," Razier said with a smile on his face. Once
Lavonda was seated next to Tracy on the couch, Razier
said, "This is what I need to come up with. I need to make
a questionnaire of sorts for eight different women. This
questionnaire is for the sole purpose of getting to know
what the ladies are into. I don't want it to be too long, so
let's say, ten questions. Tracy, since your horny ass is
so excited, you go first."

Tracy gave a wicked smile and said, "Do you like oral
sex?"

Razier wrote down the question, then looked at
Lavonda and said, "Your turn."

"What type of music do you like to listen to?"

Razier liked that one as he added her question and
then said aloud, "Are you open to be submissive, or do
you prefer to be dominate?"

"Ooh, that's a good one, Razier," said Lavonda.

"My turn again," said Tracy. "What's your favorite
sexual position?"

Shaking his head and laughing, Razier said, "You are having too much fun right now, aren't ya?"

"You damn right. Now, add that one to the list, fool."

Razier glanced at Lavonda, indicating it was her turn, and she said, "Are you into role play?"

Rubbing her thick thighs, Tracy said, "I like that, baby. Makes me think we need to get our role play on later."

"Anything for you, babe, but come on, let's be serious here while we're helping Razier. This is kinda neat."

"That was a good one, Lavonda. It made me think of this next question that I feel will be important," Razier said as he wrote down his question. "Have you ever been with another woman sexually?"

"Wow, that's hot!" Lavonda giggled and fanned herself.

Tracy stared at her and smiled. "Please tell me you've been with a female before, baby. Please, tell me that."

"You keep being good to me, and you'll see."

Tracy groaned.

Razier laughed and shook his head. "Your turn again, Mad Dog."

"Are you open to having sex outside in the open or around others?"

"Good one. Now, Lavonda, I need something off the sex track, something more feminine or romantic. You know, girly like stuff."

She nodded as she thought for a moment, then said, "Flowers . . . What kind of flowers do you like? We as females are suckers for some roses, but we all have different tastes."

Razier nodded and said, "That's exactly why I asked you to join us," he said as he wrote down her excellent question. When he finished, he said his next question aloud. "Name the wildest thing that you would want to try sexually."

"Damn, you stole my last question, clown," laughed Tracy.

"Well, it's your turn, so make it a good one."

Tracy stared at his best friend for a moment and smiled. "Would you be open for a threesome with me, you, and another woman, or me, you, and another man?"

"Yeah, that there is a good one, Mad Dog, with your nasty ass," Razier said as he wrote the last question down.

"Okay, so when do you think you're going to be ready to ask the old birds these questions? I'm dying to know their answers."

Razier stared at Tracy and his girlfriend and said, "Me too. I told Olivia to get at them and let them know I'll be calling within an hour, so it's time to get at them and see what they have to say."

Tracy smiled, rubbed his hands together again, and said, "Make it happen, Razi."

Lavonda laughed, shook her head, and said, "I done went and fell for a damn freak, for real."

"You better say it," Tracy said, and they started laughing.

Chapter Eight

Razier grabbed his phone and began scrolling through his contacts to pull up the first number of his clients so he could start his interviews. He was somewhat nervous but excited all the same. Just as he was about to press the send button to make the first call, Lavonda said, "Wait. I think we should add some more questions, Razier."

"Why?" Razier and Tracy asked in unison.

"Trust me here, fellas. It's a woman thing. Women are more into simple things, and so far, we mostly focused on sex stuff. I understand that this is basically what it's all about, but we should make it more intimate. You know, like you're not only trying to find out their fetishes per se but more about getting to know them as women. Trust me, getting to know them this way will make every encounter more personal. It will take you a long way with each of them, and in the long run, they will appreciate that touch."

"Makes sense. What do you have in mind, Lavonda?" asked Razier.

She shrugged and said, "I think you need like five or six more questions."

"Okay, baby, since you're the only woman in this here suite, you give us the five or six more questions we need to add," said Tracy. Razier nodded in agreement.

Lavonda sat there for a moment in thought, then said, "Let's do it like this . . . What's their favorite perfume? What cologne do they like their men to wear? What are their favorite foods? What do they prefer to drink if they drink alcohol? What's the name of their favorite movie? Who's their favorite actor or actress? I think this would be the best way to start the questionnaire. It will serve to relax the ladies and make them comfier. After that, you can ease into the other questions and take it from there."

Razier smiled. "Mad Dog, you definitely found yourself a winner here. You came up with a brilliant idea, Lavonda. Let's roll with it."

Lavonda smiled proudly and said, "This is going to be really interesting."

"You better say it. Now, can we please get this damn ball rolling here? I'm ready to see how this will go down," said Tracy.

Razier smiled as he picked up his phone again and hit the send button, calling Mrs. Willow. When she answered the phone, Razier wasted no time with a greeting. Instead, he went right into the spiel he decided to use for the interviews.

"It's time for the process of our stolen moments to begin, Mrs. Willow. To make our stolen moments as memorable as possible, I'm going to need some personal information from you, so I came up with some questions I need you to answer for me. Since I'm going to be writing while I ask these questions, I'm going to have you on speaker, so I can be comfortable while taking down your answers. I assure you that everything you reveal will be held in the strictest of confidence and will not be repeated to anyone—ever."

"Understood," Mrs. Willow said, sounding somewhat nervous.

Sensing her discomfort, Razier said in a soothing tone, "Calm down, mami. It's all good. I got you." He heard her sigh, and he smiled.

"Okay, Razier."

"Tell me, what's your favorite perfume?"

"DKNY."

"What about colognes for men? What scent do you like best to have a man wear?"

"Eternity."

"What's your favorite food to eat?"

"I love seafood."

Feeling as if she were relaxing some, Razier continued. "What is your favorite drink, alcoholic or not?"

"Umm, I don't drink much, but when I do, I like brandy. E&J preferably."

"Tell me, what's your favorite movie?"

Mrs. Willow smiled into the receiver she held in her now-sweaty palms and said, *Pretty Woman.*"

"Your favorite actor or actress?"

"Denzel Washington and Julia Roberts."

"That's cool. Not so bad, huh?"

"If you say so. I'm sitting here feeling like a nervous teenager, Razier."

"It's all good, mami. Trust me. You ready to continue?"

"Yes."

"Let's turn it up a little now. Do you enjoy oral sex, both receiving and giving?"

"Yes. To both."

"Mmm . . . What kind of music do you like to listen to?"

"Jazz or some good R&B from the late sixties or early seventies."

"Are you open to being submissive, or do you prefer to be the dominate one sexually?"

"Submissive," she answered shyly . . . "totally."

"What's your favorite sexual position?"

"I love it from the back, Razier."

"Are you open to role-play?"

"Yes."

"Have you ever been with another woman sexually?"

"No."

"Are you open to having sex outside or around others?"

"I've never done anything like that, but, yes, I'm open to trying that."

"What kind of flowers do you like?"

"Yellow roses."

"Name the wildest thing you would like to try sexually."

"I would love to make love to you outside in the rain."

"Mmm, okay. Last question. Would you be open to a threesome with either two men, including me, or two women, including you?"

"I've never been interested in women, so I would say, yes, I would be open to trying you and another man."

Tracy pumped his fist and mouthed the word, *Wow!* Lavonda shook her head and frowned at him.

Razier ignored them and said, "Okay, Mrs. Willow, that's all I need. Once I've finished interviewing the others, I'll be in contact with you because you, mami, are the first in line for the beginning of the stolen moments."

"Oh my God, I am so damn horny for you, Razier. This has been such a turn-on for me. I can't wait to be able to spend time with you."

"Neither can I, Mrs. Willow."

"Please call me Louise."

"Louise, it is. I'll be in touch soon. Stay ready, mami."

"I will, Razier. Believe me, I will. Bye," she said and hung up the phone.

When Razier set the phone down, he smiled and said, "One down and seven more to go."

"Man, you got to make sure you handle those broads the right way. They expect to be handled by a man—a real man. This shit is off the fuck meter, Razi, for real, for real."

"You need to calm down, babe. You act like you're the one who's going to be spending time with them,"

Lavonda said with a tad too much attitude in her tone for Tracy.

"You need to go on in the room if you have a problem with anything I'm saying. Don't overstep your bounds, Lavonda," Tracy said in a stern voice.

"You two need to chill. Let's get back to the business," Razier said as he grabbed the phone and made the next call. When Mrs. Beckman answered, Razier went right into his spiel and began his questions. "Give me the name of your favorite perfume."

"CK."

"What cologne do you like on men?"

"Polo Black."

"Favorite foods?"

"Soul food."

"Tell me your favorite drinks, alcoholic or not."

"I don't drink liquor. I love freshly squeezed juices."

"Favorite movie?"

"*The Godfather Saga.*"

"Who's your favorite actor and actress?"

"Al Pacino and Halle Berry."

"Are you very oral sexually?"

"Yes, and I cannot wait to lick all over your luscious body."

"Mmm . . . What type of music do you like?"

"Gospel. I can do some R. Kelly when it's time for soul *12 Play.*"

"Like that. Are you open to being totally submissive, or do you prefer to be dominant?"

"I'm a take-charge kind of woman, but I want to be the one who's dominated by you, Razier."

"What's your favorite sexual position?"

"Every way imaginable, honey."

"Are you open to role-play?"

"I'm open to whatever you want to do."

"Have you ever been with another woman sexually?"

"Yes."

"Would you be willing to have sex around others or, say, outside?"

"Yes."

"What kind of flowers do you like?"

"Daisies."

"Name the wildest thing you would like to do sexually."

"I want you to bend me over and spank me real hard, rub my body down with some warm, scented oils, then fuck me long and hard in every position you can think of."

"Last question. Would you be up to a threesome with another man and me, or with another woman and me?"

"Both. I'm with it all, honey. Now, can you answer a question for me?"

"Sure, ask away, Mrs. Beckman."

"Erica, honey, call me Erica. We're way beyond personal with each other now, so there's no need for the Mrs. Beckman crap."

"That part. Your question?"

"When are we going to get this party started? I'm so damn ready for your young, fine self that it don't make no sense how wet you got me."

"That's a good thing, yes?"

"You damn right, yes, so when?"

In a stern tone, Razier said, "When I say so, Erica. I'll be in contact with you after I've finished my interviews with the other ladies. Stay ready, and you won't have to get ready. Feel me?"

Feeling as if she'd been scolded and loving every minute of it, she answered sheepishly, "Yes, Razier."

"Good," was his reply as he abruptly ended the call.

"Now *that's* what I'm talking about, Razi. You checked her bold ass and put her in her place. I can tell she's going to be hell on wheels for you, buddy boy. I got to hurry up and get you started on some of that Horny Goat Weed," laughed Tracy.

"Whatever. This is some crazy stuff, but the more I think about it, the more I'm like, damn, these women are really about to get at me and pay me for this wicked stuff."

"You better believe it. So come on, clown, and get your Jay-Z on and get on to the next one."

"You're stupid, but right . . . on to the next one," Razier said as he grabbed his phone and made the next call. Forty-five minutes later, he completed his questionnaire with all eight ladies. And to say he was shocked at what he'd learned about them would have been an understatement. He was so turned on that he felt as if he needed to go in the restroom and jack his dick to relieve the pressure he was feeling from speaking to the ladies. From the way Lavonda and Tracy were eating each other alive with their eyes, he could tell they were thinking the same thing he was, so he stood and said, "All right, you two, I'm about to go to the pad and lay it down so I can let all this information marinate. I got to come up with something really good for Mrs. Willow to kick this off right."

"Do you have anything specific in mind?" asked Lavonda.

He smiled at his best friend's girlfriend and said, "Yes, I do, Lavonda."

"Well, give it up. Come on, tell me."

His smile brightened when he told her, "I'm going to give her a stolen moment she will never forget."

Tracy laughed aloud, and Lavonda frowned, frustrated that Razier didn't give her any details of what he had planned for Mrs. Willow.

Chapter Nine

Razier left the hotel, but instead of going home to take a nap like he told Tracy and Lavonda, he decided to go home and get the Visa Debit Card Olivia left him so he could start putting the money on the card to use. After getting the card, he went to Penn Square Mall and searched for the things he needed. He pulled out the stationary he used from the Skirvin and went over his notes to see what he needed to purchase. The music wouldn't be a problem. He would be able to download everything he needed thanks to TIDAL and iHeartRadio, so the first stop was to Victoria's Secret for some sexy lingerie for each of the ladies. He was glad Lavonda recommended that before he left, so he called the ladies back and got their sizes.

As he browsed through the different skimpy outfits in the store, he was getting more and more excited about this stolen moment stuff. Not only was he about to get his freak on with some pretty decent-looking older women, but he was also about to get paid while doing so. Wow. He was smiling as he checked his notes and began picking out the different types of lingerie for the ladies.

Twenty-five minutes later, he left Victoria's Secret with his purchases. He bought sixteen sexy outfits, two for each lady. Some short and skimpy, some sheer and ladylike, but all super sexy as hell. He could damn near see the women in the outfits he chose, and that mental visualization led to him becoming extremely horny.

After leaving the mall, his next stop was the liquor store, where he bought the ladies' drinks of choice. He reminded himself that he would have to remember to get freshly squeezed juices for Mrs. Beckman. Once acquiring the ladies' preference of liquor, he went home and pulled out his laptop, and began downloading the music the ladies said they liked.

When that was complete, he hit Netflix and began browsing through the many movies on their selection and picked the movies the ladies liked. He didn't have a clue how that would play out, but he wanted to make sure he touched every base and didn't miss a thing on his list.

After he finished, he took a long, hot shower and decided, why not get started tonight with the first stolen moment? He didn't have to work because Sunday was the one day of the week that he had off. With his mind made up, he checked the time and saw it was a little after five p.m. He hoped that Mrs. Willow didn't have any plans because he wanted to start with her first.

He slapped himself on the forehead when he realized he forgot to get the perfumes and colognes the ladies told him they liked. He threw on some sweats, grabbed his keys and phone, and hurried out of the apartment, headed back to the mall. When he arrived back at Penn Square Mall, he went to the Dillard's department store and sought out the perfumes the ladies liked. DKNY for Mrs. Willow, CK for Mrs. Beckman, Fendi for Mrs. Bin, D&G for Olivia, Angel for Mrs. Salley, Obsession for Mrs. Simmons, Chanel No. 5 for Mrs. Wilkins, and Paris for Mrs. Collins.

After that, he went to the men's cologne section and bought himself eight bottles of cologne that the ladies said they liked. He left the mall and hurried home. It was now after six p.m., so he decided to make the call to Mrs. Willow. He was ready for her, and he wasn't taking no for an answer. They wanted him to take charge, and that's *precisely* what he intended on doing.

He took a deep breath as he sat down on his sofa and dialed her number. When Mrs. Willow answered the phone, he said, "Hello, Louise, it's time for us to have our first stolen moment. I know you're ready for me, right?"

She inhaled deeply and whispered, "Yes, yes, I am Razier."

Yes! "Good. Very good. I want you to do exactly as I tell you to, am I understood?"

"Yes."

"In twenty-five minutes, I want you to leave your home and come to my place. Do not waste time getting dolled up for me. Come as you are now. We will take care of all of that when you get here."

"Okay."

"Have you had dinner yet?"

"No."

"Good." He told her the address to his apartment and said, "Remember what I said. Do not leave your place until twenty-five minutes after we hang up."

"Okay."

"If time will be a problem, let me know now so I can make the necessary adjustments to my plans for you."

"Time won't be a factor. My husband is gone to the casino with business associates. I can stay out as late as I want. Odds are, he won't be home until the morning anyway," she said in a disgusted tone.

"Great. That gives us all the time we need for a *very* special evening. See you when you get here, Louise." He ended the call and dialed Red Lobster restaurant and ordered a seafood platter full of shrimp, lobster tails, crab legs, and an assortment of different seafood dishes. They told him that his order would be ready for pick up in twenty minutes. *Perfect,* he thought as he got up and went into his bedroom and began straightening up the place. He put clean sheets on the bed, quickly vacuumed, and finished tidying the bedroom.

Razier lit some sweet-smelling incense, then went into the living room and made sure everything was straight in there. He placed candles strategically around the living room to give off the proper ambiance for a romantic setting. He checked the time and saw that he was on schedule. He grabbed his keys, went to the Red Lobster located on Northwest Expressway, and picked up his order. By the time he made it back home, he had just enough time to set up the dining room table with the seafood dishes.

Razier grabbed the bottle of E&J Brandy he purchased for Louise and poured her two fingers in a glass and set it on the coffee table in the living room. Afterward, he went into his room, took a quick shower, and put on a pair of slacks and a silk mock neck T-shirt. Just as he was slipping on his loafers, he heard a soft knock on his front door. He took a deep breath and said aloud, "OK, Razi, here we go." He marched to the front door with a determined expression on his face. This was definitely about to be the start of something special as far as he was concerned, and he was not going to blow this opportunity. He had a smile on his face as he opened the door.

"Hi, mami."

"Hi," Louise said as she stepped into the apartment. When she saw all the seafood on the dining room table, she smiled and said, "Is all of that food for us, or do we have company?"

"Nope. Just us, mami. Trust me. What we don't eat, we will put to good use. Come and have a seat with me." He led her to the sofa and gave her the drink. She accepted the glass of brandy and took a sip.

"Mmm, I see you seem to have everything I told you I liked thus far."

"Yep, that, and much more," Razier said as he stood and went into the bedroom. He returned with a black, sheer, short nightie and said, "Bring your drink in here with me, mami."

She did as she was told, and once they were inside the bedroom, he told her to finish her drink. She downed the rest of the E&J and set the glass on the nightstand next to his bed. He smiled as he reached toward her head and pulled out the hairpins. Her long blond hair fell past her shoulders. "I love your hair. You don't know how many times I've fantasized about running my fingers through it," Razier said seductively as he did just that. He could feel her trembling. He told her to relax as he began to undress her one piece of clothing at a time until she was standing nude in front of him. He stepped back and admired her slim body and perfect size C-cups. Though they showed a little sag, they were pretty firm. He knew he had to be patient with this, but it was taking every ounce of control he had to not lay her down on the bed and fuck the shit out of this sexy, older white woman.

He grabbed her hand and led her into the bathroom. He leaned against the sink and told her to take a shower while he watched. Louise stepped tentatively into the shower and began washing herself. Though the water was hot, she still shivered. She couldn't believe how excited she was. It had been decades since she'd experienced something so sensual and erotic. She felt her juices oozing out of her sex as she continued to wash her body. Her nipples were so hard that they hurt her ooh, so good.

A few minutes later, she stepped out of the shower and right into Razier's arms, where he was holding a huge terry cloth bath towel. He wrapped the towel around her, scooped her into his arms, and carried her back into the bedroom, then proceeded to dry her off. Once she was dry, he gave her the sheer black nightie he bought her and watched as she slipped it on. After that, he led her barefoot back into the living room and told her to sit while he went and poured her another drink.

After that, he grabbed the platter filled with the variety of seafood and brought it to the coffee table, where he took off his shirt so she could get a good look at his well toned abs and chest. She sipped her drink dreamily as she stared at his smooth brown skin. Soon, he took the glass from her hands and asked, "You hungry, mami?"

"Yes."

Razier grabbed a piece of shrimp scampi, dipped it into the cocktail sauce that came with the platter, and fed it to her. She accepted the shrimp, and never in her life has eating a piece of shrimp felt so damn intoxicating. When she finished, he gave her another and watched as she chewed slowly. He smiled and said, "You look absolutely gorgeous, Louise. I cannot wait to make your body shiver and tingle all over."

Laughing and feeling relaxed thanks to the hot shower and the effects of the brandy, she said, "You've been making me shiver and tingle all over ever since I stepped through that door, Razier."

"Good." He stood and went to the stereo system and turned on some of the music he downloaded and put the selection on shuffle, so for the rest of the evening, nothing but smooth R&B music from the '60s and '70s would be crooning to them. Marvin Gaye was first, followed by Al Green. He could tell that he was hitting on all cylinders so far, which made him even more brazen.

Razier reached and pulled the left strap of the nightie Louise was wearing and let it slide down her arm, exposing her left breast. He bent forward and began kissing the top of her breast, slowly working his way down until he had her erect nipple inside of his mouth. Louise moaned and let her head fall back on the sofa and enjoyed how hot his mouth was on her chest. She inhaled his scent and sighed because the Eternity cologne she loved to smell on men seemed to make her pussy even wetter than it already was.

Just as quickly as he started the foreplay, he abruptly stopped and pulled away from her breast and stood. He went to the bedroom and returned with a remote control to his flat screen and turned on the television to Netflix, then selected the movie *Pretty Woman*. Once done, he went to the dining room and grabbed some more of the seafood and set it in front of them on the coffee table. After that, he sat back down next to her and pulled her into his arms so they could watch her favorite movie while cuddling. He had no intentions of them watching the entire movie. He wanted her to be so turned on by the time they got down and dirty that the sex would last all night long, and he had no doubt that this lovely, older woman would not disappoint him one bit.

She lay her head on his shoulder and was smiling like a little girl because she felt extremely happy. This had turned out even better than she ever dreamt it would be. She wanted to tell Razier to shut the TV off and fuck her senseless. But she knew he had everything planned, and she didn't dare disrupt his perfect evening.

Halfway through the movie, Razier stood and reached his hand out to Louise and led her into his bedroom. Once they were standing at the foot of the bed, he slipped the straps off her shoulders and watched as the nightie fell to the floor. She stepped out of it and smiled shyly at him as he began to undress.

He stood there naked for a few seconds, and then in a stern voice, said, "Drop to your knees and suck this big dick, baby." Without saying a word, she obeyed, being totally submissive to his command. She put his dick inside of her mouth and began to suck it slow and tenderly, but the hunger for him took control, and she started deep throating him vigorously and made him feel so damn good that he couldn't stop himself from exploding inside of her mouth in under two minutes. She knew her head game was wicked but feared since it had been so long since she sucked a dick that she may have lost her touch. Razier coming so quickly showed her that her skills were still up to par.

After swallowing his cum, she looked up at him while still on her knees, awaiting his next command because she dared not move until he told her to do so. She didn't want to ruin this moment. It was so damn hot.

He pulled her to her feet and gently pushed her onto the bed. He grabbed a condom off the nightstand and told her to put it on his still very hard dick. When the condom was secure, he pulled her to him and began to kiss her tenderly. He worked his tongue deep inside of her mouth and showed just as much hunger for her as she had for him. He could taste his cum inside of her mouth, and that only served to turn him on even more. He pulled away and began to lick down her body until he made it to her pussy. He smiled and inhaled her scent as he began to lick and suck her clitoris. He ate her pussy slowly until she came so hard that she lost her breath for a moment.

"My God! I love this, Razier. I love it. Yes, yes!" she screamed.

He removed his face from between her thighs, grabbed her by the waist, and pulled her toward him. With ease, his dick slid inside of her warm, wet pussy, and he slowly began to stroke in and out of her. Her pussy was loose yet still had a tight grip to it, and that was all he needed as he began to pick up the pace and pound her sex hard.

He reached up and rubbed each of her titties, making those erect nipples continue to hurt so good to Louise as she moaned and groaned from the pleasure he was giving her . . . a pleasure she hadn't felt in years. She felt another orgasm mount and began bucking into him, trying her best to consume as much of his dick as she could take.

He noticed that she was about to come, and he knew he was close too, so he stopped thrusting inside of her and pulled out of her pussy, much to her disappointment. He pulled her off the bed and picked her up. He carried her back to the living room and took her out to the balcony. He bent her over the railing of the balcony as the rain lightly hit them and inserted his dick back inside of her pussy from the doggie-style position, then began pounding her relentlessly. He slapped her ass hard and asked her if this was how she wanted his dick.

"Yes! Yes, Razier, yes, baby! Fuck me! Fuck me good!" she screamed as he did just that. He grabbed a fistful of her long, blond hair and pulled it tightly as he continued to bang away in that pussy with all he had until they both exploded with their orgasms in unison. Now soaking wet with sweat and rain and dazed from two powerful orgasms, Razier scooped her back into his arms and carried her back to the bedroom, where he picked up the towel and dried her. After drying himself, he brought her back to the living room and turned on the TV so they could resume watching the movie.

"You've made this a perfect evening, Razier. Thank you. You didn't miss anything. This couldn't have been more perfect."

He smiled and said, "I'm aiming to make sure every time we're together, our stolen moments are even better than the last."

"I don't know, baby. This will be kinda hard to top."

"There's plenty more for us to do. Trust, after the movie is over, we got more work to put in. This will be a stolen moment to remember, yes, but we got a whole bunch we will still do."

She snuggled close to him, smelling of sex and feeling as if she were dreaming. She kissed his shoulder and said, "You've started something I damn sure hope you can finish, Razier."

He smiled but didn't respond. The start of something special had begun, and he loved it and knew he would love it even more as time progressed. Yes . . .

Chapter Ten

Razier spent the rest of the evening making love to Louise as if they were two people madly in love with each other. He kissed her so passionately that she felt as if she were caught up in a whirlwind love affair. She stopped herself from screaming, "Razier!" so many times that she lost count. When she came for what she thought was at least the fifth time of the evening, she finally fell into a deep sleep.

She woke up around four in the morning, realizing she'd better get home. Reluctantly, she climbed out of bed and went and took a shower. While she was showering, she couldn't stop smiling. She couldn't wait to call the other ladies and let them know that the money they were investing in Razier was worth it—and much more.

Just as she began to rinse herself off, she heard Razier enter the bathroom and watched as he relieved himself. When he finished, he joined her in the shower and started kissing her so tenderly that her heart rate skyrocketed. His tongue felt so divine inside of her mouth that she moaned as he rubbed her all over her body. Before she realized what was happening, he was kneeling in front of her. She instinctively raised her right leg, draped it over his shoulder, and shuddered as he began to suck and lick her pussy until she had another orgasm. She held on to the wall and screamed, "Yes yes yes, baby!"

When her orgasm subsided, he stood and kissed her again and let her taste her juices on his tongue. She kissed him back with so much passion that she hated for the kiss to end, but she knew it had to. She had to get her tail home. Razier squeezed her ass, grabbed the washcloth, and began washing her gently as if reading her mind. When he finished, she returned the favor and washed him and smiled when she saw his manhood start to rise. She sighed because she had to have him one more time. He saw the hungry look in her eyes and shook his head no.

"It's time for you to get home, baby." He turned off the water, stepped out of the shower stall, and grabbed a towel. She stepped out behind him and let him dry her off. After he finished, she took the towel and dried him. They went into the bedroom, and he slipped on a pair of shorts while she got dressed. When she was ready, he walked her outside to her car. He leaned against the driver's side of the car staring at her as she smiled at him.

"I hope you enjoyed yourself as much as I enjoyed you, Louise."

"I did. I never felt so alive. I can't remember the last time a man made me feel this good, this special. Thank you, Razier. Thank you so much," she said as she reached inside of her purse, grabbed a white envelope, and gave it to him.

"There's a thousand dollars inside of that, but I want to make sure you check your debit card because there will be something extra added to it in the morning. I want to do so much for you, Razier. I hope you will let me. You are so—"

"Shh, enough of that, baby. Go home. Get rest and think about the next time we'll have another stolen moment."

She nodded and tears almost formed in her eyes as she said, "Thank you, Razier."

"Talk to you soon, Louise," he said as he turned and went back into his apartment, feeling unbelievable. "I did

that shit! I did that shit!" he screamed as he jumped on
his bed, feeling as if the world were now in his personal
possession. He was so amped up that he couldn't go
to sleep. He jumped up and went and got the Skirvin
stationary pad, pulled out his laptop, and started trans-
ferring all the answers from the questionnaires into a
personal file for each of his clients.

When he finished, he stared at the laptop for a moment
in thought, then nodded. "I'm definitely about to make
the best of my day off," he said as he tapped the keys
and pulled up Mrs. Bin's file. The sexy little Asian was
next on his list. He smiled when he saw that she too liked
seafood, so since he had plenty of leftovers from the food
he ordered from Red Lobster, his plan started forming
for Mrs. Bin's stolen moment, and he intended to make
it just as memorable as Mrs. Willow's had been, if not
better. Since he had the food and the liquor she preferred,
as well as a sexy outfit for her from Victoria's Secrets, he
needed to make sure he came up with the right atmosphere to give the somewhat aggressive lady precisely
what she craved. He smiled when he made up his mind.
He closed his laptop and feeling a little tired, decided to
go back to bed, and get some rest. He fell asleep smiling
because he knew he was going to have one hell of a day.

Razier woke up a little after eleven a.m. feeling good.
He got out of bed and went and brushed his teeth. When
he finished, he called Tracy and gave him and Lavonda a
play-by-play recall of the events the night before but left
out the actual sex acts, much to Tracy's disdain.

"Come on, Razi, give up that shit, clown. Did you blow
her back out or what?" Tracy asked and laughed.

"You know how I do. I did my thing, for sure. But, man,
she gave me that band. I mean, we did have a hell of an
evening, and I had just as much fun with her as she did
with me, and she actually gave me a thousand dollars. I
still can't believe this is happening, Mad Dog."

"Your ass needs to believe it 'cause it's real. So what you gonna do today?"

"I'm about to give Mrs. Bin a call and set up a stolen moment for her. I might as well since this is my only day off."

"Your only day off? Fool, are you nuts? You'll be taking plenty of days off now that you have this sweet play poppin'."

Shaking his head as if Tracy were in the room with him, Razier said, "Nope. Not going to happen. I got a steady clientele, and I will still handle my business. I'll find a way to get at the ladies, you better believe that. Remember, my work is going to be lightened a little because you're going to be helping me, right?"

"Yeah, I got you. What you got up your sleeve for the Asian broad?"

Razier smiled and said, "A picnic."

"Aww, that sounds so romantic," Lavonda said, who was listening to their conversation since Tracy had Razier on the speaker of his cell phone.

"My thoughts exactly."

"Kinda corny, though, 'cause I thought the Asian broad was on some aggressive shit. She won't be feeling all the romantic shit if she trying to get rough with it," said Tracy.

"We're going to do it *my* way, but it will end up going the way she wants it. Trust me 'cause I got this."

Laughing, Tracy said, "Just make sure you get at me when you're done, and this time, I want the gritty details fuck that you sexed her good shit."

"You stupid. What are you getting into today?"

"We're going to go out and get some shopping done and get my gear right. Once that's done, we'll pick up those things so we can start what I told you about."

"Okay, I'll hit you up later."

"You do that, playboy," Tracy said and ended the call, laughing.

Razier took a deep breath before dialing Mrs. Bin's number. She answered on the fourth ring just as he was about to hang up. "Good morning, Mrs. Bin. How are you this morning?"

"Jealous as hell, young man. But happy as hell to hear your voice. Does this call mean I'm up next?"

"Yep. Are you ready for your stolen moment?"

"Was Bruce Lee an Asian? You better believe I'm ready. We all are. Louise has been bragging to us since seven this morning about how good you made her feel. You made that white woman feel like slapping the shit out of her husband, ready to start the divorce procedures." They both laughed.

"Well, I'm glad she gave me her stamp of approval, and I hope I'll be able to earn your positive endorsement as well."

"From what I've been told, I have no doubts about that. Where are we going, and what do you have in store for me, baby cakes?"

"Meet me at Lake Hefner. We're going to have a good time at the lake."

"The lake? Outside?" she asked and smiled. "Me like."

"I figured you would."

"When?"

He checked the time and said, "Meet me at Lake Hefner in an hour."

"I'll be there in forty-five minutes," she said, laughing and hung up the phone.

He laughed as he set the phone down and proceeded to get dressed. Next, he went to Walmart and bought a nice-sized picnic basket along with some more items he felt he would need for the afternoon. Razier returned home with enough time to fill the small ice chest he bought at

Walmart and packed the seafood leftovers into the picnic basket. He was just about to leave when he realized that he hadn't put on the cologne Mrs. Bin preferred. He remembered that it was Cool Water, so he went and grabbed the bottle of cologne and gave himself three quick squirts on the pressure points on his body. With that taken care of, he grabbed his stuff and was on his way. Less than fifteen minutes later, he arrived at Lake Hefner to see Mrs. Bin sitting inside her black-on-black Lexus SUV.

He pulled next to her and climbed out of his truck. Mrs. Bin got out of her SUV, wearing a pair of short shorts that fit her small frame like a glove. He thought he could see her pussy print in the jean shorts she was wearing. *Damn, this one is aggressive,* he thought as he smiled at the pretty Asian.

"Hi, baby, you're looking edible right now, you know that?"

"I sure hope you're hungry because I want and expect for you to eat me, and I do mean that literally, sexy man. Me want the good sex likie you gave Louise."

"Shh, no talking about Louise. This is about us now. Come," Razier said as he went back to the truck and grabbed the items he brought. He then led Mrs. Bin to a nice spot on the grass not too far from the lake.

He spread out the thick blanket and set everything up for them. Mrs. Bin smiled as she watched Razier pull out a bottle of Absolute Vodka along with cranberry juice and poured her a drink in one of the glasses he brought. After that, he pulled out the shrimp scampi along with some crab legs and lobster tails and set it all up. They began to nibble on the cold seafood and sipped some vodka. The conversation was light, too light for Mrs. Bin's taste, but she refrained from saying anything. She was going to let Razier lead . . . for now.

Razier could tell by the hungry look in her eyes that she felt as if she were a caged tiger ready to be set free in the jungle. He smiled because he knew it was time to turn things up. When they finished eating, he removed the food and drink from the blanket and told Mrs. Bin to lie down on the pillow he placed on the blanket. She sighed as she followed his instructions. Next, he reached inside of the picnic basket and pulled out a bottle of Fendi perfume, and, much to Mrs. Bin's delight, squirted some on her body. They both inhaled the expensive fragrance and smiled at each other. Razier stared at her for a full minute without speaking and then said, "Take off your shirt, Mrs. Bin."

She did as she was told and said, "Call me Lia."

Razier's mouth started to water at the sight of her perfect B-cup breasts encased in an expensive black lace bra. "The bra too, Lia."

Now she suddenly seemed shy, and that was exactly what Razier wanted. She looked around and saw a few people near the lake, but where they were located, no one could see them unless they really focused their attention on them. She stared at Razier for a moment to see if he was serious. What she saw in his eyes told her he was dead serious. Determined to follow through, she boldly took off her bra and tossed it aside. Her braless breasts looked even more divine to Razier.

He lay down next to her and began to feast on them slowly while sliding his fingers inside of her jean shorts, fingering her silky smooth pussy. He whispered as he pulled his mouth from her left breast, "Your wildest fantasy was to be fucked in public, correct?"

"Yessss," she hissed, enjoying the pleasure that his fingers were giving her.

"I'm about to give you everything you want, Lia." He pulled out his dick and quickly put a condom on, then rolled on top of her and began kissing her softly.

She wrapped her arms around his neck and hungrily returned his kiss. Removing her shorts, he eased all of his dick inside of the five-foot-one Asian. He was on top of her but didn't put any of his weight on the small woman. He slowly fed her the dick and gradually increased the pace, driving her crazy with lust. She wrapped her legs around his waist, trying to get every delicious inch of his chocolate dick as deep as she could inside of her.

Knowing that she preferred to be on top, this was going to be the coup de grâce for this stolen moment as far as he was concerned. He wanted to see if this sexy older woman was as bold as she let on to be. He pulled out of her, lay on his back, and stared at her without saying a word.

Puzzled—stunned—actually, Lia returned his stare, waiting to see what his next move was going to be. When he didn't move and continued to stare at her, she realized what game he was playing. He was letting her dominate. He was calling her bluff, and Lia Bin didn't care to be challenged. She stared at him boldly as she rolled on top of him, put his dick back inside of her, and began to bounce up and down on it as if she were jumping on a damn trampoline. Thank God she wasn't a loud woman, thought Razier as he watched the small woman continue to hop up and down on his dick. Her B-cups were bouncing wildly, and that made the sex that much more exhilarating. If someone was paying them any attention, neither of them noticed because they were too caught up sexing.

When Lia came, she sighed loudly, bent forward, and kissed Razier passionately while still rotating her hips, grinding her pussy on his dick, causing Razier to fill the condom with his semen. They lay there totally spent, sweating and panting.

After a few minutes, Lia rolled off him and slid down to his dick and removed the condom. She proceeded to suck his dick back to attention. She wrapped her small hand on his nice-sized joystick and stroked him while sucking him off. The harder he became, the faster she sucked until he exploded in her mouth. "Mmmmm, you taste good, Razier," she said as she reached for the bottle of Absolute and poured herself another drink.

Razier stood and grabbed her clothes and told her to get dressed. Once she had her top back on, he said, "I hope you enjoyed your stolen moment, Lia."

"I did. Thank you, Razier. I love how we did that. It made me feel kinky."

"That's cool, 'cause now, we're about to go to my place so we can *really* make this stolen moment special."

Her eyes grew wide because she thought they were finished. Shit, she was content with what they already did. The thought of receiving some more of that good dick made her pussy begin to wet instantly. "There's more?"

He nodded and said, "Yes, Lia."

Chapter Eleven

Lia followed Razier to his apartment, and as soon as they stepped inside and closed the door, he grabbed her by her slim waist, pulled her into his arms, and gave her a long French kiss that left her breathless when he took his lips off of hers. "Wow," she said and smiled.

He smiled and led her to his bedroom, where he removed her shorts and top, leaving her standing there in her black lacy thong and matching bra. "You look scrumptious, baby, but I need you to take that off because I have something I want you to put on for me."

She stared at him with hunger in her eyes as she removed her bra and thong. "I'd rather remain like this, Razier, but there's no way in hell I'll deny you anything, baby."

"Good, I like that," he said as he went to the closet and grabbed the pink sheer halter top with matching crotchless panties. He gave them to her and said, "Put this on, baby, because this is what I want you in while we fuck for the rest of the afternoon. I'm about to fuck you silly, and you're going to love every minute of it."

The aggression in his tone turned her on so badly that she felt as if she would come at that moment without him even touching her. She sighed as she put on the sexy outfit he bought her. She did a pirouette as if she were a ballerina and asked, "You like, Razier?"

He nodded, grabbed her by her hand, and led her into the living room, where he told her to have a seat on the sofa while he grabbed the remote control and turned on the TV. He went to Netflix and chose the movie *Speed,* starring her favorite actress, Sandra Bullock. Lia smiled and put one foot under her bottom and made herself comfortable as she watched Razier go into the kitchen and pour her a drink. He brought the glass to her, and she took a sip and watched as he took off his clothes down to his boxer briefs and sat down next to her with a drink in hand.

They sipped their drinks and watched some of the movie with Razier's head lying on Lia's lap. She stroked his smooth, bald head and felt as if she were at home with her man . . . a man who made her feel like she craved to feel . . . Wanted. Loved. Sexy. Adored. *Wow,* was her thought as she stared down at him while he watched the action-packed movie from the '90s. Her pussy was so wet it was leaking down her legs.

Enough of this damn movie. I got to have that dick back deep inside of me, she thought as she bent and kissed the top of his head. Next, she kissed his forehead and said, "You got to fuck me before I bust right now, Razier. I need that dick, and I need it *now.* I want it hard, baby. I want that dick for a long time, and I want it bad."

He rolled off her lap, got to his feet, and cut off the TV. Then he turned on his sound system and put the selector on her favorite rappers, turned around, and told her to follow him just as B.I.G.'s "Hypnotize" started playing.

Once they were in the bedroom, he climbed on the bed and watched as she walked to him, mounted his chest, and eased her pussy up to his face so he could suck it. She rode his face until he brought her to a heavenly orgasm that seemed to last forever. Panting, she slid off his face as she kissed and licked all her juices from his lips and chin.

Lia saw him reach for a condom and grabbed it for him from the nightstand. Quickly, she slid down to his dick and began to suck him real fast. She had her hair tied in a long ponytail, and he grabbed it tightly as she was sucking his dick so fast that he felt as if he would explode any second from her tiny mouth. The pressure she was putting on his dick drove him crazy as she got the result she was feverishly working for. He came long—and hard. She pulled back just as his orgasm squirted right onto her face. She licked some of his cum off her lips and smiled as she rubbed the rest on her face as if it were expensive lotion. He groaned, and she growled.

"Grrrrr, this is dick belongs to *me,* Razier. Do you hear me?"

"It's all yours, baby. What you gon' do with it?"

She answered his question by securing the condom on his dick and mounted him. Once she had him inside of her, she began to bounce on top of it so hard that it was as if she were trying to stay in tune with the beat of Tupac's "How Do You Want It" that was playing in the background. She would rise almost all the way off his dick, then impale herself as hard as she could on him, making it feel as if his dick were touching her deep in her chest cavity.

"Gimme, gimme this dick! Gimme all of it, dammit!" she screamed over and over as she came hard.

When her orgasm subsided, she sighed, slid off him, and lay down breathing hard, trying to catch her breath. Razier was so hard that he felt like his dick had turned into a piece of steel. He got up and turned her onto her stomach and lay on top of her, putting all his weight on her small frame as he guided his dick inside of her and started fucking her slowly. The friction on her clitoris from his weight on her drove her crazy as she tried to back that ass into his every thrust. Her pussy was so tight and good that Razier felt he could stay inside of her forever. But when he pulled her to her knees and started pounding into her from behind in the doggie-style position, it was a wrap. He exploded and filled the condom with his semen. He didn't realize that he had pulled out of her and lay down with her wrapped in his arms as he fell into a deep sleep.

He didn't know how long he had been asleep when he opened his eyes Lia was gone and the apartment was silent. Razier got out of bed and went to use the bathroom. When he finished, he went into the living room and saw a white envelope on the coffee table under the remote control. He smiled as he grabbed what he knew was his payment for another job well done. He was shocked when he opened the envelope and saw not a thousand dollars but $3,000 inside the envelope and a note from Lia.

You rock, Razier. I felt a thousand dollars would have been an insult to you, so here's two more because that dick was worth every penny. Thank you so much for our first stolen moment. I will be anxiously waiting for the next one.

Lia Bin.

Laughing, he went back to the bathroom and took a long, hot shower. When he finished, he dressed and called Tracy to see what he was doing.

"Man, fuck what I'm doing. What the hell you been doing with the little Asian broad? And don't give me that fucking, G-rated version either, Razi," Tracy said seriously.

"All right, fool. Get ready. I'm about to get you, and we can go out and get something to eat, and I'll put you and Lavonda up on my hell of a time with Lia Bin."

"Don't worry about Lavonda. She went back to Boley. She has to get ready for work tomorrow. So it's just gon' be you and me. What you trying to go eat?"

"Let's go out to Midwest City and get some Cheddar's."

"That's what's up. Hurry your ass up. I'm hungry," Tracy said and ended the call.

Thirty minutes later, they were seated at Cheddar's restaurant eating some hot wing appetizers and laughing as Razier gave his buddy a play-by-play how the afternoon with Lia Bin went.

"Man, I'm telling you, that small woman was like a freaking tiger on the dick. She wouldn't let up. I didn't think a woman that small could take dick like that."

"That's wild. I heard small broads got some deep pussy. Never had an Asian broad, so I can only imagine how good that pussy was. Was it super tight and right? Does she have some miles on her old ass? What is she, like 50?"

"Fifty-two. Let me tell you this, though. That pussy felt as if she were a 22-year-old woman. Tight isn't the word I can use to describe that pussy, bro. More like a super gripper. She gripped this dick and went nuts on it for over twenty minutes. She came like crazy, and, man, let me tell you, her head game is just as great as the pussy. When I got balls deep in that pussy from behind, she actually was growling as I served her the dick until I busted a monster nut and passed out. I woke up a few hours later, and she was gone. All I could do was smile and inhale the sweet-smelling Fendi perfume scent on my sheets. I went into the living room to see that magical white envelope, and you already know I was smiling because of that."

"I know that's right. Another easily earned stack, huh?"

Shaking his head, Razier raised three fingers and said, "Nope. *Three* bands this time."

"What? You lie. She gave your ass three stacks for blowing her back out?"

"Yep. Left me this note saying if she had only given me a band, it would have been an insult," Razier said as he passed the note to Tracy.

After reading the note and giving it back, Tracy was smiling and shaking his head. "You are one lucky sum-bitch for real, Razi. I mean, man, this is a fucking dream come true, bro. You got to push this for all it's worth because these old broads will make you fucking rich. On top of that, you won't ever have to waste your time with any other bitches because you'll be getting that mature pussy whenever the fuck you want it. Plus, getting paid for that shit. This is fucking crazy."

"I know. It's surreal, for real. I'm going to have to space these ladies some because there's no way I'll be able to hit them all like this on a regular."

"I told your ass you're going to need to get some of that Horny Goat Weed," Tracy said as he checked his watch. "It's too late to hit the mall now, but first thing tomorrow, we'll hit the GNC store and get you stocked up. That way, you can get it in your system so that by the time you're ready to get with the next in line on your fuck list, you'll be even more ready to break them old broads off real proper like."

"I'm with that. So, you'll be ready for me in the morning to get to work?"

"Might as well. I don't have shit else to do. I'll need to go get at my parole officer before five, though."

"That's cool 'cause Mondays are fairly light. I only got like eight yards, and they're small ones. With your help, we can finish before two. After that, we can go to the GNC store and grab something to eat. Then we can look at some catering trucks because, with these ends I got, it's about time to make that move now. I'm ready to get in on the H&8th Street stuff, so a catering truck is a must."

"I feel that. What about the pool service thing?"

"I'm taking these three bands I got from Lia and using that to pay off the last bit I owe for the pool cleaning equipment, so I'll be good to go on that as well. It's all starting to fall in line for me, bro."

"Yes, it is. For both of us, for real. Me and Lavonda went and bought ten phones. Once she gets them inside to the dudes I hooked her up with, that money will be used to get more phones for the inmates. That's some good money right there—not as good as the money you getting, but good all the same."

Razier knew better to speak on Tracy's business, so he shook his head and laughed. "That's right."

"What's so damn funny?"

"Thinking about copping me something foreign. You know how big I dream, bro. But now this stuff seems as if all of my dreams are about to come true."

Tracy stared at his best friend and smiled. "All of your dreams are about to become a reality, Razi. And I'm going to be right by your side, making sure we win all the way, bro, just like we always planned. Business partners, getting rich, rolling foreign, and having the very best of everything. Me and you all the way."

Razier smiled and said, "I know that's right. But we have to do something before we cop foreigns and all of that stuff. We got to get your ass a place to stay because I already know your ass thinks you're about to move into my place, and that ain't happening, bro. I love your ass to death, but I know you would be all in my mix with the ladies, and I can't afford to risk messing this up. We're getting you a spot tomorrow as well."

Laughing, Tracy said, "Damn, Razi, I thought you loved ya boy, for real. I still got the suite at the Skirvin paid for two more days."

"Good, that gives us plenty of time to get you a one-bedroom spot. I'll check and see if they have any available in my apartment complex, but don't make me regret having you that damn close to me, bro."

"Fuck you."

"No, F. *you*." The best friends both started laughing as they finished their meals.

Chapter Twelve

Razier knew that with Tracy's help, the workdays would be easier, but he didn't expect it to be this easy. They finished the eight yards much sooner than Razier expected, and that was a definite plus. Tracy was all business and didn't slack once. Razier felt that everything was falling right in place; perfect. With Tracy's help, they would be able to get more done on a daily, which would leave more time for him to make the other moves he wanted to make. He was now thinking about hiring some help. That way, he would be able to focus his attention on the catering truck business and the pool cleaning service. All of that, combined with the money he would be making with the ladies, he knew they would be sitting lovely financially, really quick, and that thought put a huge smile on his face as he dropped Tracy off back at the Skirvin after they left the mall, getting him some of that Horny Goat Weed from the GNC store.

Since it wasn't even two o'clock, Razier decided to call Mrs. Beckman and give her a stolen moment. When he made it home, he took a long, hot shower. Afterward, he checked his laptop to make sure he had everything on her list. Realizing that he didn't have any freshly squeezed juice, he threw on some clothes and went to the grocery store and bought some fresh lemons and oranges. When he made it back home, he made some orange juice and lemonade after tasting the juices, making sure they were OK. He placed the two pitchers of juice into the freezer to chill them by the time Mrs. Beckman arrived. Then he grabbed his phone and called her. When she answered the phone, she laughed nervously.

"Hiya, Razier. I've been wondering when I would receive a call from you. Is it my turn?" she asked, sounding anxious.

Razier was staring at his laptop, seeing if she was one of the ladies who liked to be dominated or not. With that information, he answered her question in a stern voice. "Yes, it is, Mrs. Beckman."

"Please call me Erica."

Ignoring her, he said, "Have you eaten anything yet?"

"A light breakfast earlier."

"Good. Meet me at Mama E's Soul Food Restaurant on the East Side in twenty minutes. Don't be late," he said and hung up the phone, then started laughing. He couldn't believe he was doing this craziness. It was crazy, but the money was serious, so he had to make sure he kept to the script and kept everything on point to please the ladies. This stolen moment stuff was going to put him in an extraordinary financial situation. *Damn,* he thought as he went into the bedroom to get dressed.

He chose a pair of Levi jean shorts, polo sandals, and a polo shirt. He went back to his laptop to check and make sure he put on the right cologne for Erica. Walking into the bedroom, he squirted some Anucci cologne she liked on his body and grabbed his keys. Before he left, he made sure he had a few gospel songs selected on the stereo for the music he would use to start their stolen moment. Smokie Norful, J. Moss, and Yolanda Adams should suffice, he thought as he set the stereo for the music. Afterward, he smiled as he added some R. Kelly for when it was time for them to get busy.

Along with R. Kelly's classic 12 Play CD, the Black Panties CD would do the trick, he thought as he left the apartment. He would give her the outfit he bought her when it was time for them to chill and watch a little of *The Godfather*. Confident everything was in place, he climbed into his truck and drove toward the Northeast Side of town.

They enjoyed some of Oklahoma City's best soul food at Mama E's, as well as some good, flirtatious conversation. Erica was still slightly nervous, but the more they conversed, the more relaxed she became. Razier was utterly mesmerized by her double-D breasts. They had to have been worked on, he thought as he chewed delicious collard greens. She noticed how he kept glancing at her buxom breasts and smiled.

"You like my girls, I see. That's good, Razier, really good. God knows I love a man who appreciates my size. I'm a *whole lot* of woman." She started laughing as she sipped her lemonade.

"I'm going to make sure I give you a whole lot of me, baby, so you make sure you drink plenty of water along with that lemonade because we're about to get it in real serious."

"Normally, that would have come across as being really arrogant, but from what I've heard, your words serve to make the ladies intensely aroused."

Razier gave her an expressionless look and said, "That's exactly what my words were intended to do. You finished?"

His straightforwardness caused her to squeeze her legs tightly under the table. She was so turned on that she felt as if she were having a mini orgasm at that very moment. "Yes, I'm ready, Razier. I've never been more ready for anything in my life."

He stood and told her, "Go get in your car and wait for me. I want you to follow me to my place so you can get the best fucking you've ever had in your life." Twenty minutes later, they were sitting on his sofa watching *The Godfather,* sipping some of the freshly squeezed orange juice Razier made for her. "I can't believe how detailed you are. The ladies you've seen so far told me you are on point in every way, but this is very flattering. You've seemed to go out of your way to make certain you have everything I like. That makes me feel special. I really appreciate that, Razier."

He smiled but didn't speak as he stood and reached his hand out toward her. She accepted his hand and let him lead her into the bedroom with chills running through her entire body. Once they were in there, he stopped, turned, faced her, and said, "Strip. I want you naked so I can take you in the bathroom and shower with you."

He turned and went into the bathroom, took off his clothes, and got into the shower. Less than a minute later, she joined him in the shower, and once again, he was amazed at how firm her huge breasts were. He began washing her body, paying extra attention to those magnificent breasts. He couldn't hold out any longer. He had to have one of her erect nipples inside his mouth. When he dipped his head to her chest and began sucking her nipples, she moaned loudly and held his head to her breast as if she were nursing a newborn.

"Yes, suck 'em for me, baby; suck 'em good," she cooed as he continued to give equal attention to both of her lovely titties. His dick was so hard that he knew he had to stop because he wanted to get balls deep inside of her right then and there but knew he couldn't rush things.

He wondered as he removed his mouth from her breast if his dick was this hard because he was so turned on by this older woman, or was it the effects of the Horny Goat Weed he had taken when he came home. He reminded himself to ask Tracy about that later. Right now, he was only concerned with sexing this attractive older woman.

After they finished showering, he led her to the bedroom and sat her down at the end of the bed and began drying her off, starting at her feet and working his way to her chest, but he just couldn't keep his hands off her titties.

"My, you really do like my girls, don't ya?"

He stared at her as he put his finger to his lips and said, "Shhhh." He went to the closet and came back with a long, sheer, black nightgown. He told her to stand as he put the nightgown on her. He grabbed a bottle of Calvin Klein's CK perfume and gave her a few squirts on all the pressure points on her body. She sighed, loving the smell of her favorite perfume.

He then led her back into the living room and had her sit. He grabbed the remote, turned on the stereo, and watched as she smiled when J. Moses came on singing a song about how he wanted to rebuild his life. They sat there, silently enjoying the good gospel music, sipping their juice, and cuddling together as if they were boyfriend and girlfriend. Razier knew he was setting everything up perfectly. This one was going to be extra special because he couldn't remember how many times he fantasized fucking the Amazon-like older woman. At five foot nine, she was not only statuesque, but she was also fucking gorgeous. Her dark skin seemed to shine, and her pearly white teeth made her smile seem like she was an African queen. Yes, this would be really good, he thought, just as R. Kelly's song *12 Play* came on.

"I sure hope that's our cue to begin, Razier, because you have me so excited right now that I'm scared I'm going to explode as soon as you touch me," she said breathlessly.

"Shh. Stand up." She did as she was told and stared at him, scared her legs would not hold her up from the amount of trembling she was experiencing. "Turn around and flip the back of your nightgown over your waist and hold it there."

She complied and, with her back to him, bent over without him telling her to, placing one hand on the end of the sofa while holding her nightgown as he instructed with her other hand. He smiled as he stared at that big, firm ass and the pink pussy that was peeking at him. He knelt behind her and began sucking her pussy from that position, driving her insane with lust. He grabbed her shapely ass cheeks and spread them as he ran his tongue up and down between the crack of her ass back to her soaking wet pussy. She squealed as he stuck a finger inside of her asshole and kept right on eating pussy.

When she came, she screamed and tightly squeezed the end of the sofa. Her cum came streaming out of her, sliding down her long, smooth, dark legs. Razier pulled back and watched it for a moment before he lapped up her cum, all the way back to her pussy. Shuddering but still holding on to the sofa, Erica sighed loudly and thought, *What the hell is this young, freaky man doing to me? My God, I can't remember the last time a man made me cream as much as I just did. Shit.*

Razier stood behind her and slowly put a condom on his superhard dick and eased inside of Erica, causing her to moan in pleasure as he filled the large woman with his massive dick. He started slowly and gradually picked up his pace until he was banging inside of her hard and deep—so deep that every time he hit her, she would scream out.

"Yes . . . Fuuuck . . . Yessss."

"Shhhh" was all he said as he continued to hit that pussy real good from the back until he felt his nut rising out of him. Right before he started to come, he pulled out and turned Erica around. He quickly snatched off the condom and ordered her in a stern voice, "Suck it and swallow my cum."

She dropped to her knees without hesitation and did precisely as she had been told. He grasped those two lovely titties and pinched her erect nipples as he filled her mouth with his seed. When she had siphoned every last drop of his cum out of him, she sighed, smacked her lips, and looked up at him with questioning eyes. She knew not to speak, so she just stared at him.

He liked how she was obeying, and that only served to turn him on even more. He pulled her to her feet and kissed her, softly at first, then passionately as he tongued her, tasting his cum on her tongue. She moaned in his mouth because she felt as if that act was extremely kinky to her. No man had ever come in her mouth and kissed her afterward. This young man was too much, and she loved it.

He pulled from their embrace and led her into the bedroom, where he laid her onto the bed and took off the sheer nightgown. He grabbed another condom, put it on, and began sucking her toes while working his way up between her legs. He was sucking her pussy with so much vigor she exploded instantly. He sucked her juices for a minute or two as he eased on top of her and put one of her long legs on his shoulder, then bent it back until the tip of her toes were touching the headboard.

He went inside of her swiftly and mercilessly began giving her the dick. He raised her other leg, so he had both of them bent back and was balls deep inside of the Amazon, giving her more dick than she'd ever had in her life. Her pretty, dark titties were bouncing wildly as he gave her the best sex she had ever experienced. When he started to come, he yelled, "Tell me this pussy belongs to me—tell me!"

"Oh God, yes, yes. This pussy belongs to you. You own this pussy, Razier," she screamed as she came so hard she felt faint. She actually saw stars. The words he asked her for did him in as he too began to come like crazy. They were totally in sync as their bodies shook and shivered until their orgasms subsided.

Razier slowly let her legs down and lay next to her, then sighed. "Now you can talk."

She lay there, staring at the man who had just fucked the shit out of her, and smiled. "The only word I can think to say is *damn*. If you're going to fuck me like that every time we get together, I need to make sure I eat my Wheaties." They both started laughing.

Chapter Thirteen

Olivia came loudly as she was riding Razier in the reverse cowgirl position and slid off his dick, feeling exhausted after the two-plus-hour sex session they just completed. She sighed heavily as she inhaled the Black Polo cologne Razier wore. He gave her a perfect stolen moment just as he gave the rest of the ladies. She was a little perturbed that Razier chose to make her wait for her turn the more she heard the glowing reports from the ladies about how good he had been. She wanted to have him again. She slapped him lightly on his chest and said, "You do know I'm sorta pissed at you, right?"

"Why? What did I do?"

"You made me wait and have to be the last to get a stolen moment," she answered and pouted as she began to rub his right nipple, causing his manhood to stir to her liking.

He moaned and said, "Always save the best for last. Plus, it wasn't like you hadn't already ridden this ride at my amusement park."

"True. But I felt like you held back on me because the ladies have been driving me nuts telling me about all the special attention you gave them. I mean, jeez, I felt like, damn, he really held back with me, which made me pissed, sir. All they keep repeating to me is how good you made them feel, how special they felt by your attention to detail, and how you met their every need, every desire."

He smiled. "Jealous?"

"This may sound childish, but, yes, I am. I was like, *ugh*. Why is he torturing me this way?" They both laughed.

"I thought it would mean more to you if I did them first to show you that I was following the script you laid out for me to a tee. So by the time it got to your turn, you would be able to see that I was definitely what you expected me to be."

"Oh, lover of mines, you have to know better than that. I knew after our first time that you were made for all of us. I will say that I didn't expect all the ladies to be so smitten over you. I mean, the way they talk about you would make one think they're madly in love with you."

Laughing, he said, "I sure hope not. That could cause some serious problems down the line with their current marital status."

"Baby, let me tell you this about these ladies. They are living a life of comfort and comfort only. Each of them is being neglected so much sexually by their husbands that there is no way in this world that they would ever do anything to risk losing the special attention you've given them, and that is a good thing for you. Your pockets are about to get deeper, Razier . . . really deep. It's obvious by the amount of money you've had added to your debit account. If my calculations are correct, you should have well over fifteen thousand added to the original five thousand that was put on there."

"True. When I checked it the other day, I couldn't believe that the ladies had been so generous."

"I don't know why you couldn't believe it. You've brought them out of a sexual funk and breathed fresh air into their lungs, sexually. You made them feel wanted, special, and most of all, desired. You didn't make it seem as if you were just fucking them, and that's what makes the stolen moments so special for them."

"Mmmm. What about you? Did you feel special by the attention I gave you this evening?"

"Definitely. Even though I expected everything you did, it was still flattering to know that you went out of your way to make sure everything was set up to my liking. From the perfume I love to the cologne I love for a man to wear, down to the food and drink I prefer. The chicken fettuccine was divine, by the way. You even had my fave movie, *Boyz N the Hood,* and that was a nice touch because I loves me some Ice Cube. Making love to me with my fave blues and R&B so did me in, though. I was floating when I came as Marvin Gaye was singing 'Sexual Healing.' You, my man, have outdone yourself. My question to you now is, how are you going to maintain this for your encore performance because the ladies are anxiously awaiting your call for their next stolen moment."

"There's plenty more I can do. I will let it come to me when the time comes for me to please each of them. There are several questions on the questionnaire that I haven't addressed yet, so it will get better each time. I just wanted to give you all a little taste. Trust me because it will be even more intense every time," he said confidently, feeling like a king.

"Mmmmm, I know I better not be last to receive the intensity you're talking about."

He smiled and said, "You won't. Promise."

"Good."

"One thing confused me, though."

"What's that, baby?"

"Mrs. Wilkins. She enjoyed all the attention I gave her, yet she refused when it came time to make love to her. All she wanted to do was enjoy the movie, meal, drink, and just talk afterward."

"Really? She didn't say anything like that to us. In fact, she made it seem like you blew her back out like you did us all."

"I wish. I was so horny that it felt like I was going to burst. She saw this and gave me a hand job that got me off. After that, she showered and left."

"Mmm, that's interesting."

"Don't say anything about it, though. I get the feeling that she really didn't want to cheat on her husband. Yet, she still needed my attention."

"I'm sure that will change because she absolutely wants to see you again."

He shrugged and said, "I'll make sure to jack off before I get with her so that I won't be tortured like that again." They both started laughing.

"What about Mrs. Collins? Did you enjoy her as much as she enjoyed you?"

He smiled as he thought about how he had Vera's legs bent back and went as deep as he could inside of her over and over for forty-five minutes. She blew his mind when she told him to ease his dick inside of her asshole from that position. He came like he'd never come before after a few short strokes inside of her ass. "Vera is a wild one. In fact, she's the wildest out of all of you."

Laughing, Olivia said, "Don't I know it. You went deep in that ass, Razier, and she loved that shit, no pun intended."

"I can't believe y'all be talking about how I sex each of you. That's kinda weird, for real."

"We all don't go into *every* detail, but Vera does because she's outspoken like that. The other ladies may mention certain things but not every detail, so don't be embarrassed."

"I'm good. It is sort of strange, though."

"I can imagine. So, what about Mrs. Salley and Mrs. Simmons?"

"Making love to Marie was like making love to a woman who's been starved sexually for years. She was insatiable.

She was rushing through the dinner I prepared for her and didn't want to watch the *Titanic*. All she wanted to do was drink and fuck. So drink and fuck we did."

"Don't I know it. She told us she damn near spent the night with your dick inside of her because it felt so good."

"Now, Mrs. Salley was a slow burn, but once she got going, she too turned into a firecracker. She kept me giving it to her doggie style for over an hour straight before we switched positions. She blew my top, though, when she asked me to get to the end of the bed and asked me if I'd ever had my asshole licked and sucked. Before I could answer her, she went at it, and I've never felt so ashamed in my life."

"Why? Because you didn't like the new experience?"

Laughing, he said, "No. I *loved* that stuff. I've never been so turned on in my life. The more she licked and sucked my asshole, the harder I became. When I got back inside of her, I think I lost it because I went nuts in that pussy. No pun intended."

"See, you've learned something from us old ladies, and you liked it. Trust, there's plenty more you will learn from us. All you need to do is make sure that you keep Mr. Happy there ready at all times. It would be disappointing if you weren't able to perform for any, and I do mean *any*, stolen moments."

"Trust, that's one thing we will not ever have to worry about. One thing for certain is I will make sure to keep an ample amount of time in between each stolen moment."

With her lips stuck out, she said, "I sure hope not too long a time in between."

"I was thinking like one every other day should suffice."

"I agree. So, what are you going to do with your new-found financial status? Any extravagant spending coming?"

He smiled as he thought about the catering truck he and Tracy went and priced the other day and said, "I'm going to start a catering business. I've found a truck that I want, and I'm going to get it next month. That way, I'll be able to go down to Harvey and Eighth Street and do my thing there. That money will be good for me, as well. I also paid off the last of my pool equipment."

"You're turning into quite the businessman, I see. I'm happy for you. I am concerned that with all of this new work you'll be doing, are you sure you will be able to service all of us?"

"I'm positive I will because I'm hiring some help for my pool service, and with my best friend, Tracy, helping me with the yards, it will be all good. I'll handle the truck because that will be like three times a week. As for the pool service, that's only for the warmer months, and since summer is almost over, I won't get that going until late spring. By that time, I should have found some workers, as I mentioned. The winter concerns me, but I think if I can round up some new clients to cater parties, I'll be fine there too."

"You won't have to worry about any business there. I'm sure the ladies and I will have no problems introducing new clients to you for all you got going. Six of us have pools, so you know you'll get that business. As for parties to cater, we all entertain, so that should be easy to set up for you as well."

"But won't their husbands become suspicious when they see that I not only do their yards but their pools *and* cater their parties?"

"Their husbands care only about themselves, and they do whatever their wives want. Don't you worry about that. As long as the ladies don't request sex on a regular, the husbands could care less what their wives do with their money."

"That's crazy. I could never see myself treating my wife like that, no matter how old we got. When a man marries a woman, it's a lifetime commitment that he should respect."

"Aaah, only if all men thought like you, Razier. You are a rare breed, and I hope you remain that way."

"One thing for sure, I won't be getting married anytime soon. Dealing with you ladies is more than enough for me. Who has time for falling in love and getting married?"

"Great. That means you belong for sure, and we can keep you as long as we want. Now, my stolen moment has been put on hold too long. I'm not through with you yet, Razier. You gave me an idea when you told me how much you loved it when Dionne licked and sucked your asshole, so I've decided to take you there too. You ready, baby?"

His answer to her question was a moan. "Are you serious?"

Her answer to his question was her sliding down between his legs and inserting his semierect dick inside of her mouth. She sucked him until he was hard while lightly rubbing her fingers between the crack of his ass. He hoped and prayed that she wouldn't insert a finger inside of it. He didn't think he would dig that at all. Sucking and licking his ass was one thing, but putting anything in it was an alarming thought.

When she put her mouth on his testicles and began humming while sucking them, he felt like he would immediately explode. She was giving him a top-notch head. It felt so good that it was causing him to squirm. His squirming increased as she dipped her head lower and slid her tongue over his asshole. He sighed loudly, and she smiled as she grabbed him by his right thigh and raised it a little so she could have better access to his asshole. She made her tongue as stiff as she could, pushed it in his ass, and started sticking it in and out of it, causing him to shake from the chills that ran throughout his body. A tongue going in and out of his ass wasn't a finger, he thought, but it felt strange. Yet, he was so caught up in the experience that he didn't have time to complain because she was driving him crazy with her multitasking . . . stroking his dick with her right hand while sucking and licking all over his asshole. She rose from between his legs and smiled.

"Now, I'm going to show you a trick I learned many moons ago, young man. You have to make sure that you keep your eyes open, no matter what. Don't you close them, no matter how good it feels to you, okay?" she asked as she continued stroking him slowly.

He could only nod as he was too caught up in it all. The feelings he was experiencing were so great that he couldn't speak, so he just nodded.

"That a boy," she smiled wickedly as she dipped her head back to his dick and began sucking him off with such force that he knew that he was about to bust a monster nut. She sensed this too and stopped sucking his dick and held her hand at the base of his dick, holding it there as if holding his cum inside of his balls. The sensations that ran through him were so foreign that he cried out.

"My! God! Olivia, what are you *doing* to me?"

She gave him that wicked smile again as she lowered her head and went back to sucking his asshole, sliding her wet mouth and tongue all over and inside of it. Then she returned to his dick and looked up at him and knew he was about to explode. She removed her mouth from his dick and said, "Remember, keep those sexy brown eyes open and on me, Razier."

He nodded and stared at her as she returned to his dick and suddenly picked up the pace, sucking him so fast that her head looked as if she were a machine instead of a sexy, older woman. Just as his orgasm started, she pulled her mouth three inches from the head of his dick, and he watched as he came. Globs and globs of his cum shot right into her mouth. It felt as if he would never stop coming. That was the most exciting sexual experience he ever had in his life. *"Olivia!"* he screamed at the top of his lungs, positive that everyone inside of his apartment complex heard him.

Olivia smiled as she swallowed every delicious drop of his cum and climbed up next to him, then kissed him on the cheek. "Rest now, my lover. This stolen moment still ain't over yet. I'm punishing you for making me wait." She lay her head on his heaving chest and smiled. *Damn, this young man is going to get so much pussy, he may never leave us. That's absolutely fine by me,* she thought and snuggled closer to him, genuinely enjoying her stolen moment.

Chapter Fourteen

Friday, being Razier's heavy workday, was a piece of cake, and he thanked God for Tracy. They breezed through every yard and were able to make it to the Wilkinses' home two hours earlier than expected. Razier told Tracy what he needed him to work on in the front yard while he went to the back to trim the bushes to Mr. Wilkins's specifications. While he was working, he couldn't help but think about Mrs. Wilkins and how sexy she looked in the two-piece silk nightie. Her long, bronze legs and pretty feet turned him on like crazy, and he was sick that he didn't get the chance to have sex with her. He knew he had to bide his time, and the day would come for them to *really* have a special stolen moment. Special to him, at least, he thought while he continued working.

By the time he finished trimming the bushes, Tracy had finished the front yard and came to the backyard and mowed the lawn there. Razier looked up and saw Mrs. Wilkins standing on their back deck, staring at him with a smile on her face. She had her long, luxurious hair braided in one long ponytail draped over her shoulder. She was looking casually sexy in a pair of jeans, sandals, and a white blouse. She saw him looking her way and finger waved. He waved back, and she gave him a nod of her head, requesting him to come to her. He set down the large trimming shears he had in his hand and went to see what the beautiful Mrs. Wilkins wanted.

"Hi, Razier. I see you hired some help finally."

"Yes, and that was the best decision I ever made. I've been able to finish my work much faster, and that gives me more time to start my other business ventures."

"I've been told about your pool service and catering business. You're a very determined young man. That's impressive. You've impressed us all, especially me. Thank you again for a lovely time. I really enjoyed our stolen moment."

"It was truly my pleasure, Mrs. Wilkins."

She frowned and said, "I thought I told you to call me Carmela."

"I know, but I figured since we're here at your home, I'd better keep it strictly business."

"I appreciate that, but my husband isn't home, so Carmela will be fine."

"Okay."

"I won't keep you long. I wanted to say hi and ask you a question. I know you had a good time with the others, and I wanted you to know that even though we didn't have sex, I enjoyed how you made me feel. Thank you for not pushing the sex. I'm going to need some time to take it there." She stared directly into his light brown eyes and said, "But I *will* take it there, Razier. God knows I wanted to jump your bones the other night, but—"

He shook his head and said, "No buts, Carmela. If you aren't ready, I'm good. When you *are* ready, it will make it that much more special for both of us."

"You're so mature for your age. I appreciate you, and I love how you respect me. I wish I had that kind of respect here in my own home."

"Wow, your husband is a jerk like that?"

She raised her eyebrows and smiled. "Normally, I would be offended if anyone spoke about him in that manner, but you're right. He is a complete jerk in the highest order. I've never once mouthed those words to anyone, though I think of them daily. That shows me how comfortable I am sharing things with you. You have my complete confidence, Razier. Please don't ever betray the trust I have for you."

"Never. All I want to do is give you smiles and some memorable times. You deserve that."

She nodded in agreement and said, "Yes, I do. I've tolerated so much with my husband, and it's only served me pain and more pain. He's a good man, a great provider, but ever since our daughter left our lives, he chose to take it out on me at times."

"What happened to your daughter?"

She shrugged. "Your guess would be as good as mine." She changed the subject, obviously uncomfortable with the topic. "My husband has been so distant with me that the only time he pays me any attention is when we argue."

"He doesn't hit you, does he?"

"I wish he would. I'd have his ass in jail so quick his head would spin. No, he abuses me with words."

"Sometimes, words hurt more than the physical."

"True. I'm so unhappy, Razier. I want more. I deserve more," she said as her eyes started to water. "Excuse me for this burst of emotions. This isn't what I wanted to discuss with you."

"It's okay, I understand. Look, why don't you let me finish my work so I can get home and freshen up. After that, I'll give you a call and maybe we can have a stolen moment. I think you need some companionship. We can get some good takeout Mexican food from this spot I know, then watch *Die Hard 2* since you love you some Bruce Willis. We'll sip some Rémy and talk some more if you like."

"Just talk? Don't you want me, Razier?" she asked and stared at him with hunger in her eyes that served to make his dick rise instantly.

"Whatever you want to do, Carmela. I'll let you lead."

"No. It's important that you control our stolen moment, Razier. I'll do everything you want *and* some, much more than just jerking you off."

"In that case, you must let me hurry up and get back to work because we're in for one hell of an evening."

She laughed and said, "'K. I'm going to call Olivia and arrange a girls' night out so I can have a good excuse for staying out late. I may just tell my husband I intend to stay over at Olivia's for the night. I'd love to wake up in your strong arms, Razier. I need that."

"I'd love to have you in my arms when I wake up, Carmela."

"What time shall I come?"

They both started laughing at her words.

"I'd say something crass, but why bother? You and I both know you will be coming a lot tonight."

"I sure hope so," she breathed.

"Be at my place at seven. Don't be late."

"I'll be there at 6:55," she said and softly kissed him on his lips, turned, and went back inside of her home.

Razier went back to work, and he could feel Tracy's eyes staring at his back, but he refused to turn around and say anything so he could avoid the crazy statement he knew would be coming. Tracy shook his head and laughed as he continued to mow the backyard.

When they finished work and cleaned off the equipment, they went and washed the truck. Once that was finished, Razier drove them to their apartment complex. Tracy was able to get a one-bedroom apartment in the same complex as Razier, thanks to Razier's good standing with the apartment manager. The good thing about that move was he could get Tracy an apartment on the *other* side of the large apartment complex. He didn't need or want his besty too close to him because that would only serve to have him being driven out of his mind with Tracy's antics whenever he knew Razier had company.

When Razier pulled into their apartment complex, he told Tracy, "Looks like it's going to be a long night for me."

"Yeah, I could tell ole girl had the dick on her mind. She looked like she wanted to fuck your brains out right there on the damn back deck. I thought she was the one who didn't want to get her fuck on."

"That's the one."

"Well, she sure as fuck done changed her mind. So what you got up for her tonight, bro?"

"I'm going to give it to her as best as I can because out of all of the ladies, she's the one I'm feeling the most. She's not only the sexiest of them all but the sweetest. I mean, bro, you seen her. She's a dime for real, for real! She is in her 50s and looks like she could be in her late 30s."

"Yeah, she is a bad ol' bird, for real. Is that Horny Goat Weed doing you right, or what?"

"Yep. Good looking on that. But, man, I can't even think about a female without my piece starting to rock up. That gets kinda irritating."

"I feel you. At least you don't have to worry about standing up when it comes time for you to do your thang."

"I know, right? Anyway, what you got up for the weekend?"

"I'm waiting for Lavonda's funny-looking ass to get here from Boley so I can break her off and keep her smiling. Feel me? She's a cool broad, but you know that ain't my type of get down. The money she's making me is keeping her in my life, but what's so crazy is she knows it and ain't tripping about it. What's even crazier is I'm actually feeling her a li'l bit."

"Now, that *is* crazy. I never thought I would see you with a female less than a nine. She's a nice girl, though, and that can make up for the lack in the looks department. She sure isn't lacking anywhere else, that's for damn sure, so that's a plus for you."

Laughing, Tracy said, "That part. She's a stone freak too, so you know I'm loving that shit. Let me tell you, bro, she has to be the freakiest broad I've ever met in my life."

"*That's* what's up. Looks aren't everything, bro. She is down for you and your schemes and willing to accept her place in your life. You have to keep her in your mix."

"I feel you. I'm about to put you up on something that you will not believe."

"What?"

"Since I've been home, I haven't thought about getting at another broad. What's crazy is Lavonda doesn't even believe me. She swears I'm out here getting my freak on with other bitches. I told her with the combo of you working the fuck outta me on a daily, I don't have the time or energy to get at broads. I genuinely look forward to seeing her freaky, thick ass on the weekends. I think the pen fucked me up for real."

Shaking his head, Razier smiled at his best friend and said, "Nah, bro, you're maturing. You like what you like, but you're no fool. Lavonda may not be all that easy on the eyes, but she's a good woman who is down for you, and that makes you look past what she looks like and appreciate her."

"You may be right. But you do know the first chance I get, I'm going to get me that nine you were talking about and post her up somewhere."

Laughing, Razier said, "No doubt. Now let me get ready, so I can get some grub for Carmela and set the tone for tonight's stolen moment. I'll give you a call in the morning. If you want, since Saturdays are light, I can handle it on my own so you can spend more time with Lavonda."

"Yeah, that would be cool because we need to make some runs and get more phones. Some of the dudes I hooked her up with want more of them, so that will make us more bread. After that, I need to check on Pops. Moms hit me earlier and told me they took him to the emergency room because he wasn't feeling right."

With genuine concern in his voice, Razier asked, "Why didn't you say something, fool? We could have cut things short and gone to check on Mr. Briggs."

"Moms said she would call if things were serious. She texted me and said they were running tests on him, and he was resting comfortably, so I kept it to myself. By the time we finished the last yard, she hit me and told me they were back home and that it was just gas." They both started laughing.

"Okay, cool. But don't do that no more. You get a call like that, you make sure you get at me, jerk. I should make you body up for that goofy stuff."

"I feel you, bro. All right, let me roll. You know I'm copping that brand-new 'Vette next week. You need to step up ya game and cop that foreign you been bumping your gums about. You got the catering truck getting ready, you got the pool service equipment paid for, so what the fuck you waiting on? You know damn well you're not hurting for money. Shit, how much money you got on that Visa now?"

"Close to fifteen bands. What's so crazy is Olivia told me that any one of the ladies would gladly cosign for me for whatever whip I want."

"So what the fuck you waiting on?"

"I've been thinking about it a lot, but there's one major thing in my way."

"What?"

"A little slim, old lady who will swear to Jesus I'm into something illegal and would blame it all on *your* ass, bro—especially when she sees your new 'Vette and my new foreign. What you think she'll say?"

"Damn, didn't think about that. Mrs. Coleman will fry both our asses because there wouldn't be nothing we could tell her that would make her believe we're totally legal . . . well, almost totally."

"Exactly."

"What if we told her about what you're doing? You know they say the truth will set you free," Tracy said and started laughing.

"Yeah, right. The prison system *did* mess up your head. If you think I would ever tell my mother some stuff like that, you're plum stupid. I think I'll wait a few more months before I tell her the businesses have been solid and good enough for me that I can afford it. In the meantime, you do you, and when I want to get flossy with it, I'll push your 'Vette and do me."

Laughing, Tracy said, "Yeah, I bet your ass will. Okay, bro, get at me before you head out to work in the morning to let me know how good that ole sexy bird's snapper is."

Shaking his head, Razier gave his best friend some dap and said, "Don't worry about a thing. I will make sure that I'll tell you *nothing*."

Chapter Fifteen

Carmela was sitting in front of the mirror in her dressing room, applying her makeup, feeling giddy as she thought about her upcoming evening with Razier. She never once cheated on her husband, but tonight was the night. Instead of being scared, she looked forward to the sexual release she knew she would receive from Razier. To know that he was willing to please and make her feel like a woman was something she was yearning for. She wanted it. She *needed* it. She wanted her husband to make love to her too, but he hadn't touched her in that way in over seven months, always complaining that he was too tired or just not in the mood. She didn't deserve that, and she let it be continuously known, only to be scolded on how hard he worked every day to keep them living the good life. What he thought was the "good life" was a miserable life to her, but all of that was about to change. She was about to make love to a vibrant, sexy, handsome young man, and she was dead set on making sure he enjoyed her just as much as she intended on enjoying him. At that moment, her husband entered the room and saw she was applying her makeup, so he asked her where she was going.

"I'm going out with Olivia. We're going to have dinner at the Riverwind Casino and do some gambling . . . a girls' night out. I called your office, but your secretary said you were in a meeting and told her you weren't to be disturbed."

"Why didn't you leave a message? You should have let me know what your plans were, Carmela."

"My evening plans aren't your secretary's business, Walter. I told her to tell you to call, but you didn't, so, oh well."

"Whatever. Did you make me something to eat?"

"No. I didn't know whether you would be home."

"Well, I'm home, and I'm hungry. Cook me a steak and some mixed vegetables."

She checked the time and said, "I'm running late as it is. I don't have time to make your food. You can go out and get something or order a pizza."

"You must be out of your damn mind, Carmela. I've been at work all day, and if I want my wife to cook me a damn meal, you're going to cook me a damn meal."

She turned in her seat and faced him with anger flaring in her eyes. "There's a lot I want and expect from my husband, Walter. But guess what? I don't get any of it. I don't complain any longer, so you shouldn't start. You want something to eat, so I suggest you fend for yourself. I'm going out, and I'll be home late." She turned back toward the mirror and finished the final touches of her makeup.

He stared at her in shock for a moment because he couldn't believe she had the nerve to talk to him that way. "What if I told you I didn't want you to go out tonight?"

She laughed and said, "Why? So you could go into your office and burn the midnight oil working until I fall asleep? Don't you understand that I'm tired of being alone in my own home? You better get used to meals not being prepared for you when you get home. You better prepare yourself for a lot of changes, Walter. Either that or start acting like my husband again." She stood, went into her closet, grabbed a pair of form-fitting skinny jeans, and put them on. She then grabbed her black blouse and put it on when she felt her husband standing behind her. Without turning to face him, she asked, "What do you want, Walter?"

He stared at her back for a moment and said softly, "I don't want you to go out tonight. Especially angry. You might do something you'll regret."

She turned, faced him, and laughed. "Really? If I were going to do something I'd regret, I would have done it a long, long time ago. I need an evening out so I can feel free and enjoy myself. I've become trapped within my own home, and I don't care for that feeling at all. If me going out worries you, why don't you join Olivia and me? We can go out and enjoy the evening together if you like. That way, you can get plenty to eat at one of the various restaurants inside the casino."

"You know I don't care for gambling or being in a smoky casino."

"That's not what you said when you had those business associates in town trying to get them to sign with your company."

"That's different. That was business."

"Right. Business is more important than putting a smile on your wife's face. Got it."

"It won't be just with you. You said Olivia is joining you."

"Whatever, Walter. This conversation is over. Good night," she said as she grabbed her purse and started walking out of the bedroom.

"Carmela, are you cheating on me?"

"No, Walter. I am not cheating on you, nor have I ever cheated on you."

"Do you want to cheat on me?"

"If I did, I would've cheated on you a long time ago. Good night, Walter," she said and left the bedroom. Once she was inside her cute one-year-old Toyota Prius, she laughed out loud as she started the car. "*Now* you want to worry about what I'm doing? What a joke." She pulled out of the driveway and turned on the radio, chose one of her favorite salsa songs, and started nodding her head to the beat. She was determined to have a great evening with Razier, and nothing was going to spoil her plans. Not even her husband, trying to act as if he gave a damn what she did, knowing damn well he could care less with his selfish ass. As far as she was concerned, he could do what he always did. . . . Go in his office, snort some cocaine, and act like he was working while talking on the phone to whatever woman he was sleeping with. Tonight was her night, and she was about to have sex and enjoy *every* tingling moment of it.

Razier was inside the kitchen setting plates on the counter to place the steaming enchiladas on them that he bought from Ted's Mexican Restaurant. Once he had the food ready, he took it and set the plates on the dining room table when Carmela knocked on his door. He smiled as he went and let her in. Carmela entered his apartment smelling sweet, wearing her favorite Chanel No. 5.

"Mmmm, you smell really good, Carmela."

"Thank you, handsome," she said in a flirtatious tone that made Razier instantly horny for her. "Ummm, the food smells delicious."

"I hope you like it. I got some enchiladas from Ted's. To me, it's the best Mexican restaurant in the city."

"I've heard of that place. Isn't it off Sixty-Third and May?"

"Yes. A small place, but the food is excellent."

"I'm sure it is because it certainly smells good," she said as she set her purse on the coffee table and went and sat down at the dining room table. After they blessed the food, they began silently eating. Razier was staring at Carmela and wondered how good it would feel to be inside of her. She noticed the lustful look in his eyes and smiled. "Is it the spicy food, or am I having a certain effect on you this evening, Razier?"

"Trust, it's not the food." They both laughed as they finished eating.

"We have the rest of the evening to watch *Die Hard 2*, Razier. I love me some Bruce Willis, but right now, I need you to touch me. Kiss me. Lick me. Hold me and fuck me long and slow. Make me feel special, please."

For some reason, her words had an effect on him that confused him greatly. He wanted her bad, really bad, but it wasn't like the other ladies. He didn't want to just fuck her. He wanted to make love to this sexy, older woman . . . a woman old enough to be his mother . . . a woman that was paying him for sex and a good time. He wanted and intended on making love to her as long as he could. It was like he had feelings for her, and that was what was so confusing to him.

He stood and grabbed her hand and pulled her into his arms. Then he hugged her tightly as he kissed her neck and licked her earlobes. She sighed heavily and held him tightly. He shocked her when he let his kisses go from her ears and neck to her lips. She was somewhat hesitant, but she opened her mouth, and their tongues began a passionate dance that turned them both on greatly. Her hunger for him took over, and she knew there was no turning back now. She had to have him . . . and have him she did.

They made love off and on for two hours straight, stopping only to get a drink of water. Refreshed, they were right back at each other's body, licking, sucking, and having the best sex that either of them ever had in their lives. When they came for what felt like the tenth time, they stopped and lay down next to each other, panting, trying to catch their breath.

"Wow," said Razier.

"No. *Double* wow," she added, and they both laughed. "I didn't know it was humanly possible to have that many orgasms."

"Me neither. You were incredible, Carmela, and it took all I had to be able to keep up."

"You're such a passionate and skilled lover, Razier. What have I gotten myself into with you? I don't ever want to let you get away from me now. My God, that sounds so crazy. But it's so damn true." She started laughing as she got out of bed and walked into the bathroom naked, without any shame. Her body was still tight and sexy, and she was totally confident as she went into the bathroom. She returned with a warm washcloth in her hand and began to wash off their sex from Razier's manhood. He moaned when she placed the warm cloth on him and felt himself start to get hard again. "Whoa, now, give an old lady a break, will ya? I don't think I'm quite ready for more of that monster inside of me, at least not yet." She checked her watch and saw that it was barely ten p.m. "We have plenty of time, okay?"

"Don't blame me. *You're* the one who's seducing *me*, lady."

Laughing, she slapped him playfully on his chest and said, "Stop that, Razier. You're so bad. You're making me feel like I'm taking advantage of you."

He grabbed her hand and started kissing her again, this time softly and with such ease that they felt as if they were a couple of long-standing. She pulled from their embrace after a full minute and sighed.

"What's wrong, Carmela?"

She turned and lay her head on his chest and said, "Nothing. My life is so confusing right now. I have never been with another man since marrying Walter. I feel as if I've disappointed God. I broke my wedding vows, and though I feel guilty for what I've done, I don't regret it at all. I've been the best wife I can be to that man, and all he does is ignore me and make me feel as if I'm nothing but a good housekeeper instead of a loving wife. I don't deserve that, Razier. I deserve to feel special. I deserve to be able to have the man I married love me the way I need to be loved."

"Yes, you do. You shouldn't regret what we did because the number one rule in life is self-preservation. Always take care of self, and that's exactly what you did tonight. You don't strike me as a woman who would decide hastily to cheat. You proved that the first time we were together. Please don't feel guilty because that will only serve to make me feel guilty too."

"You're so sweet. You made this hard decision easy for me, Razier. You made me so comfortable that I was lost in it all. Lost in you. Only if you would have come into my life twenty years ago."

Laughing, he said, "Twenty years ago, I was only 8 years old, Carmela."

"Ugh. Don't you go and remind me. You're making me feel old."

He gave her a peck on her forehead and said, "Don't feel old, mami. Live and enjoy our stolen moment."

She stared into his eyes and said, "'K." Then she proceeded to take his solid advice by sliding down to his semihard dick and put it in her mouth, and for the first time in over twenty years, had another man's dick inside of her mouth. They made love for another hour or so before falling into a peaceful sleep.

Carmela opened her eyes and saw that it was almost four in the morning and sighed. She got out of the bed and went and took a long, hot shower. When she came back into the bedroom, Razier was still sound asleep. She tiptoed into the living room, grabbed her purse, and pulled out a white envelope, which she set on the coffee table. Silently, she slipped on her shoes and left the apartment, feeling content and satisfied sexually. She got into her car and started crying as she left the apartment complex. Why couldn't her damn husband make her feel as good as Razier just did?

Why?

Chapter Sixteen

The past two months had been so productive for Razier that he was the happiest he'd ever been in his life. His money was right. He made over $20,000 from the ladies giving them stolen moments, plus his businesses were flourishing. The H&8th catering truck was bringing him more than he dreamed it would, and he owed that success to Olivia with the bright idea she gave him of having fried turkey legs made on his truck, along with fried chicken wings and fries. It seemed like every time he opened up at the H&8th event, his truck received more attention than any of the many other food trucks there.

The pool cleaning service was working out as well. He hired two of Tracy's friends who had been recently released from prison, and thanks to their hard work and dedication, he was able to stay on his yard work with Tracy. Everything was perfect.

What was even more surprising to him was his relationship with Carmela Wilkins. Not only were they making love to each other as often as they could, but they also formed a friendship that was getting stronger by the day. They spent time together outside of their stolen moments. They enjoyed lunches whenever he had the time from work. They had dinners and walks in the park and even went out to the movies a few times. They shared deep conversations, talking about everything from their past pains and failures to their future goals. Razier shared the hurt he experienced by getting caught having sex with a woman on the battleship and ruining both their naval careers. She admitted that her husband had been abusive with her on both the physical and verbal side. She told him about her husband's addiction to snorting cocaine. He shocked her by his reaction to her words. His anger and how protective he became over her served to only make her care for him even more.

The direction their relationship was headed was confusing to them, but one thing was clear . . . They cared for each other, and neither wanted what they were building to end. Now that Razier's money was right and his businesses were doing well, he felt it was time for him to enjoy some of the hard earned money he made, and as far as he was concerned, making love to eight mature women was arduous work. The ladies were becoming more and more demanding of his time, so he was seeing them as fast as he could. Carmela teased him about how she was jealous, but he knew she wasn't, and that only added to their closeness, strange as it sounds. She felt that as long as he continued giving her friends stolen moments, she could never be jealous or have to worry about some younger, prettier woman stealing him from her. Crazy.

Razier loved how all this craziness had worked in his favor. So today, he was on his way to the car lot, and thanks to Olivia and Vera Collins, he was about to cop that foreign whip he'd been dreaming of getting, the brand-new Audi A7. When he sat inside of the white Audi, he instantly fell in love with it. After ordering the upgrades, they left the car lot with Razier feeling as if he were on top of the world. Olivia and Vera used their connections at the dealership, and he got a great deal, plus a few extras thrown in. It felt good to have the right people on your side, and these ladies had proven that all eight of them were the right people for his life.

After he dropped off Olivia and Vera, he called Carmela and told her that he would be free for the afternoon because he was not giving any of the ladies a stolen moment. She agreed to meet him at his apartment because she had a surprise for him. He knew better than to ask any of the ladies what they had for him whenever they told him they had a surprise for him. It meant some form of a gift or more money than he expected, and he was OK with that. He had to admit that he felt some kind of way about what he was doing because he was having sex for money and assisting women in cheating on their husbands. But he convinced himself what he was doing was giving some temporary happiness to some women who were caught up in a miserable marriage, so he was doing a good deed.

The more he thought about it, the more he realized that it was time for him to do something he dreaded. He had to have a conversation with his mother. They were too close for him to keep this from her any longer, especially when he was about to be driving a brand-new, expensive Audi. Once his mother saw his new car, she would flip out and swear he was up to something illegal with Tracy. She already knew Tracy bought a new Corvette and asked him several times if Tracy was back to his old hustling ways. He couldn't explain Tracy's business with Lavonda because that was his personal stuff, and though she loved Tracy as her own, it wasn't her place. As far as he was concerned, though, it was time for the talk.

Ugh.

When he pulled into his mother's driveway, he saw Mrs. Hopkins in a pair of shorts and a wife-beater sitting on her porch look too damn sexy, and he wondered if she would be interested in a stolen moment. As he got out of his car, he had to shake his head at that thought. *Damn, what's up with you? Are the only women you digging now the older ones? Stop it,* he scolded himself as he waved at Mrs. Hopkins's sexy ass and quickly went into his mother's house.

"Well, well, look at the businessman. I was wondering if all of your success was going to go to your big head and keep you from spending some time with your lonely mother," Mrs. Coleman said as she gave her only child a warm and tight hug.

"You know better than that, Mama. No matter how much money I get or how busy I am, I will never be too busy for you. As a matter a fact, I'm here to take you to lunch."

Shaking her head, she said, "Sorry, Charlie. I got me a hot date, and I'm going to the mall to find me a nice outfit for the evening."

"A date? With whom?" Razier asked with a frown.

"A friend of mine. Actually, it's my doctor's brother. She introduced us a few weeks ago, and we've been getting at each other in our DMs, kicking it a li'l, getting to know each other. We've decided enough of that DM stuff and decided to go on our first date. He's very nice, and I like him, so I want to see how things go."

"You need to miss me with the DM stuff, Mama. Jeez. You are acting way too extra again. But anyway, I'm glad you're going out and all that, but you do know I need to meet this cat before you even think about getting into anything serious, right?"

"Am I not *your* mother, child? Did I *not* give birth to you?"

"Yes and yes."

"So when did I have to ask your permission for me to get involved in a relationship? Since when do I need your approval for anything regarding my personal life?" Before he could answer, his mother continued. "I know you care for me and my well-being, son, and I appreciate that. However, I don't need your approval because I'm grown, first and foremost, and I'm in total control of my life. I *do* know how to pick a man."

She saw the hurt expression on her son's face and her tone softened. "I love you, Razier, and that will never change. No man will ever interfere with our relationship, son. I'm not getting any younger, and it's time for me to find someone who wants to spend time with me and maybe give a go with being with me in a relationship. Right now, Carl is interesting to me, and I want to see where this leads, if anywhere at all."

"I understand, Mama, but it's kind of hard hearing you even thinking about being with another man. That's the little kid in me, I guess. You're a grown woman, and I know you're no fool. I feel some kind of jealousy because it's like Daddy's gone, and you're going to be with another man, and that thought sucks, for real."

"As hard as this sounds, it's the truth. Life goes on, Razier, and one thing for sure that I know is true is your father was never a selfish man. He took the very best care of me. He always wanted me happy. He always wanted me to have whatever made me happy. I don't doubt in my mind that he wants me to continue to be happy now. Really, I feel he's been frowning down on me for taking so long to move on with my life. I've been ultra loyal, and I felt if I got with another man, I would be betraying my husband, the man I loved since I was in high school.

"You are a grown man now, living your life and finally showing me you can be a mature man who can think with your head instead of that little head between your legs, and I'm so proud of you. That's really what helped me decide it was time for me to move forward with my life and to give this a go with Carl."

Oh my God, I wonder what she's going to say when I tell her what I've been doing, he thought as he stared at her. "You know what? Why don't you let me take you shopping so we can get you something real fly so this Carl cat's mouth will water when he sees how good you're looking."

"Now, you already know my taste is expensive, son. Are you sure you want to put yourself out there like that? You not bringing in that much loot, especially with men on your payroll now. I'm good. I can handle it."

"No, I insist. Let me handle this for you, Mama."

She shrugged and said, "Okay. I'm from the old school, son, and we don't turn down nothing but our collar."

Razier shook his head and said, "There you go. But before we leave, I need to talk to you about some things that are going on in my life."

She stared at him and tried to read his facial expression but saw nothing that would give her a clue about what he was going to say. "Let's have a seat because I have a feeling I need to be sitting down when you tell me what's on your mind."

Once they were seated, he wasted no time with any preamble and went straight in and told her what he was doing besides the yards, pools, and catering truck. When he finished, he stared at the shocked expression on his mother's face and instantly regretted telling her about his business with the ladies.

"Please, Mama, don't go off on me. This was a decision I made, and I'm good with it. You may disapprove, but it's my life, and so far, it's helped me achieve some of my goals way faster than I ever imagined."

"Boy, you and that tender dick. Only you could find a way to stumble into some damn gigolo stuff. I can't believe you even told me this," she said, shaking her head.

"I had to. I bought a brand-new Audi A7 today, and I knew when you saw my new whip, your mind would have all types of questions, so I wanted to let you know ahead of time what's what. The catering truck, the pool service van, and equipment, all of that have come from my hard work, Mama."

Laughing, she said, "Hard work? You call freaking off with eight older women—women my age or older—hard work? You are out of your damn mind, boy. I sure as hell hope you're wearing protection when you be with those horny old women."

"Come on, Mama. You know me better than that. Of course, I'm staying safe. These women are nice and respectable, and they all care for me, for real. They have helped me in more ways than I can even begin to tell you. Olivia and Vera signed off on my car and gave the down payment for me. What's even crazier, Mama, is they agreed to work it out with the other ladies to pay my monthly car note. That gives me the room to save my money and put it toward the condo I want downtown. You know, the ones where all the Thunder players be staying. For once, everything is going my way. It may not be the way I ever envisioned, it but it's happening for me, Mama, and I got to keep pushing this thing."

"I understand everything you're saying, and honestly, I can't blame you, Razier. This has to be any young man's dream come true to have women falling over them to have sex with women and get paid for it. It's like, wow. But it sickens me because I'm worried somehow you're going to get hurt, which is something I will not stand for. Because if that happens, I *will* reach out and touch every last one of those old freaks, do you hear me?"

"Yes, Mama. I honestly don't see how any of this can come back and hurt me, though."

"Humph. You wouldn't because you're too damn busy having sex with those women and counting your money. And a damn Audi. Brand-new at that. Boy, you better be careful because somehow, someway, this will come back and bite you in that tail of yours real hard. I have never wished any ill will your way, son, but this is a scary situation, and I can't see where this will end. I can only pray that it ends well in your favor. Tell me, what part does your partner in crime have to do with all of this mess? Please spare me the details if it has anything to do with him assisting you with sex with those women. I don't think my stomach could take that."

He laughed and said, "Nah, Mama. Tracy has helped me with the yard and catering truck business only, and honestly, his help has made things easier for me to make more moves. He's doing well on his own moves."

"What moves, Razier? You know that boy don't need to go back out there in those streets. He'll be back in prison before the year's out."

"He's not in the streets, Mama. He has a hustle, though, but it has nothing to do with drugs or any street stuff. I don't want to put his business out there, but I will tell you it's pretty cool and has no risk to his freedom being taken."

She rolled her eyes and looked up at the ceiling. "Lord, please keep your hands on these two young fools." She stood and said, "Come on, boy, let's go to the mall so we can go get me something expensive and cute. Might as well spend some of your money. After all, you're getting your American Gigolo on, so you might as well treat the woman who helped create you and that 'magic stick.'"

"Mama!"

She turned and faced him and said, "What? It's true, ain't it?"

He smiled. "Yep. And my magic stick is making it do what it do, for real, for real. They loving it, Mama."

She raised her hands in front of her face as if trying to block his words and screamed, "TMI, son. TMI. Come on, boy, let's go."

Chapter Seventeen

Razier went back to his place feeling good yet somewhat worried about his mother pursuing a relationship with this new friend of hers, but he shook that thought out of his mind because life goes on, and his mother deserved to be happy. She was his world, and as long as she was happy, and that guy didn't do anything stupid, everything would be all good. The thoughts of his mother were quickly put to the back of his mind when he received a text from Carmela telling him that she would be at his apartment within the next ten minutes. He smiled as he set the phone down and went to the bathroom to freshen up before she arrived. Since Carmela didn't have any preference when it came to the flowers she liked, he stopped and got her a dozen red roses, positive that they would put a smile on her lovely face.

He loved making the ladies smile because they damn sure kept him smiling. The sex was great, and so far, he had been maintaining strong erections to please them all, even if he was bone tired. Thanks to that Horny Goat Weed, he'd been able to perform like a true stud. Every time one of the ladies came through for a stolen moment, he was turned on instantly. He was starting to wonder if it was all the Horny Goat Weed because each woman possessed a certain sexual quality that made him want them badly. Some were freakier than the others, and that was something that aroused him intensely. Some were tender and loving and made him feel as if they were meant to be together sexually. Some even were demanding, which added another dimension to their great sex. Sex and money were what his life had become all about, and he loved it.

Carmela knocked softly on the front door and waited anxiously as her young lover came to let her inside. When Razier opened the door smelling good, wearing her favorite Givenchy cologne, she smiled and kissed him.

"Hi, Razi," she said as she stepped inside. She stopped suddenly, turned, faced him, and smiled. "Are you ready for your surprise, Razi?"

"Now, you know I'm always ready for any surprise from you, Carmela. What you got going on in that gorgeous head of yours?"

She gave him a devilish smile and said, "You'll see. I need for you to have a seat because I want to give you something." She led the way to the couch and sat down as she waited for him to join her. She reached over and began to unbuckle his belt until she had his pants opened and pulled out his soft dick, which instantly began to harden.

"Ooh, looks like this nice piece of man meat wants some attention. God, I love how you're always ready for me. That's such a turn-on, Razi," she said as her mouth watered just as she put him in it and began to give him a sloppy blow job. The slurping sounds she made as she gave him head drove him to the point of coming much faster than he wanted, but he enjoyed every minute of the oral love she was giving him. When he came, she swallowed every drop of his cum and moaned as she savored his flavor. "I don't know what it is about you, Razi, but you keep me so hot for you. You make me feel like a randy teen."

"You make me feel like I'm the luckiest man in the world, Carmela. I never thought anything like this would or could happen to me. This is like a wonderful dream."

"This is a dream come true for you, Razi, and I never met a man who's more deserving of everything that comes your way." She kissed the head of his dick and put it back inside of his pants, then said, "Now, let's go."

"Where are we going? I'm cool if we chill here for the rest of the evening."

Shaking her head, she said, "No way. You're about to get the surprise of your life, young man. Now come on."

Twenty minutes later, Carmela pulled into a neighborhood called The Hill in the Bricktown area of Oklahoma City. It was a two-block section of new town houses where several Oklahoma Thunder players resided. The newly built town houses had the look of an East Coast brownstone. Razier's curiosity was aroused, but he remained silent as Carmela pulled into the driveway of a two-bedroom town house. She got out of the car, and he followed. She opened the door, and they went inside the town house. Razier looked around the lovely home, genuinely impressed, and again, wondered what was going on and why were they standing inside of an empty town house.

"Okay, why are we standing inside of an empty place, Carmela?"

"It won't be empty for long, Razi," she said as she held the keys in her hand she used to open the door and tossed them to him. "This is your town house. Remember when you told me you wanted to get a place out this way?"

He stared at her in amazement and couldn't find his voice to answer her, so all he did was nod his head.

"Well, the ladies and I concluded that if you're going to be driving a hundred thousand-dollar vehicle, you shouldn't be living in an apartment. So, welcome to your new home."

Before he could say a word, the rest of the ladies came out of the upstairs bedroom screaming, "Surprise!"

Erica, Olivia, Lia, Vera, Marie, Louise, and Dionne came down the stairs, smiling at him. Each of the ladies came to him and kissed either on the lips or his cheek. He was still so shocked, he couldn't speak. After a moment, he finally found his voice and asked, "What did I do to deserve this from you all?"

Touched by the sincerity in his voice, Carmela spoke for the ladies. "You've given some old women their groove back, Razi. You've made us all feel alive again. For doing that, we wanted to make sure no matter what, you are adequately taken care of. You now have a new car which we will pay for monthly.

Along with your new car, you have your own home. This place is yours, Razi; all yours. No matter what happens, you will never lose any of the gifts we've given you."

"That's right. On top of that, we've also taken the liberty to buy you a new wardrobe. We want you to have the best of everything because you've given us the very best of you," Lia said with a smile. Each of the others smiled in agreement with their friend.

Razier felt so blessed at that moment that he damn near started to cry. Instead, he shook his head, smiled, and said, "Y'all have lost your minds. I can't accept this. It's too much."

Olivia started laughing. "Shut up. You're going to accept our gifts and not say another word about them. This is your housewarming of sorts, so enjoy." She turned and went into the kitchen, then returned with several glasses and a bottle of Dom Pérignon and gave everyone a glass before popping open the bottle of expensive champagne. "A toast." She raised her glass in the air and continued, "A toast to the man who came into our lives and made us all feel alive again. A man who knows how to please a woman. To Razier. Our Razi."

The ladies all raised their glasses in the air and yelled, "To our Razi. Cheers."

Razier downed his drink and grabbed the bottle from Olivia. He quickly poured himself another. After downing that glass, he sighed and shook his head. "I really can't believe you did this for me."

"Believe it, buddy. This $350,000 town house is all yours. All you have to do is take care of your monthly bills. We've taken care of everything from the taxes to the insurance, yearly. You're good, and it's all yours," said Dionne.

"That's right. You've earned this, Razi, and trust me . . . We do plan to make sure you keep right on earning everything we give you. That is, if you can continue to handle giving us our stolen moments," said Erica.

"If you choose to move on and stop our special treatment, everything we've given you is all yours, regardless. We're no Indian givers, baby," Lia said with a smile on her face.

"Damn," was all he could think to say.

Laughing, Louise said, "I sure hope you'll let us furnish your place for you, baby. No offense, but I think you *need* us in that department. Your apartment is a nice, macho bachelor place and all, but this place needs a classy ladies' touch."

"I don't even know why you said that mess, girlfriend. You know we've already taken care of that as well," laughed Marie.

"Y'all got me furniture too?" Razier asked, well beyond shocked now. He was flabbergasted.

With a wicked smile on her face, Marie said, "Kinda, Razi." She turned toward Erica and Lia and said, "Come on, ladies, let's show him." Marie led the way upstairs toward the bedroom, followed closely by Lia and Erica. The rest of the ladies came to Razier and kissed him.

With a smile on her face, Olivia said, "Enjoy this stolen moment, Razi, because it's purely for your enjoyment."

"I hope I can hear from you later in the week, Razi, because I think you're going to need some recuperation time," Dionne said as she planted a kiss on his lips and slid her tongue inside of his mouth as she moaned.

Vera smiled at him and said, "Mmm, I cannot wait to feel you again, Razi. See ya later, babe."

Louise kissed him and winked. "You're so damn hot, you've actually made me start back sexing my husband, Razi. You've earned everything you've gotten, *and* some, baby. Enjoy your night."

Last, Carmela stepped to him, smiling. She leaned close to him and kissed his right earlobe, then whispered, "I wanted to be daring and be a part of this, but I chickened out. You make sure you tell me all about it."

"About what?"

She smiled, gave him a tender kiss, and said, "You'll see."

He stood there and watched as the five ladies left his home. He was still standing there staring at the front door, trying to make himself believe that this was his home. *Man, when I tell that fool, Tracy, this, he's going to flip his wig,* he thought as he poured another drink. He wasn't a big drinker, but at that moment, he felt he needed the spirits to help him realize that he wasn't dreaming.

Lia Bin, Marie Simmons, and Erica Beckman came out of the bedroom and stood at the top of the stairs, each of them completely naked. Razier turned and stared up at them and almost dropped the glass of champagne he was holding.

"Come on, Razi, so you can come and come all night long," said the sexy Asian Lia. "Tonight, we love you a long time."

"That's right, Razier. Tonight, you're going to have the night that men across the world have only dreamed of," said Marie.

"That's right, baby. You're about to make old Hugh Heff do flips in his grave from jealousy with what's about to go down," Erica said as she grabbed one of her large breasts, turned toward Lia, and said, "Give him an example of what he's about to experience, Lia."

Lia shyly smiled as she stepped next to Erica and kissed her, and then let her push her head toward her erect nipple. Lia sighed as she began sucking and licking Erica's tit.

Marie moaned and began rubbing her pussy as she watched this erotic sexual act taking place next to her. Before long, she stepped to the ladies and began tongue kissing Erica while Lia was still savoring Erica's mammoth breasts. She pulled her lips from Erica's and told Razier, "Come. Come upstairs to your bedroom, Razi. We bought you a California king-size bed, baby. Let's give it the proper christening." She didn't wait for his answer. She turned and led the ladies back inside of the bedroom.

When Razier climbed the stairs and entered the bedroom, he couldn't believe what he saw. Erica was lying on the bed with her legs spread wide open while Marie was between them sloppily sucking her pussy. Lia was sitting on Erica's face getting her pussy sucked as well. Razier started stripping, feeling as if he were about to come in his pants without even touching himself. His dick was so hard he felt as if it were about to burst through its skin.

The sucking and slurping sounds the ladies were making as he stepped toward the bed were making him dizzy with lust. He knew that this was going to be one night that he would never forget. When his skin touched the ladies, the heat generating from them made his body tingle as it never had in his life. Lia smiled at him and made him kiss her. They tongue kissed each other passionately as she continued to grind her pussy on Erica's face.

She pulled from his lips and smiled. "You ready to join us so you can experience the ultimate pleasure, Razi?"

He pulled Lia off Erica's face and began kissing Erica passionately while tasting Lia's juices from Erica's lips. "Damn, your pussy tastes so good, Lia."

She moaned and said, "Come taste it for yourself, Razi. Come lick me good, baby." As he rolled over and began eating Lia's pussy, Erica screamed that she was coming, and Marie lapped her pussy faster. The rest of the night was a blur to Razi. Orgasm after orgasm of pure bliss all night long filled with their moans, grunts, and screams of passion. Razier Coleman finally fell asleep, feeling as if he died and went to heaven because heaven had to be this good. It had to be. If it didn't, he indeed must have just experienced heaven on earth.

Chapter Eighteen

Tracy made a horrible mistake when he decided to roll through Club Avenue 101. He was bored after having dinner and chilling out with Lavonda, so he thought it would be a good idea to roll through the club and get his floss on right when everyone was exiting the club. He knew instantly once when he saw Sunny that he made a major fuckup. Sunny was his longtime girlfriend before he went to prison. Being the man he was, he chose to let her go because he didn't need the added pressure and stress while doing his time, worrying what she would have been doing, so he felt that decision would be best for both of them. She, however, thought he dogged her by letting her go. When he saw her leaving the club, all of the feelings he suppressed for her came rushing back to him big time. He was standing next to his brand-new Corvette with all eyes on him and his new toy. All eyes and the one pair of eyes he wished hadn't seen him did.

Sunny smiled and started walking toward him, and his heart began beating faster, not only because he was happy to see her still looking so good but also because he knew she would flip her wig when she saw Lavonda sitting in the front seat of his car. There was nothing he could do, so he stepped away from the car to cut her off.

"What's good, Sunny? Looking good as always, I see," he said with a smile on his face.

Sunny frowned and looked right past him at who was sitting inside of his car and said, "I must not be looking too damn good, Tracy Briggs. I see your ass got a boo thang with you tonight. I heard you been out for a few months, and I was wondering when you would give me a holla. When you didn't, I already knew you had something going on with someone else. And that is real fucked up, Tracy Briggs."

"Dead that and don't even think about tripping the fuck out right now. I didn't get at you because I figured you'd moved on with your life."

"Oh, now, aren't you ever the considerate one, Tracy Briggs. Always looking out for me and my little feelings. You ain't shit, Tracy Briggs. I wish I would never have fucked with your ass. As for me tripping on you, uh-uh, booboo, not my style anymore. I hope you're happy with your new boo thang there. I see you're getting your paper. I'm happy for you. Hopefully, you'll be able to stay out of prison. Bye, Tracy," Sunny said sadly as she turned and started walking toward her car, feeling as if her heart had been crushed by the one and only man she'd ever loved. It took all of the control she could muster not to snatch that female out of his car and beat her ass. She was being mature and doing the right thing, but a part of her told herself to go back and fight for what was hers. Because as far as she was concerned, Tracy Briggs belonged to her. Now wasn't the time to act, but she would act soon— sooner than anyone expected, that was for damn sure.

Tracy shook his head as he watched Sunny walk away. "Damn." He turned and got into his car and sped away, hoping Lavonda didn't start with him because he wasn't in the mood for none of her slippery lips.

His hope was in vain.

"So who was that? One of your females from back in your big playa days, Tracy?"

"Yep," he said, hoping his honesty would dead the conversation. Again, luck wasn't in his favor.

"You're lucky I didn't jump out of this car and check that bitch."

"Check her or what? She was coming to say, 'What's up?' You need to calm your ass down and let that one go, Lavonda. She's the past."

"I'm yours now as well as your future, so I have the right to speak on this shit."

"Fact: I don't have a problem with you speaking on shit. But I told you what it is, so dead that shit."

"I know while I'm working and handling *our* business, you be out here in the city doing your thang, Tracy. I'm no fool, so don't try to play me like that."

"You may not be a fool, but you're talking foolishness because there are not enough hours in a day for me to be working with Razi all damn day and then find time to be fucking with any broads. I told you I'm doing right by your ass, but for some reason, that's not registering in your fuckin' head. That's not good because your insecurities will only bring us to an end, so you need to shut the fuck up and dead that weak shit. Don't think for a minute that the business we got going will stop me from ending this shit. No one—*no one* dictates my moves or how I get down. My word is my word, and I gave you my word. I will be true to you, believe me, or not. If you don't, when we get back to my spot, you can get your shit and take your country ass back to Boley. The money we making, you can have that shit. I can do me and keep it moving, Lavonda, and don't you ever fucking forget that shit."

"Damn, Tracy, why you so mad at me? You're my man, and if I think a woman is trying to get at mine, I have every right to speak my mind."

"You already said that shit, and I agreed with you. You spoke on it, and I told you what it is, so that's that. Now, do you want to go get something to eat or head back to my spot and call it a night?"

"Go on home. I'll cook us something when we get there, baby. Don't be mad, Tracy. I'm for you 100 percent, and all I want is to see you win, baby."

He gave a slight nod of his head but remained silent as he drove home, thinking about Sunny the entire ride to his apartment. *Damn, Sunny, why you had to be looking so damn fine? Fuck,* he thought, clearly confused now because though he cared for Lavonda, his heart belonged to Sunny, and the look of pain on Sunny's face was killing him on the inside. His money was right from the cell phone stuff with Lavonda, and he knew she was using that to her advantage to keep him locked in with her. He was working hard with Razier every day, and that made his money clean with the business they were doing with the yards and pool service. Razier even cut him a piece of the action with the food truck, so it was all good. He may not be pushing the new Audi and living in a fly town house like his bestie, Razier, but he was happy and living right. At least he thought he was happy. Seeing Sunny proved that he wasn't as happy as he thought he was. He would never be truly happy without Sunny in his life.

Fuck.

Razier and Olivia were lying on his bed, cuddled up, relaxing after an intense stolen moment. Olivia wasn't in the mood for any wining or dining. All she wanted was some good old-fashioned fucking, and that's precisely what Razier gave her.

Now that they were relaxing, he thought about how good everything had continued to go for him. He was expecting to wake up any moment from this wonderful dream. Feeling Olivia's heartbeat on his chest made him realize this wasn't a dream. It was his life, and he loved it tremendously. He was so grateful to the ladies for making everything he wanted to happen so quickly for him. Never in his wildest dreams did he expect to have so much in such little time. He had reached all his goals, and then some. He not only had his own foreign car and a town house fully furnished but also the ladies made sure that he was decked out properly with an entirely new wardrobe. Not just any new wardrobe . . . Nothing but top-of-the-line designer *everything* from suits to his shoes. Tailor-made shirts with his initials monogrammed on each . . . Stuff any man dreamed of. Who would ever have thought he'd be decked out in suits by Kiton, Stefano Ricci, Isaia Napoli, Tom Ford, and Ralph Lauren's Purple Label?

Added to the expensive clothing, he was now rocking some very costly pieces of jewelry. Watches by Audemars Piguet, Chopard, Franck Muller, and an ultraexpensive watch by Rotonde de Cartier. The ladies refused to tell him how much they spent on everything they got him, so he hit old faithful Google and damn near choked on the piece of fruit he'd been chewing when he saw that the Rotonde de Cartier cost over $185,000.

Damn, was his dick *really* that good? He smiled when he answered his question. Had to be. Here he was, living it up and having all the sex he could handle *and* getting paid for it. The ladies were well off. He knew that, but never did he think they could afford all of what they had done for him. He was so grateful that he felt there had to be something he could do to show them how much he appreciated what they did for him. But what? That was the question. His money was right and steadily growing day by day. His work ethic had paid off because as winter was soon approaching, he would still be able to make it through the slow season with the business they were doing with the yards and the food truck. Razier even cut Tracy a piece of the catering food truck, so it was all good.

He was thinking about doing some catering to help bring in some extra coins during the winter months. But why bother? All he had to do was continue making sure the ladies were straight, and he'd be OK for sure. Damn, he was one lucky man.

"Penny for your thoughts, Razi?" Olivia asked as she stared up into his light brown eyes.

"I was just thinking about how grateful I am to you and the rest of the ladies. Y'all have changed my life in a few short months, and I feel like I need to show you how much I appreciate everything you've done for me."

Shaking her head, Olivia said, "You don't have to do any such thing, Razi. You've made some very lonely women feel alive again in every facet. You've touched us all in one way or another. You've given us a reprieve from a life of extreme boredom. You've breathed a breath of fresh air into our lungs, and we are so very grateful to you for that. There's a lot that you don't know about us and what our lives have been like. I know some of the ladies have shared some personal stuff with you, but trust me when I tell you that there is much that you don't know. It took a whole lot for the ladies and me to approach you. We needed you, Razi, and you came through big time. The gifts we've bestowed upon you are our way of hopefully keeping you as happy as you're making us. We don't want to lose you any time soon, baby. So go on with that nonsense of showing us how much you appreciate us. We know that. We know you are grateful. You know what impresses us most about you, Razi?"

"What?"

"The fact that you remain dedicated to your work. You still get up every morning even after sexing one of us all night long. You get right up and stick to your plan. You are a good man, a good, hardworking man. Any other man that had women paying him for his services sexually, along with giving him lavish gifts like we've given you, would've quit working and lived the rest of his life off of us. Not you. You remain dedicated to what you do, and believe me when I tell you this, that has made us feel like everything we've given you is well worth it. You're a good man, and that turns us on even more. We know we made the right choice by choosing you, Razi."

"Wow. Thank you for that compliment."

"Trust me when I tell you this, Razi. I speak not only for myself but also for all of my girls. You are very special to us, and we look at it as an honor and privilege to have such a handsome and respectable man in our lives this way."

"That really means a lot to me, and as crazy as this situation is, I feel like it's just . . . just right, you know what I'm saying?"

She smiled and rubbed his chest. "Yes, baby, I know."

"It's sort of weird because it's like I care for each of you . . . like y'all are all my girlfriends in a way."

She laughed and said, "Baby, we are. You got us all. We are all yours."

"That settles it. I got the perfect idea for how I can show my appreciation to y'all for what you've done for me."

"What do you have in mind, Razi?"

"A long weekend, for all of us together. To make this work, I'm going to need your help, Olivia."

"If I can help, you know it's done, baby. Now tell me what you have bouncing around in that handsome head of yours?"

"Branson, Missouri. I want to drive us all down there so that we can spend a long, relaxing weekend together. No stolen moments, though. Just us enjoying one another's company. My mom took me out there last year for a weekend, and we had a nice time. I think y'all will enjoy it out there. Do you think you can get your girls to agree and be able to get them away from their husbands for a long weekend?"

"That shouldn't be too hard. We'll make it look like a girls' trip for the weekend. I think it can happen. When are you trying to do this, Razi?"

"Next weekend. We'll leave early Friday morning. It's a five-hour drive, so we'll arrive in Branson by noon and spend the entire weekend out there and leave Sunday morning."

"Mmm, sounds like a plan. I like it. Well, I like everything except for the 'no stolen moments' part, and I'm sure the girls will feel exactly as I do."

"Tough. I need a break, so this will be a weekend of relaxation and fun. No sex. And one more thing."

"Yes, baby?"

"Tell your girls that the entire trip is on me. I mean, after all, I *can* afford it."

They both started laughing.

"Yes, you most definitely can afford it, Razi. Now, can we get back to *my* stolen moment, baby?"

His answer to her question was him sliding his hand between her legs. She moaned, and he smiled.

Chapter Nineteen

"So you mean to tell me you're taking all of those old birds outta town for the weekend, and their husbands are going for that shit?" Tracy asked as he sat down on the plush leather sofa inside of Razier's town house.

"Yep. The thing is, their husbands won't know they're going with me. They have it set up as an all-girls' trip for the weekend to Branson. Olivia got at all of the ladies for me, and they're excited about spending the weekend with me out there. They think they're slick, though, because each one has called me and tried to get me to agree to sneak away with them and give them a stolen moment, but that's not happening. I told them no, and that this trip is on me to show my appreciation for all that they've done for me."

"What? Are you actually going to spend all that loot on thoze ole birds? Fool, you tripping. This thing you got going with them is for you to make the dough, not blow the dough, fool."

Shaking his head, Razier said, "You don't get it. These women have changed my life, bro, and it's only right that I give back a little. Trust me, the little I give back will only make the ladies give me more because they feeling ya boy, for real, for real."

"Yeah, I hear you. So what you gon' do, rent a couple of SUVs to take them down there?"

"Nope. I have a friend who has one of those Mercedes Sprinters. He's agreed to let me use it for the weekend.

It seats twelve comfortably. It's hooked up with TVs, leather bucket seats, and a fully stocked bar so that we can have a smooth ride on the drive to Missouri. I was thinking about taking the ladies to breakfast at Jimmy's Egg before we hit the highway. What you think?"

"More money is what I think, but since you saving some change with the Sprinter, it sounds good, bro. Shit, with all the drama Lavonda has been dishing my way, I wish I could roll out there with your ass. I'm telling you, bro, this shit with her is about to end. The broad is too damn jealous, and it's driving me fucking nuts."

"You told her you not messing with anyone else, and she's still going left on you?"

"That part. What's worse is ever since I saw Sunny's badass at the club, all I've been thinking about is getting at her. You know, that's my ride or die, for real."

"Yeah, I thought she was. Why did you shake her like that?"

"I couldn't focus on doing my bid, worrying about what she would be doing while I was on lock. She would have fucked up my head with that type of stress and shit. I wasn't having that, so I let her go."

"And now you want her back?"

"For a minute, I was good and was trying to really feel Lavonda's vibe because it was all good with the business and all. It was more than money, though. She's a real one, and I was trying to do right by her. I even thought I was starting to love her crazy ass. But all of that shit came to a fucking halt when I saw Sunny. That woman still owns my heart, bro."

"Looks like you got yourself in a mean jam, bro."

"Don't I know it. I hit up Sunny on her Facebook page, and she in-boxed me back, asking me where was that ugly-ass girl I had in that clean-ass 'Vette."

Laughing, Razier said, "That sounds just like the Sunny I remember."

"I didn't hit her back. I logged off and was like fuck, what have I gotten myself into? If Sunny gets started, there will be only more drama because she will get at Lavonda in a heartbeat. You know Sunny don't play no games."

"I know. I'm surprised she didn't act a damn fool with you and Lavonda at the club."

"Me too."

"You know what? I think you need a little vacay yourself, bro. Why don't you join the ladies and me?"

"Are you serious? Don't be playing with me, bro."

"Nah, for real. You can be my driver and drive us to Branson and enjoy the weekend with us. That way, I'll be able to chill and entertain the ladies during the ride there. You can share a suite with me, and we'll have a ball down there with the ladies. Never know, you might turn one of the ladies on and get chosen for the weekend, especially since I'm not serving them any dick."

Laughing, Tracy said, "You better be careful. You know if I give them some of this dick, you may be put out of business."

"I wouldn't even be mad at you, bro." He raised his arms wide with his palms open and said, "Look at how much I already got. If I lost the ladies, I'm still good. None of that will pop off, though. Those mature women belong to me—and me only," Razier stated in a cocky tone.

"Check your ass out, all cocky with it and shit, bro. I feel you."

"So are you with it, or what?"

"No question, bro. A free trip to get some rest and chill while being able to duck this storm that's headed my way, I'd be a fool to pass that up."

"OK, it's settled. We're outta here this weekend, bro."
"Yes, sir. Branson, Missouri, here we come."

Friday morning, Razier and Tracy met all the ladies
at Olivia's place, and they all loaded up in the Mercedes
Sprinter and went and enjoyed a hearty breakfast at
Jimmy's Egg. Once they finished eating, they boarded
the luxury vehicle, and Razier served them all mimosas
as Tracy eased into the early-morning traffic. The ride to
Branson didn't seem like a five-hour drive to any of them.
They laughed, flirted, played cards, and talked the entire
ride, thoroughly enjoying themselves. The ladies seemed
like excited teenagers on a school field trip.

When they made it to Branson, Missouri, they checked
into the Hilton Hotel and were escorted to the suites that
Razier had reserved for them. They were each paired up.
Erica and Louise, Marie and Lia, Dionne and Olivia, Vera
and Carmela, and, of course, the two men, Razier and
Tracy. Razier told them that he would give them an hour
or so to freshen up and meet him in the lobby so they
could start having some fun.

The first day went by extremely fast. They checked
out a few local attractions, the Hollywood Museum,
Silver Dollar City, White Water, Mount Pleasant Winery,
and the Stone Hill Winery. By the time they made it back
to the hotel, they were beat. Razier was happy and tired
at the same time. He was really having a good time. Tracy
was having a ball and seemed to hit it off with all the ladies. They were all comfortable with him since they knew
that Tracy was Razier's best friend and business partner.
Razier could tell the ladies were a little concerned about
if Tracy knew about their private affairs with Razier.
Razier assured each of them that Tracy would never betray him. The ladies relaxed because they trusted Razier

totally, and if he said they didn't have anything to fear from Tracy, that's what it was.

The evening was just as pleasant as the day had been. They dined at a nice restaurant, drank, and had a good time. At the end of the evening, Razier and Tracy walked each pair of women to their rooms and wished them a good night. Tracy could tell that each of the women had sex on their mind—big time. The looks he caught each of them give Razier made him feel as if he were in the way. He had to give it to his best friend because Razier played it nice and cool and remained firm. No sex. He gave each of them a kiss on the cheek and wished them a good night. When they made it back to their suite, both Razier and Tracy burst into laughter.

"Damn, bro, did you see how those ole birds were looking at your ass? They looked like they wanted to gang-rape you or some shit."

Still laughing, Razier said, "I know. Do you think I'm tripping by not getting with them?"

"Hell yeah, I think you're tripping. You might as well pick the ones you want to get with tonight and get your late-night creep on and break they ole ass off."

"I wanted this trip to be no sex and all about fun and enjoying ourselves. If I got with one or two of them, then all the ladies will expect to get it, and Horny Goat Weed or not, there is no way I can fade all of them, bro."

"Well, bro, I sure as fuck wish I had that type of dilemma in my life. I wish I could help you fade those ole birds."

Razier stared at Tracy for few seconds and laughed. "You know what? You may be able to help me. Gimme a minute," Razier said as he went into the bedroom of the suite, grabbed his laptop out of his bag, and brought it back to the living room. He turned it on and pulled up the questionnaire he had on the ladies. It took him a few minutes until he found what he was looking for. After that, he closed his laptop, grabbed the phone, and called Erica Beckman and Louise Willow. Tracy was staring at him with a confused expression on his face as he listened to Razier's conversation with the ladies.

"Okay, this is how it's going to go down. I know I told you all that this trip would be no sex, which was my original intention. But the looks of hunger y'all gave me has made me change my mind. Are you and Louise ready for a special stolen moment?"

"As hard as these big old nipples are right now, you damn right we're ready. What do you want us to do, Razi?"

"Give me thirty minutes, then come to my suite."

"What about Tracy? Where will he be?"

Razier stared at his best friend and knew that he was going to love him even more after he heard what he had in store for him for the rest of the night. "Tracy will be joining us, Erica. He's going to assist me in giving you and Louise a stolen moment you two will never forget." He hung up the phone and stared at Tracy, who looked like he was about to start hyperventilating. "Breathe, bro. Breathe and talk to me. You with me on giving these ladies the double dose?"

For the first time in his life, Tracy Briggs was speechless. All he could do was nod his head in agreement with his best friend's question. He started laughing as he went to the bar and poured himself a stiff drink, downed it, poured another, then said, "It's about to be one hell of a night, Razi."

Thirty minutes later, the ladies arrived at the suite. Both were wearing the complimentary terry cloth robes from the hotel with slippers on their feet. They entered the suite and sat down on the couch while Tracy poured them each a drink.

"Okay, ladies, this is how it's going down tonight. You both answered that you were willing to have a threesome with two men, so, tonight, we're going to make it happen. Tracy and I are about to serve you all the dick you two can handle . . . that is, if you ladies are interested." Razier stared at the women waiting for their answer.

Erica and Louise stared at each other with bright eyes and smiled. Quickly, Erica stood and boldly took off her robe and put her hands on her hips so both men could get a good look at her tight body and big tits. "I can't speak for Louise here, but I'm more than ready for all of that dick you two talking about serving us."

"Damn," Tracy said as he quickly poured himself a third drink and downed it.

Louise stood, disrobed, and smiled. Her long, blond hair was hanging past her shoulders. To say she was looking sexy would have been an understatement. She looked like a sexy model, but right now, she was feeling like a slut and was ready to be treated as such.

"I want all of that black cock deep in me all night long, so let's stop with the chitchat shit and get this party started."

Razier smiled as he started toward the bedroom, taking off his clothes as he walked. Tracy poured himself one more drink, took off his shirt. The only word he could think to say was, "Damn." They all went into the bedroom, and the men gave the mature ladies a night they wouldn't forget any time soon.

Chapter Twenty

The next morning when Razier opened his eyes, he looked to his left and right and saw that he was alone. He sighed as he got out of the bed and went to the bathroom. When he finished relieving himself, he went into the other bedroom and saw Tracy sound asleep with a smile on his face. He shook his head as he thought back to the sexcapade they gave Louise and Erica. Thinking about that great sex caused him to get an early-morning hard-on. He checked the time and saw that it was a little after seven a.m. He went back to the bedroom and called Marie's cell phone. When she answered sleepily, he said, "I'm sorry for waking you, but I woke up with you on my mind, baby. I want you. Is Lia awake?"

"I don't think so, Razi."

"I want you to slip out of your room and come to me, baby."

"But I thought you said this weekend there would be no sex?"

"True, but right now, I'm hard as a rock, and I need to be deep inside of you. I want to give you a stolen moment in Branson that you will never forget. Do you want that?"

"Yes," she whispered, feeling her juices start to slide down her legs just from the sound of Razier's voice. "I'll be right there, Razi."

"Hurry, baby, hurry," he said as he hung up and went back into Tracy's room and woke him. "Get up and get yourself together. Marie is on her way, and I want to give her a double dose like we gave Erica and Louise. She wanted to experience having sex with two men too, so I figured we might as well break her off proper like to start the day right. You with it?"

Tracy was laughing as he jumped out of bed and went into the bathroom. When he returned, Marie was knocking softly on the door of their suite.

"This is what I want you to do. I'm going to take her into my room and get her fired up. After that, I want you to come in a few minutes later and join in."

"You know I'm with that. Damn, two sexy white broads in less than a few hours . . . You making me feel like the luckiest man in the world, bro."

"Whatever, clown. Get ready, bro," Razier said as he stepped into the other room and went and let Marie inside. He pulled her into the suite, grabbed her tightly, and gave her a passionate tongue kiss. She moaned in his arms and trembled as he stuck his hand inside of the shorts she had on and started slowly to finger her. "You ready to come like you've never come before, Marie?"

"Yes, Razi. I want you to fuck me good. Fuck me long and hard so this day can start better than I ever dreamed it could."

He scooped her into his arms and carried her into the bedroom. He laid her on the bed and pulled off her shorts while she took off the T-shirt she wore. He dipped his head between her legs and began eating her pussy, much to her delight. While he was busy eating her, he could tell that Tracy had entered the room because he felt Marie jump and heard her gasp.

"What-what are you doing in here, Tracy?"

Razier raised his head from between her legs and said, "On the questionnaire, you said you would be open to a threesome with two men. We're about to give you that. If you don't want it, then Tracy will leave, and we'll proceed."

She smiled. Her cat-green eyes seemed to glow when she raised her index finger and motioned for Tracy to come to her. Razier smiled and went back to eating her pussy while Tracy walked toward the bed. When he was standing on the side of the bed, Marie turned her head to the right and opened her mouth wide so Tracy could stick his now-very-hard dick inside of it. She began to suck him hungrily, and their threesome began. So did their morning.

Two hours later, Marie went back to her suite on wobbly legs feeling as if she just finished the most intense workout she ever experienced in her life. When she entered her suite, she went straight to the bathroom and took a long, hot shower, reliving every juicy moment of what had taken place with Razier and Tracy. Once she finished her shower, she saw that Lia was still sound asleep. She wanted to scream and wake her up so she could share what happened, but Razier made her promise that she couldn't tell the ladies what had occurred. She felt so special that Razier had chosen to give her that extraordinary stolen moment. She climbed into her bed and lay down with a satisfied smile on her face as she drifted to sleep.

Back in Razier and Tracy's suite, both men were knocked out. After sexing three women in less than a few hours, they were both beyond tired. Razier knew the ladies would be ready for some more fun for the day, so he called the front desk and left a message for each of them that they would meet for brunch in the hotel's restaurant by 11:30 and told the front desk he needed an eleven a.m. wake-up call. After accomplishing that, he closed his eyes and went straight to sleep.

When the telephone started ringing, he felt as if he had only been asleep for a few minutes when actually, it had been three hours. He climbed out of bed and went to wake Tracy to shower so they could go meet the ladies for brunch quickly. To his surprise, Tracy was sitting in the living room talking to Lavonda on the phone. Razier motioned to him that he was about to take a shower. Tracy gave him a thumbs-up and continued with his conversation. By the time Razier finished showering and dressing, Tracy was already ready to go.

"Damn, you sure do got a lot of energy, bro."

"Let me tell you something, bro, that shit last night and this morning was the wildest shit I've ever been a part of in my fuckin' life. You got them broads loving your ass like crazy and keeping it real with you, bro, for real. I'm jealous as fuck. After being balls deep inside those three sexy ole birds, all I want to do is get back with they ass. Damn, this is wild, bro."

"Well, I'm glad you enjoyed it, but the other ladies ain't with that type of get down, bro, so you have to hope Louise, Erica, or Marie will be down for another round before we go home. You never know. They may request another double dose before we get back."

"I'll be praying for that shit every single night from this point on, you lucky sonofabitch." They both laughed as they went to meet the ladies for brunch.

After they finished eating, Razier and Tracy took the ladies to the Dolly Parton's Dixie Stampede, Ziplines, Cave Tours, and National Tiger Sanctuary. Then they went and rode the go-carts, played minigolf, and went to Ripley's Odditorium housed in a building made to look as if it had cracked wide open by an earthquake or other disasters. The Titanic Museum is a half-scale replica of the famous ship and iceberg. By the time they returned to the hotel, the ladies were exhausted. Razier could tell that each of them had thoroughly enjoyed themselves, and that made him feel proud. He told them to get some rest. They would meet in the lobby for dinner much later that evening.

He made reservations for them at a nice restaurant that served the best steaks in the state of Missouri. They agreed that they all needed a good nap so they would meet at eight p.m. for a late dinner. Once Razier and Tracy were inside of their suite, Tracy told Razier that he was beat and to wake him around seven p.m. so he could get dressed and that he needed a nap something terrible.

Razier went and took a shower while Tracy napped. Once he finished with his shower, he slipped on a wife beater and some gym shorts and was lying down to take a nap himself when he received a text from Carmela. He smiled as he read it, telling him that she wanted to come and have a few words with him for a moment. *A few words, my ass,* he thought as he texted her back, telling her to come to his suite. Ten minutes later, she was knocking on the door.

He let her inside and led her to his room. She sat on the end of the bed and smiled shyly at him for a moment, and then said, "I know you said no sex this weekend, Razi, but I must have you inside of me even if it's just a quickie. I've been yearning for your touch all damn day. Can you please give me some, *please?* I promise I won't tell the others. I need you so bad," she said as she stood and peeled off the form-fitting sundress she was wearing.

"Now, how could I ever resist or deny you, Carmela?" he said as he slipped off his shorts and stepped toward her.

Their sex was amazing. It was as if they were making love. Their rhythm was as one, and the sex was explosive, as always. What was supposed to have been a "quickie" turned into a forty-five-minute sex session that ended with Carmela holding back her screams from the several orgasms that ripped through her core.

After regaining her breath, she kissed Razier, slipped out of bed, and went and took a quick shower. She left the suite and went back to hers, leaving Razier feeling extremely tired yet invigorated at the same time. Marie, Louise, Erica, and Carmela . . . Four of the eight ladies had been taken care of so far, and he felt it was only right that he took care of the other four before they left the next afternoon. He was worried if he would have the energy needed to handle Olivia, Lia, Vera, and Dionne.

By the time they were all loading up the Mercedes Sprinter to head back to Oklahoma City, he was incredibly proud of the fact that he had been able to service all eight of his mature ladies. He smiled at the thought that they each thought they were the only ones who received a stolen moment during their trip to Branson, Missouri.

During the ride back to Oklahoma City, the Mercedes was silent because everyone was knocked out cold except for Tracy, who was happily listening to music with a smile on his face. He wasn't able to get any more sex, but he still enjoyed his trip and was reliving how he shared two women at the same time with Razier. They even double penetrated each of them, and that was on some porno shit for real. Thinking about the incredible sex they had was turning him on as he felt himself get a hard-on. He checked the rearview mirror and couldn't help but feel a twinge of jealousy when he saw that Carmela and Olivia both were sleeping soundly with their heads lying on Razier's shoulders.

"You lucky sonofabitch," he whispered as he continued to drive. He grabbed his phone and called Lavonda. When she didn't answer, he checked the time and realized she must still be working at the prison. He wanted to talk to her, but since he couldn't, he did something without giving it a second thought. . . . He called Sunny.

When she answered the phone, Tracy said, "Don't say shit. Just listen to me, Sunny." He went on to tell her everything about Lavonda and what they had going on with the cell phone business inside of Boley State Prison. He kept nothing from her concerning his business or his relationship with Lavonda. He told her how strongly he felt for Lavonda and was really trying to make it work between them because she was being his ride or die, and everything was good.

"If everything is so damn good, why are you calling, telling me all of this, Tracy Briggs?" Sunny asked with a smile on her face because she knew damn well that her man—the man she never stopped loving—was on the verge of being back where he knew he belonged. With her. She knew not to push Tracy. She knew him better than anyone next to Razier, so she had to let him feel as if he were the one in control of things. Patience was the key here, so she would let things come together with him leading the way.

"I'm calling you because I'm on the highway on my way back to the city, and for real, Lavonda didn't answer the phone when I hit her. She's still at work. Plus, I needed to talk to you, Sunny."

"You needed to talk to me about what? Your new bitch and all the money y'all making together? Come on with that, Tracy. This is Sunny. You know I know better. What's *really* on your mind, booboo?"

Tracy sighed heavily and said, "You're on my mind in a major way, Sunny. You've been on my mind ever since I saw you at the damn club looking 'Kill Bill' in that tight-ass dress. I miss you, baby. But before I get into all that, I have to apologize for doing the goofy by letting you go. That was the worst mistake I've ever made. Now I'm in this with Lavonda, and we're locked at the hip for the time being because of my ends. I can't blow this loot, at least not right now. I got to get where I need to be before I can make another move. I got things going right with Razier, and it's all good, but I need to secure this bag before I switch up and shake Lavonda. You feel me?"

"Yeah, I feel your ass. You're trying to have your cake and eat it too, Tracy Briggs, and you should know better. You know there is no way I'd ever share you. Either you're mine or not."

"I'd never diss you like that, Sunny. I'm letting you know what it is and how it's going to be for the time being. I'm coming to get mine."

"Humph. What's yours to come get, Tracy Briggs?" she asked with a smile on her face.

With a serious tone in his voice that left no room for any misunderstanding, Tracy said, "You. You are mine, Sunny. Always have been and always will be."

Sunny's smile brightened when she said, "Well, hurry your ass up and get that bag so you can come and claim what you say is yours, Tracy Briggs."

Chapter Twenty-one

Tracy was lying on the bed with Lavonda next to him. She was watching TV, and he was sending Sunny a message through Facebook Messenger. For the last few weeks, he conversed with Sunny either on Messenger or texting whenever he was around Lavonda. He knew for sure that it was only a matter of time before he shook Lavonda and got back with the one and only woman who owned his heart. He felt terrible because he did care for Lavonda. He just didn't love her like he did Sunny.

Lavonda was being as thorough as ever handling the business with the cell phones inside the prison, and he made sure they split the money she brought him equally. He wanted her to be well compensated for her time and illegal efforts. If Sunny hadn't gone to the club that night, things would've gone a totally different direction with them, but fate made him go to the club to see Sunny, and now, all he thought about day in and day out was Sunny. He yearned for her touch, her kiss, her body—all of her. He wanted her so badly that he didn't give it a second thought whenever he chose to text her or send her a message in her DM.

When Sunny told him that she loved him more than life, that made him make his decision. Tonight was the night that he would tell Lavonda they needed to end what they had because he had to move in another direction with his life. His money was right. He had close to seventy thousand in the vault and close to seventeen thousand in the bank from the hard work he'd put in with Razier. The food truck was an enormous hit, and the pool cleaning and lawn service were bringing in more and more money every month. Since he joined Razier, they had hired more men to help with the lawns they did weekly, which allowed them to add more clients to their list. It was demanding work, but it made him feel good to earn an honest living.

The cell phone money made everything else gravy for him. It was time for him to get out of that one-bedroom apartment and step up his game like Razier. He wasn't the town house type of guy, though. He wanted to get a fly-ass condo downtown and have Sunny lying with him night after night. He smiled as he thought about that because he was entertaining the thought of asking Sunny to marry him. *Yeah, it's time,* he thought as he logged off Facebook and put down his phone.

Lavonda was so caught up in the reality show she was watching that she didn't pay him any attention when he left the room and went and poured himself a drink. He came back and stood in the doorway of the bedroom and stared at her. She wasn't easy on the eyes, but she was a sweet woman. Her sex game was right, and the body was definitely tight. The flaws meant nothing to him. His feelings were not as strong as they should have been that made him realize that it was all about Sunny. He sighed as he downed his drink.

"Lavonda, I need you to listen to me for a few. I got something we need to talk about."

"Aw, come on, babe. Can you give me like ten more minutes? My show is at the best part."

He shook his head and left the bedroom and went and poured himself another drink. He sat down in the dining room and wondered if this was the right move he was about to make. He would definitely miss that easy money coming in from the cell phones, but he wasn't happy, and the money wouldn't ever change how he felt about Sunny. He nodded as he sipped his drink. *Yep, this has to be done. I wonder if Lavonda would still be down to keep the money going with the cell phones,* he mused. He shook his head again and laughed because he doubted she would be with that.

Lavonda came into the dining room, sat down at the table next to him, and said, "Okay, I'm ready for you to dump me now."

Tracy was taking a sip of his drink and almost spit the liquor into Lavonda's face. He grabbed a napkin, wiped his mouth, and said, "What did you say?"

"You heard what I said, Tracy. If you think I don't know what you're about to tell me, then you really don't know how transparent you are. You've become more and more distant every time I come down here to spend time with you. Whenever we spend time together on my days off, you've tried to make it seem that things haven't changed, but it's crystal clear to me that things have changed . . . for the worst. So let me make it easy for you. Before I ever let a man dump me for another woman, I will gracefully step aside. We've had some fun and enjoyed good times over the last seven months. We've made some serious paper too, more money than I thought we would make. I know what you said in the beginning, but never did I think I would have $70,000 saved. I love you, Tracy, and I would love to continue to be together, but it's over, and I accept that."

"Damn, baby, you got me speechless here, and that shit don't happen too damn often. I don't know what to say other than you're right. We've had some good times and made plenty of coins. We've won, baby, so I think it's best if we take the money and run with it. You can keep working at the prison and let that stuff go and be good without further jeopardizing your job and live good. No need to continue to push that line or push our luck. Let's let it all go."

"That's funny because I just knew you were going to try to come at me with some lame shit like 'We can still do the business stuff and remain friends.'"

"Nah, that would be weak, and there is no weak shit with me. I've never tried to take advantage of you, baby. You've been special to me from the beginning, and I genuinely care for you. I can't run from my past, and it seems to have caught up with me in a major way."

"I understand. It's that female from the club that night, huh?"

"Yeah. Her name is Sunny. We go back like dinosaur piss. She's the only woman who I ever really loved, Lavonda. What's so crazy is if she had never come to the club that night, we would have still been good."

She smiled at him and put her hand over his. "We *are* still good, Tracy. I know I'm not all that in the looks department, but I still feel I can hold my own with the prettiest bitch. Remember what you told me when we first started talking when you were in prison?"

"What? I told you a lot of stuff during that time, baby."

"You told me that as long as I played my position right, we would win, and everything would be all good."

He smiled and said, "That's right, and you've played your position better than I could have ever imagined, Lavonda."

"I'm willing to continue playing my position, Tracy. You go on and get with your Sunny. Just know that you still got me whenever you want me. We can still keep the business going if you want and keep everything right. I'm no fool. That money is too damn good to let go. I need you on this end to keep it right. Your connections with the inmates help me and give me the security needed to keep everything running smoothly." She smiled at the shocked expression on Tracy's face and continued.

"I'm playing my position, and I'm willing to play it all the way out for you, Tracy. You can still have me whenever you want me. I don't have a problem with being your side piece. You break me off from time to time, and we still get the coin. That way, you can be with your Sunny and have your cake and eat me too. Oops. I meant have your cake and eat it too," she said, laughing. "The money, your girl, and me all wrapped up nicely."

"Damn." Tracy poured himself another drink and tried his best to process what Lavonda just hit him with. He smiled as he sipped his drink, then said, "That's some heavy shit you getting at me with, baby, and that raises the level of respect I have for you, Lavonda. But that's not how I want to get down, baby. Now, the old Tracy would've jumped on that shit in a heartbeat. That's not a good look, for real, and it would be unfair to Sunny. I love her, Lavonda. I love her more than I've ever loved a woman in my life. When we hook back up, it's going to be right all the way around. She doesn't deserve to be cheated on, and I refuse to do her dirty. And you don't deserve to be second to any woman. You deserve better than that. Your looks have absolutely nothing to do with anything. You are beautiful in so many ways, baby. It's been a pleasure being with you and helping you get your pocket full of coins. But we got to end this and move on with our lives.

"As for the business, I want you to promise me you will let it go. That money is good, but it's not worth you losing your job or getting caught up. Yeah, it's been lovely, but anything can switch up, and it can get real ugly fast. I say we dead everything and take this W. instead of ending up taking an L. That way, we can win and live our lives without the stress of worry about you getting caught up. You know what I'm saying?"

"I do, and I don't. I mean, you're actually passing up the chance to keep me and get all that money, all in the name of love?"

He stared at her and started laughing.

"What's funny?"

"You saying that to me made me realize that I've matured in ways that no one who really knows me would ever believe. Hearing those words come out of your mouth was the best compliment I ever received in my life. Yes, I'm doing all of this in the name of love. Not only the love I have for Sunny but for the love I have for you as well, Lavonda. So promise me you will dead that business and move on with your life."

"I'll make you that promise if you can do something for me."

"What's that?"

With her eyes watering and tears slowly sliding down her cheeks, she said, "Make love to me one last time, Tracy. Make me feel as good as you've made me feel the last seven months. Take me in your bedroom and make love to me off and on for the rest of the night, babe. Let me have you one more time before I let you go. You've been so good to me, and I respect you for your honesty. I respect you even more for looking out for my best interest. It's obvious that you do care about me. You're the realest man I've ever met in my life, Tracy. So can you bless me, babe? Bless me to make love to me all night long."

He downed his drink, stood, and reached for her hand. He pulled her to her feet and into his arms. He kissed her and wrapped his arms around her real tight. He let his hands slide down to her firm ass and gave it a good squeeze. "You got that, baby. You got me for the rest of the night. You promise that you're not going to be greedy and will dead the phone shit in the pen?"

She gave him a peck on his lips, smiled, and said, "I promise, babe. Now, take me in the room and fuck me like you've never fucked me before."

Razier was lying down with Lia wrapped in his arms, feeling as if he were recovering from an intense workout. Lia never ceased to amaze him with her stamina. For a small woman, she had the sexual appetite of a whore in the busiest whorehouse in the city. She was insatiable. He loved sexing her, but every time they finished, he felt as if he couldn't move.

Once his breathing returned to normal, he turned and saw her staring at him with a wicked smile on her face. She checked the time on her Cartier and said, "That's right, Razi. Catch your breath because I have two more hours before I have to be home, and I intend on sucking you and fucking you some more. That is, if 'mister' there can raise back up for me," she teased.

"I honestly don't think I can do it, but if your little mouth can work that magic like it's always done, and you're willing to get on top and get your ride on, you know I can never tell you no, Lia."

Licking her lips, she smiled and slid down to his limp dick. She removed the condom and started sucking him slowly and tenderly. To his amazement, he felt himself beginning to stir, and he groaned. "Looks like we're going to make the next two hours go by the way you wanted."

"Mm-hmm," she moaned as she continued bobbing her head up and down on his now extremely hard dick.

Just as she removed her mouth from him, his cell started ringing. She frowned when she saw his erection begin to go limp as he turned to check and see who was calling him this late at night. When he saw that it was Carmela Wilkins, he didn't think twice about Lia and answered the phone. "Hello."

"Razier, can you please come over to my house and help me? This damn fool husband of mine has lost his damn mind. I think he's going to hurt me. He's been snorting cocaine all evening, swearing he's going to do something to me if I didn't talk to him. I'm terrified, Razier. Please, come help me."

"Call the police, Carmela. That's the right thing to do. If I come over there, I'll only make a messed-up situation worse."

"I can't call the police. That would ruin my husband's reputation, along with putting my business out for all to know. That's not something I want to do, Razi. I need you. Please, come get me—please."

"What will your husband think when your yardman comes to your home at one something in the morning, Carmela? You're not thinking right."

"I don't care. I have to get out of this house, at least for a little while, and the only way I'll be able to leave is if you come and get me. I thought you cared about me, Razier. I guess I was wrong. I get it now. It's strictly business with you. That's so hurtful."

The sad tone in her voice touched him deeply. He didn't even realize that he had gotten out of bed and started walking toward his closet to grab some clothes.

"You know better than that, Carmela. I'm on my way."

Chapter Twenty-two

Lia refused to let Razier go to the Wilkinses' home alone. She convinced him to let her join him. That way, it wouldn't look suspicious to Mr. Wilkins, and hopefully, he wouldn't suspect anything was going on with Razier and Carmela. Razier thought it was a good idea, even though he really didn't care after hearing Carmela's hurtful tone. He was ready to do Mr. Wilkins some serious damage.

Fifteen minutes after hanging up with Carmela, Lia pulled her Subaru Outback into the driveway of the Wilkinses' home. Lia was out of the car first, leading the way toward the front door. She banged her small fist on the door loudly and waited a few seconds before she started back banging on the door even harder. Razier's heart was racing because he had some horrifying thoughts running through his mind as he impatiently waited for someone to open the door. When he saw Carmela's face as she opened the door, he sighed with relief.

"Thank you for coming, Lia. You too, Razier," Carmela said as she cut her eyes to the right giving them the signal that her husband was behind her.

"Are you okay, Carmela? Do you want to leave with us?" asked Lia.

Tears started sliding down her cheeks as she spoke. "Yes, I think it would be best if I left for the night."

Mr. Wilkins pulled her away from the door and stood there looking like a deranged man with snot running out of his very red nose, obviously high from snorting cocaine. His eyes were huge, and he spoke so fast that they had difficulty understanding anything he was saying.

"You two aren't taking my wife any-damn-where. I'll call the police and have you put in jail before that happens. Get the fuck off my property."

"First off, you need to lower your damn tone before you put all of your neighbors in your business, Walter. You need to calm down and let us take Carmela so we can diffuse this situation. She'll give you a call tomorrow, and then you guys can talk when you're in better shape," Lia said as calmly as she could.

"Didn't you hear me? Get the fuck off my property before I call the police. I mean that shit. Now!"

Shaking her head, Lia sighed. The next thing she did shocked both Razier and Carmela. She drew back as far as she could and punched Mr. Wilkins as hard as she could, dropping him like a sack of potatoes. He was so high off the cocaine that he was too slow to see the punch coming and fell to the ground, stunned. Lia stepped over him and told Carmela to get her things. Carmela did as she was told while Lia stood over Mr. Wilkins with a look on her face that said, *If you get up, I'm knocking your ass back down.* It took all the control Razier could muster not to laugh at Mr. Wilkins, who looked silly.

Razier stared at the man with his disheveled blond hair. His crystal blue eyes looked crazed, but he was no fool. He realized now that Lia meant business, and he wasn't about to try to take on the small woman. *Damn coward,* Razier thought as he waited for Carmela to come from the bedroom. When she returned, Lia grabbed her hand and led her out of the house.

"You leave now, don't you ever come back, Carmela. You're nothing without me, and I'll make sure you don't get a fucking dime from me. You tell them you're not going anywhere and get your ass back in this house so we can deal with our problems alone."

Lia stopped and was about to turn and go back for another good whack, but Carmela put a hand on her arm and stopped her. She turned and faced her husband, who had now climbed back on his feet.

"Our 'problems'? Walter, are you *serious?* The only one who has a problem in this house is you. You need help, and you need to get some fast because I will not take much more of this abuse. As for your money, you can have your money and your cocaine and whatever else you have going on in your life. I don't want, need, or deserve any of this crap. I'll return tomorrow, and we can talk. I don't feel safe with you while you're like this. But I'm telling you right now, if the discussion we have doesn't involve you getting some help, believe me, I'll be coming back to pack my things, and I will *not* be returning. I mean that." She turned and walked quickly to Lia's car.

With a look of disgust on his face, Razier stood there staring at Mr. Wilkins. It took a full minute because he was undecided if he would say something to the husband of his lover. Instead, he sighed and shook his head. It wasn't his place to say a word, even though he wanted to give Mr. Wilkins another sock to the nose. He knew that wouldn't be a good look.

As if he'd just recognized who Razier was, Mr. Wilkins snapped, "What the fuck are you doing here, Razier? Who called you to my fucking home? You're the fucking yardman."

Razier stared at him for a few seconds before Lia called out to him. "Come on, Razier. He's not worth your energy. Let's get Carmela out of here."

"You have a lovely wife who loves you more than you deserve, Mr. Wilkins. You need to get your mind right. If you don't, you're going to lose a good woman. You need to look at what you're doing and ask yourself, is it worth losing a woman who truly loves you?"

"Who the fuck are you to give me advice? Get the fuck outta here," Mr. Wilkins yelled as he slammed the front door.

Razier shook his head and went to join the ladies inside of Lia's car. Fifteen minutes later, they were inside of his house having a drink while listening to Carmela as she told them what had taken place earlier at her home.

"We've been together for over twenty years, and Walter has never even raised his voice at me. It's the drugs. For some reason, he went overboard with it tonight, and he chose to act an ass big time. I asked him if something was wrong, thinking it was stress from work that caused him to do so much. His nose was red and raw, and he kept snorting it right in front of me, and that was also a first. I knew it was bad, but when he said he would hurt me if I ever left him, I knew I had to get the hell out of there. I don't have anyone else to call. The only person I thought to call was you, Razier. I didn't mean to put a guilt trip on you, but I was hurt because you're the only person who came to my mind. I didn't want to call the police because there is no way I would want to destroy Walter's repu-tation in the neighborhood or with any of his colleagues, who, I'm sure, would have learned about this."

"I understand, Carmela, but you have to understand the only reason why I was hesitant was that I didn't want to cause further issues with you and your husband. When you made that statement, I threw all of that out the window and came to get you. Luckily, Lia came up with the idea to join me and help us so it wouldn't look as if something were going on with us. She actually helped in more ways than one because if I would've come alone, your husband would have received more damage than just being knocked on his ass."

"I guess you're right. Thank you, Lia. You're a lifesaver, girlfriend. Where did you learn to pack a punch like that?"

"I've taken self-defense classes for years ever since I was almost mugged once while leaving the gym one evening. The one thing most men never expect is to be punched by a woman. The element of surprise is always on our side. So I hit your jerk-ass husband with all I had."

"Yes, yes, you did. When I saw Walter hit the floor, I couldn't believe my eyes."

"Neither could I. I thought he would get up and try to put his hands on Lia, and that thought caused a slow rage to build up inside of me. But when I saw him looking up at her with fear in his eyes, all my anger slowly turned to pity. Your husband needs a lot of help, Carmela," said Razier.

"I know, Razi, I know," she said as she took a sip of her wine. She sighed and stared at both of them for a moment, then said, "I'm sorry for disturbing you two. Lia, being with you this late at night could only mean you two were having a stolen moment. Forgive me," she said with tears starting to slide down her cheeks.

"You stop that. Your well-being was at stake, so don't you dare feel bad about calling Razier and disturbing some damn sex. This handsome hunk isn't getting away from us, so stop. Come here and hug me 'cause I have to get my ass home so I can take a long, hot bath and be in bed before my husband gets back. He's burning the late-night oil and should be texting me any minute, letting me know he's on his way home. If I leave now, I'll have just enough time to handle my business." She gave Carmela a tight hug and said, "You stay here with Razier and let him hold you so that you can get some peaceful sleep. Tomorrow we'll deal with tomorrow. Right now, you need some peace of mind."

"Thank you, Lia. Thanks for everything."

Lia smiled and turned toward Razier. "Take care of her, Razi. We'll finish up where we left off next time, okay?"

He smiled and said, "You know it, Lia."

Lia reached inside of her purse, pulled out a white envelope, and gave it to him. "Thank you for a great time. As always, you made me feel so good. You know how you make me feel 'cause you last a long time every time."

Razier dropped his eyes, slightly embarrassed, and both of the ladies started laughing.

"Look at him, Carmela. Been blowing out all of our backs for months, yet he's still shy. Isn't that so damn sweet?"

Carmela stared at Razier for a moment and nodded. "The sweetest."

"Okay, since you two have made me feel even more embarrassed here, can we say our goodbyes because I do have to get up and go to work tomorrow."

"Work? The only work you need to be concentrating on is working Carmela. She needs a stolen moment right now that will take away the pains she's feeling. Go take a shower with her and use that wicked tongue of yours and give her some stimulation that will erase some of the bullshit she's been through tonight."

"Lia, stop that. I'm too tired for sex. All I want to do is go to sleep and think about how I'm going to deal with that man I'm married to."

Lia shrugged and said, "Okay, if you say so. If it were me, I'd let Razi suck my pussy until my toes curled, then fall asleep with his strong arms holding me tightly all night long."

"Freak."

"You know it." Both the ladies started laughing and shared another hug. "You make sure you give me a call tomorrow so I can take you home. I swear if I even think Walter is gone on that coke, I'm bringing your ass right back here with Razi."

"Okay, girlfriend. Thank you, Lia."

"No problem. Now, go take a relaxing shower so you can wind down." She turned to Razier and asked him to walk her out to her car. Once they were in front of her SUV, she said, "She needs some serious consoling. She may or may not want some sex, but she damn sure needs you. She would have never called you if she didn't trust and feel deeply for you, Razi. This is a sticky situation here because feelings are involved. Be careful with what you say to her. Don't say anything you don't mean. She's in a vulnerable state right now."

"I understand, Lia. I'd never do anything to hurt or mislead Carmela. I care for all of you wonderful women, and any one of you can call on me anytime you feel the need to."

"This may be true, but we all see how you and Carmela look at each other. There's a deeper connection between you two. Just be careful, Razi."

"I will."

"Gimme some tongue and go take care of my friend," she said with a smile as they shared a tongue kiss. "Whew. Wish you could bend me over this front seat really quick and give me some of that dick."

Laughing, he said, "You're truly insatiable, you know that?"

"Only for you, Razi, only for you. Now, go. I'll give you a call tomorrow before I come to get Carmela."

He gave her a quick kiss and said, "Okay." Next, he returned the white envelope she had given him and said, "Tonight was my pleasure. You keep this until our next stolen moment." Before she could say a word in protest, he turned and went back inside of his home with mixed emotions. Was he falling in love with Carmela? Damn.

Chapter Twenty-three

Razier came home after a long day of work to see a fleet of cars in his driveway as well as parked in front of his home. He smiled because he noticed they were Marie's Lexus NX, Olivia's BMW X4, Lia's Subaru Outback, Vera's Nissan Murano, Dionne's Mercedes E63, Louise's Audi TT, and Erica's VW Jetta. *I guess the ladies are all here to support Carmela,* he thought as he got out of his car and went inside. He was expecting them to be in a somber mood or expressing their anger at how Mr. Wilkins treated Carmela. However, he was shocked when he stepped inside the house and saw the ladies laughing and enjoying themselves immensely. Each had a drink in her hand, so he could tell that they were well beyond tipsy. They were positively faded and looked as if they were still going strong. When they heard him enter the house, they looked at him and, in unison, screamed, "Hi, Razi."

Too tired to attempt to figure out what was going on, he waved at them and went straight into the kitchen to grab a bottled water. *I sure as hell hope none of them are horny because nothing is happening tonight,* he thought as he downed his bottled water and reentered the living room, joining the ladies of his life. Once he was seated, he said, "Okay, I see you ladies are having a great time. What's up with this?"

"This, my handsome lover, is a show of love and support for our girl, Carmela, here. We refused to let her sit here moping around, being sad and depressed, all day, alone, while you were working. She needed us, and we're here for her," slurred Dionne.

Nodding his head, he said, "So getting plastered was the best solution to Carmela's situation?"

"It may not have been the best solution, Razi, but it's what we came up with, and so far, it looks to me as if it was a pretty good decision," Louise said and burped loudly. "Excuse me," she giggled.

"Now that you're home, we can have more enjoyment," Lia said and laughed.

Shaking his head, he said, "I don't think so, Lia. I'm dead tired. All I intend on doing this evening is taking a hot shower and watching *Monday Night Football* games. It's the season opener, and I want to watch the Lions play the Giants, and the Chargers play the Cardinals since I missed the 49ers beat the Cowboys last night." He stared at Lia and grinned. "Remember, someone didn't want to let me watch the game yesterday."

Pouting, Lia said, "I would have hoped you enjoyed yourself more with me than you would have if you watched some silly football game."

"You know I did. But tonight is all about football and rest." He turned and faced Carmela and asked, "Are you okay, Carmela? Have you spoken to your husband?"

Carmela took a sip of her wine before answering. "Nope. He's been texting me like crazy and calling my phone so much that my phone is dead, and I don't have my charger to charge it back up. I was going to go by there this evening with a few of the girls and get some of my stuff."

"Some of your stuff? What, you're not going home tonight?"

She stared directly at him and said, "Nope. I'm going to stay here for a few more days, Razi. That jerk needs to realize what he has, and the only way I can make him realize that is by showing him how things are in that house without me being there. If there's a problem with me staying here a few more days, I can go get a room."

"Nonsense. And you know better than that. I was under the impression that you would be going back home so you and your husband could talk it out and hopefully find some kind of way to get back on the right track."

"The only way that prick is going to get us back on the right track is by getting some damn help for his obvious drug addiction to that cocaine," Carmela said seriously. Though she was as buzzed as the rest of the ladies, she seemed to have control of her bearings, and the anger in her tone told him that she was still pissed.

"I feel that. You should at least call him and let him know you're okay, Carmela. No need to have him more stressed than he already is."

"See, that's what I love about, Razi. You're not only a great fuck, but you're also a caring and considerate man," said Louise.

"Thanks, Louise. But for real, there's no need to keep bashing Mr. Wilkins. He has a problem. We all want what's best for Carmela, and I feel the best move right now would be to give him a call so he can know she's good. That way, he won't use her absence as an excuse to do more drugs and make things worse for both Carmela and himself."

"That does make sense, Razi," said Vera.

"I agree," added Marie.

Carmela stared at Razier for a moment and sighed. She reached out her hand toward Dionne and said, "Let me use your phone, girl." When she had the phone in her hand, she quickly dialed her husband's number and waited for him to answer. She was staring directly at Razier when she started talking to her husband. "Hello, Walter."

"Where are you, Carmela? Are you OK, darling? Please tell me you're still not angry with me. I'm so sorry. Come home and let's talk, please?"

"I'm coming home, Walter, but I won't be staying. I'm coming to get some of my things. We need some time apart. I need to think, and you need to get your mind right. You have a critical decision to make."

"What do you mean? What decision do I have to make? I know what I want. I want my wife here home with me—always."

"You have to decide whether you want me bad enough to give up using that stuff, Walter. You need to choose between that stuff and me. I will not live like this any longer. You need help, Walter, and as your wife, I will stand by your side through it all as long as I see that you are sincere in seeking help. If you think I will continue to live like we've been living, you're sadly mistaken. I don't want anything from you other than your love and treating me right. I don't want your money, the house—nothing. If you want to keep doing that stuff, I'll walk away from it all. It's not like I've never started over before. So like I said, I'm coming home in a little while to get some clothes. Then I'm leaving. I'll return in a few days to see what decision you've made," Carmela said sternly, feeling proud of herself.

"I don't need any time to make that decision, Carmela, darling. You are my everything. There is nothing in this world that I wouldn't do for you. I mean that. I'm quitting that stuff cold turkey—done. It's over. I don't need it. I need and only want you. Come home so we can talk, please?"

Shaking her head as if he could see her, she firmly stated, "No. That would be making things too easy for you, Walter. I want you to sit back and take the next few days to think while I'm not there. I want you to be your normal, calculating, and meticulous self. I want you to think about everything clearly so there will be no misunderstanding about what you want to do and what I expect you to do. The drug using stops. Period. Cold turkey isn't a good idea. You need help. You need counseling. You're a serious user, and though you've shown some control of your actions, last night showed me that you're to the point of losing that control. I will not let you hurt me, Walter. I'll leave you for good before I let that happen. You scared me, and that hurt me more than anything else. I will not live in fear with the man I love."

"You do love me, don't you? Please tell me that I haven't pushed you away from me for good."

"I will always love you, Walter. We're not right and haven't been right for a long time. It's time to get right or end this. It's time for you to be right and to do me right." While still staring at Razier, she continued as if she were speaking to him. "I too need to do right so we can make sure our marriage remains intact. We've been through a lot over the last twenty years. Neither of us is perfect, but if we work hard at it, we can salvage our marriage and get back on track. Not only do you need help with your addiction, but we also both need to see a marriage counselor. So again, take these next few days to think about what you want to do. After that, we'll talk. Please respect me enough and don't be at home when I return to get some clothes and other things."

"I'll do whatever it takes to please you, darling. I won't be here when you come by. I'll be ready to talk when you're ready."

"Thank you, Walter," she said and ended the call. Then she gave Dionne her phone.

"Wow, that was deep," said Vera.

"We all love our husbands, and though we're having our 'indiscretions,' the love we have for our men hasn't wavered," said Marie.

"True, but how long does that love hold out? How long can our love continue to keep us in a situation that has none of us happy? Our indiscretions are wrong yet justified in our eyes only because our husbands have chosen to take us and our love for granted," Louise said logically.

"I'm the only one out of us that's not married, but I agree with you, Louise. How long must a woman continue to be taken advantage of by the man she swore to love and honor?" asked Olivia.

"I meant every word I said to Walter. I have done wrong, and though I feel my actions are justified, it's still wrong. Wrong is wrong. Period," Carmela said as she sipped her wine and sighed. "If Walter is willing to make things better, I will give him a chance. If he cannot beat that addiction and get some help, I'm leaving his ass."

"I have no right to speak on any of this, but then again, I feel as if I have to speak. Listening to you talk to your husband made me realize that I'm interfering in your relationship, and that makes me feel some kinda way, for real. My feelings are conflicted in so many ways. I feel guilty because I don't want to be a part of the reason why your marriage ends, Carmela. Yet, I don't want to lose any of you, but as Carmela said, wrong is wrong, and what we're doing is flat-out wrong in numerous ways," Razier said as he stood and started walking toward the stairs.

"You stop right there, Razi, and come listen to me and listen good," Erica said sternly. "You've helped us in more ways than any of us can count. Though we have similar situations, trust, each is different. You've given us something we've needed for a long time . . . attention. You've made each of us feel special, adored, and cared for. That's something none of us have received from our spouses in ages. Don't you dare make yourself feel bad about any of this. We're some big girls, and we did exactly what we wanted to do. We enjoy you and genuinely care for you, as well. The money and everything else we've given you was to help you for helping us . . . a service needed and greatly appreciated.

"You are a hardworking young man and deserve even more than we've given you. Most men in this type of situation wouldn't care about our feelings or personal situations. They would be too caught up with the sex and money. But not you. You are a good man. Your mom should be proud of how she raised you because she did a great job, and I mean that from deep within my soul. No guilt trips, buddy, because we're not going to let your fine ass get away. If Carmela chooses to try to make her marriage work, so be it. We respect that and will do all we can to support her. If she chooses to stop seeing you, we still move forward. Some of us need you more than ever, and I'm speaking for myself here. My husband, whom I love to death, just doesn't do it for me anymore. When he tries to be loving or sexual, it's forced, and that hurts me. When I'm with you, as strange as this sounds, I love my husband even more. You're the reason why I'm staying with him. You are my stolen moment, and my stolen moments with you give me peace in my home. So again, dead the guilt, Razi. You're doing some good, regardless of whether you believe it."

"Plus, that dick is too damn good to let get away," joked Lia, and everyone started laughing.

"All of you are crazy . . . You know that?"

"*Yeah,*" they all screamed in unison.

Razier stared at Carmela and, in a sincere tone, said, "All I want is for you to be happy."

She returned his stare and said, "As long as I have you to call on when I need you, I will always be happy, Razi. I mean that."

"Okay, go get your things and leave me so I can get ready for the first game. It comes on at six, and I need to get showered and make me something to eat."

"Now you know you got *eight* lonely and horny women here, and you talking about watching a damn football game, so stop. You know damn well you're going to have to put that work in tonight," laughed Vera.

Shaking his head, Razier laughed and said, "If that's going to happen, it's going to happen *after* I watch me some football."

Each of the ladies groaned as if they were in agony.

"I bet you would enjoy the game better if you were watching it while receiving some good head at the same time," Dionne said and started laughing.

"Ugh. Don't you ladies ever get tired of sex?"

"*Nope,*" they yelled and started laughing. Even though he didn't find it funny, he couldn't help himself. He started laughing right along with the ladies in his life. Crazy . . .

Chapter Twenty-four

Tracy and Sunny had been spending all of their time playing catch-up ever since the night he called her and told her he ended the relationship he was in with Lavonda. Their lovemaking was so passionate and intense that it felt as if they'd never been separated. It was so much more than sex with Tracy. He felt as if he'd found his long lost love, and the same went for Sunny. Tracy Briggs was the only man she ever loved, and now that she had him back in her life, she was determined never to let her man get away from her again. She was proud that once he broke up with Lavonda, he didn't waste any time getting right at her. After two weeks, they decided to move in together. Since Tracy wanted a bigger place, she didn't have a problem giving up her apartment, so they found a two-bedroom condo near Bricktown, making things easier for Tracy to hook up with Razier for work. To see how Tracy had become so dedicated to working hard every day, she knew that their lives together was meant to be. He was no longer Mad Dog, the wild hustler that did whatever it took to get the money. He was now a hardworking, legal hustler, and that, in itself, was a major turn-on to her.

Razier had definitely rubbed off on Tracy in a positive way. Their food truck business and the lawn and pool service were working out well for them. Tracy put his all into his work, and every day he left for work, she thanked God for bringing her man back into her life. She had his back and would do whatever he needed her to do, and she proved that as she stood in the kitchen bottling up his Kool-Aid pickles.

She couldn't stand the smell of pickles. Tracy came up with the ingenious idea of making Kool-Aid pickles to sell on their food truck. Everywhere they went, whether it was the H&8th events or the Black rodeos out in the country, Tracy's Kool-Aid pickles were a hit. The kids loved them, and it had become one of the food truck's bestsellers. So here she stood, putting cherry and grape Kool-Aid inside of jars of pickles. She would have to let the pickles soak in the pickle jars for at least a week before they would be ready to be sold. She shook her head as she diligently did her work because the smell of the pickles was giving her a headache. Nevertheless, she knew that Tracy depended on her to assist him, so she endured the headache and kept right on working.

Hours later, after filling over a hundred jars of pickles with Kool-Aid, the daunting task was complete. She rushed to the bathroom and took a hot bath. By the time she was getting out of the tub, Tracy had come home from work and went straight to the bathroom to take his shower. When he was finished, he went into the bedroom and smiled at his woman.

"Hey, baby, what it do?"

"I'm good, how about you?"

"Tired but happy that it's Friday. What you want to get into tonight?" he asked after giving her a tight-ass kiss.

"I've been invited to a birthday party at the Russel Lounge."

"The Russel Lounge? That little spot that's inside of the old Marriot?"

"Mm-hmm. A friend I used to hang out with back in the day is having her birthday party there and asked me to come through."

"Which friend from back in the gap?" he asked as he put on a pair of basketball shorts.

"Willeta. You know, Mario's older sister. Don't tell me you don't remember them because you used to serve back when he was hustling."

"Yeah, I remember Mario. What's he up to nowadays?"

"I heard he's designing clothes. He's trying to blow up his own clothing line."

"That's what's up. Glad to see he didn't become a casualty from the game. So Willeta is what now . . . at least in her 30s, right?"

"Yeah, she turned 31 yesterday. Do you want to go with me? I know you're tired from work, so you don't have to go if you don't want to, baby. I'll stop through for a minute, have a drink or two, then come on back home so we can relax and chill for the rest of the night."

"Now, you know better than that, baby. I'm not letting your fine ass go to no party without me right by your side. These suckas out here need to see you're back home, and they have no action getting at your sexy ass ever again."

"So, you on some possessive shit with me, Tracy Briggs?" Sunny asked and smiled as she stepped to her man and kissed him. "I like that. It turns me on when you let me know you feel that way. Come here and let me show you exactly how much it turns me on," she said as she pulled him on the bed.

Thirty minutes later, after they had finished making love and taken a shower together, they were dressed and getting ready to go to Sunny's friend's party. Suddenly, Tracy received a call from Razier telling him that he needed to immediately meet him at his mother's house. Without any hesitation, he left the house and jumped into his Corvette. He broke every speeding law known to man to get to his best friend's mother's house.

When he pulled into the driveway of Mrs. Coleman's house, he saw Razier's Audi in the driveway and once again asked himself what was going on. Razier sounded mad. And that confused him because he knew it took a lot to get Razier mad. He also knew that once Razier was angry, it took a whole lot to get him calm once again. Someone was going to get hurt.

He jumped out of his car and rushed to the door, followed closely by Sunny, who had refused to let him go over to Mrs. Coleman's house alone. Before Tracy could knock on the door, Razier opened it, and he looked as if he were ready to kill somebody.

Uh-oh, thought Tracy, knowing that look all too well.

"What's up, bro?" Tracy asked as he followed Razier inside the house with Sunny right behind him.

When Tracy entered the living room and saw Mrs. Coleman sitting on the couch with an ice pack on the side of her face, Tracy's anger began to mount. He immediately knew that whoever had the nuts to touch Mrs. Coleman was not only going to feel Razier's wrath but also his own as well.

"What happened to you, Mrs. Coleman?"

"Nothing that I can't handle, Tracy. I don't know why I even called Razier. I should have known he was going to call you. I don't want you two getting into any trouble. I said I'd take care of it."

"Bullshit, Mama. You know damn well there's no way in hell I'm going to sit back and do nothing when some clown has put his hands on you," Razier said heatedly.

"You watch your mouth, Razier. Don't you dare think you are that angry that you can disrespect me, do you hear me, boy?"

He sighed loudly and started slamming his right fist into the palm of his left hand, pacing around the living room. "You know I would never disrespect you, Mama, but you also know that there is no way I'm going to let that man get away with hurting you. *No. Way.* If you don't give me a way to get in contact with him, I promise you on my daddy's grave that I will find that prick, and when I do, I'm going to do him real bad."

"Then what? You go off to jail and do time for someone who isn't worth it? You'll ruin all the hard work you've put into all of your businesses. Not only that, but you also get your best friend caught up in all of this, and he goes back to jail as well. I'm sorry, Razier. You're just going to have to stay mad at me because I'm not going to let you ruin your life behind something I can handle myself."

"Handle yourself? You're sitting here with your jaw swelling more and more by the minute, and you telling me you can handle it yourself? Come on with that, Mama. My daddy wouldn't let anything happen to you without willing to give up his life for you, so neither am I. You have no right not to let me protect you. Ugh. Would you tell her, Tracy, man, please? Help her feel me, bro, for real."

"It's all outta love, Mrs. Coleman, and you know that. You also know your child. You don't give him what he needs, he'll find a way to get that info one way or another. And, yes, you're 100 percent correct that when Razi finds that dude, we're going to beat him to a pulp for putting his hands on that beautiful face. Whatever happens after that, we're both prepared to deal with the consequences. If you give us what we need, we can maybe make this happen without anything going astray. Give us the advantage, and neither of us will be going to jail. That, I promise you," Tracy said confidently.

Shaking her head, she knew what Tracy said made sense, but she didn't want anything to happen to her son or him behind the wrong decision she made by going out and getting involved with that scumbag, Carl. He had been so nice in the beginning, always polite and super sweet. He made her feel so good. He made her feel alive again, and she hadn't felt that way in years. He never made a move on her or even hinted at anything sexual, and that made her comfortable enough to let him come to her home for a nice, home-cooked meal.

After preparing one of her special meals for him, they were sitting in the den sipping some wine and listening to some Kenny G., relaxing. When he eased his arm around her, she let him because she thought all was good. When he put his hand on her leg, she eased it off and stared at him . . . and saw a completely diffcrent person from the man she had been dating for the last month. He had a hungry, crazed look in his eyes that made her feel a fear she had never felt in her life.

She stood and told him that it was time for him to leave because she was tired and didn't want this good evening they enjoyed together to end badly. He shocked her by yelling at her how she was such a tease, and she needed to get over her dead husband and start living again. She didn't realize she had slapped him with all her might until she felt the blow to her face from Carl. Though she was a small woman, there was plenty of fight in her. She was born and raised on the Northeast Side of OKC, and ain't no punks come from where she's from. When in a fight, you fight with all you had—no matter who you were fighting.

She rushed the stunned man and began punching, scratching, and kicking him with every ounce of strength she possessed in her petite frame. He knew he was in for more than he bargained for and was finally able to grab her and wrapped his arms around her to stop her from kicking his ass. He yelled at her that he was leaving, but she had to stop hitting him. She calmed down some, and he let her go.

Wrong decision, buddy . . .

She went right back to hitting and kicking him and clawing at his face with her fingernails. He ran out of the house and was trying to get into his car—with her right behind him.

"If you ever come near me again, I'll hurt you, you bastard," she screamed at him.

"You don't have to worry about me ever coming near your crazy ass again, bitch. I got a wife any-fucking-way. Who needs your deadbeat ass? I was trying to get you to start living again. Fuck you, bitch," he yelled as he got inside of his car so he could escape. Before he put the car in gear, however, Mrs. Coleman hurled one of the loose bricks around the flower bed of her house at his vehicle and smashed the front windshield of Carl's car.

"That's more for you to explain to your wife. Explain all those scratches to her ass too, you fuck-boy-ass nigga."

The defeated man pulled out of the driveway feeling as if he'd just lost a heavyweight fight. Nope, he just got his ass beat by a proud and enraged Black woman. Shame ate him up during the ride back to his home.

After listening to her son and Tracy, Mrs. Coleman realized she messed up by calling Razier to come to take care of her. She regretted making that call so much now because the look on her son's face scared her to death. She already buried the love of her life, and there was no way she would ever risk losing her son behind the mess she created, all in the name of loneliness. No. Way.

"No, Tracy. I'm not telling either of you anything. Let this alone. I handled myself, and I'll be all right. My face is a little sore, but I'm fine. I told Razier I beat that scumbag ass, so that should be enough. We need to let this go. I mean it. Let it go. Do both of you hear me?"

Both of the men stared at her as if she'd lost her mind. They knew not to continue to argue with her because they had too much respect and love for her. Both knew that one way or another, they were going to find the man who did this to her and beat the crap out of him. She stared at both of them and knew her words were in vain.

Sunny sat down next to Mrs. Coleman and held her hands. "I understand everything you've said, Mrs. Coleman, but you know they don't. All they see is your pain, and that pain is being multiplied by fifty with them. The longer you let that pain fester, the worse it will be whenever they get their hands on the man who did this to you. I in no way want either of them to get into any kind of trouble behind this, but that man deserves to get his ass beat by men, not what you gave him. Any man who hits a woman like she's a man deserves to be beaten bad—real bad."

Mrs. Coleman stared at Razier and Tracy and saw the anger mixed with pain on their faces, and her heart beat faster. The throbbing of her jaw and the pain she was feeling made her go against what she knew was right. She stood and went and got a card from her purse and gave it to Tracy.

As Tracy read the card, she said, "Don't let my son get into any trouble, Tracy Briggs. You two go do what you feel you have to do, but dammit, don't get caught."

Tracy nodded as he stared at the card for a moment longer. "You ready to go handle this, bro?"

Razier gave him a look that asked him, *Have you lost your damn mind?* "You damn right, bro. Let's go get that jerk."

Tracy turned toward Sunny and said, "Will you stay here with Mrs. Coleman until we get back, baby?"

"You know I will. You hurry up and do what you gotta do and get back to me safe, you hear me?"

"You already know," he said as he turned and left the house.

When Razier and Tracy were inside Tracy's car, Tracy sat there stuck in thought. He had something to tell Razier, but he was hesitant after seeing the pained look on Mrs. Coleman's face. However, he knew he had to keep it real with his best friend.

"There's something you need to know before we move on this fool, bro."

"I don't need to know nothing, bro. He put his hands on my mother. That's *all* I need to know. Come on. Let's go handle this, bro."

Tracy sighed and gave Razier the card that Mrs. Coleman had handed to him and said, "You know I'm with you, bro; never against you. Read the card and tell me how you want to move, and I'll be right by your side."

Razier read the card aloud. . . . "Carl Salley, M.D. Should this mean something to me? What are you on, bro?"

"Take a look at the address, bro. The doctor works from his home office."

Razier stared at the card for a moment as he focused on the address to the chiropractor's home office. It didn't register at first, but when it did, Razier said, "Fuck."

"Exactly. So my question for you is, are we still going to go and beat the fuck out of Dionne Salley's husband?"

Razier was confused and pissed off even more now. "Fuck," he yelled.

Chapter Twenty-five

Razier pulled out his phone and sighed before dialing Dionne's number. He was now in a precarious situation, and he didn't know what he would do. Yet, he *did* know what he was going to do. He just didn't know how it would affect things with Dionne. She was important to him, as were the other ladies, but his mother was more important to him than any of them, and if he lost them while defending his mother, so be it. When Dionne answered the phone, he could tell that she was surprised yet happy to hear from him. That soon would change, he said to himself.

"Hey, Razi, what have I done to deserve this call? I sure hope it's my turn to spend some time with you."

"This isn't a good-time call, Dionne. I need to tell you something, and I hope that what I'm about to say won't damage things between us."

Puzzled by the seriousness in his tone, she asked, "What's wrong, Razi?"

"Are you at home right now?"

"Yes."

"I'll be pulling into your driveway in the next three minutes. Do me a favor and come outside to talk to me first. I'll explain everything face-to-face."

"This must really be serious if you have to see me at my home. You *do* know my husband works from home?"

"Yes, I'm aware of that. Be there in a minute, Dionne," he said and ended the call.

"How you gon' play this, bro? You know this can get really ugly," Tracy said as he turned on Dionne's street.

"The only way to play this is to tell the real. After I tell Dionne what that asshole of a husband of hers did to my mother, I'm going inside and beating his ass—period."

"You really feel it's worth messing up your business with the ladies?"

Razier faced his friend with a smirk on his face and said, "I don't believe you could ask me something like that, bro. When it comes to my mother, I will give every last penny I've made from the ladies back, bro."

"Yeah, I feel you. Damn, this is fucked up. There she is waiting for us," Tracy said as he pulled the car into the driveway and killed the engine. He sat back and watched as Razier got out of the car and stepped toward Dionne.

"Hey, you. You do know you have me a little nervous here. This isn't your day to do the yard, and I don't need Carl asking me any questions about why you're here, so be quick, Razi."

"I'm not here to see you, Dionne. I'm here to speak to your husband."

"About what? Talk to me, Razi, because you have me nervous now."

He sighed and clenched his jaws tightly before speaking. "I don't want what is about to happen to affect us negatively, but if it does, I totally understand."

"Huh? Come on, Razi. Talk to me, baby. Nothing could affect us negatively. You've been too good to me for any of that. What business do you have with my husband?"

"He's been cheating on you, Dionne," Razier stated bluntly.

She stared at him for a moment and then burst into laughter. "You are truly one good, caring, and loving man, Razier. Baby, I've been knowing my husband has been having different affairs for years. He does him and thinks it's all good. He thinks he's super sick, but I honestly could care less. So don't let whatever you've found out about him get you all upset. I'm fine, and as long as I have you and our stolen moments, I'll continue to be fine."

Shaking his head, Razier said, "You don't understand, Dionne. Your husband's private business is none of my business, and if he hadn't messed with someone close to me, I wouldn't be here now."

"What? Has Carl been messing with someone close to you? Who?"

"My mother."

Razier's answer to her question hit her as if she had been shocked by electricity. She stared at him and now saw the anger in his light brown eyes and thought, *Oh shit. He's here to beat the shit out of Carl.* She put her hand on his arm and said calmly, "Come on, Razi. Don't let this get you all worked up. Just because your mom chose to have an affair doesn't mean you should come here and do something you may regret later. I'm sure their little fling was what they both wanted. I'm not defending that prick of a husband of mine, but he is the breadwinner, and as crazy as it sounds, I do love the cheating sonofabitch."

"You still don't get it, but I understand because I haven't told you everything."

"There's more?"

"Much more. My mother's personal business isn't any of my business. She made it quite clear to me when she first told me about going out with this new 'friend' she spoke with on the phone and on Facebook. So I accepted that and let her live her life without any interference from me. That all came to an end today when she gave me a call and told me to come over to her house because she needed me. I went to her house to see her holding an ice pack on the side of her face.

"Your husband put his hands on my mother because she wouldn't give him what he wanted. She fought him off and was able to get the best of him until he finally left her home. As he was leaving, she threw a brick and smashed the windshield of his car. He hurt my mother, Dionne, and I'm here to hurt him. I don't want to hurt you or make you mad at me, but I'm not leaving until your husband feels some pain."

"Well, it looks as if this is about to be an interesting evening. Come on inside, and let's bring this to Carl and see what he has to say. This will be more than interesting because though I've known for years that Carl has been cheating on me, I've never had any solid proof. This gives me more leverage than I've ever had. To know that he has put his hands on a woman sickens me. To hear that the woman he hurt is your mom pisses me the fuck off." She put her hand on the side of Razier's face and said, "You hurt, I hurt, baby." She gave him a quick peck on his cheek and said, "Let's go get that asshole."

As she led the way into her home, Razier looked over his shoulder and gave Tracy a nod. Tracy got out of the car and followed them inside the house. As soon as Dionne opened the door, she started yelling, "Carl! Carl! You need to bring your ass to the front room right now." A few minutes passed before she yelled again, "Carl, did you hear me? Bring your ass to the front room now."

Carl came into the front room with an angry expression on his face. "What the hell are you screaming for, Dionne? You know I don't care to be disturbed while working, so this better be important."

With her arms folded across her chest and a smirk on her face, she said, "Yes, dear, it's really important. As a matter a fact, it's so important that I think I'll let Razier here tell you what's so important."

Mr. Salley turned and faced Razier with a questioning look on his face. "Hello, Razier. What's going on here?"

Razier took a deep breath, trying to calm himself, but it wasn't working. "You put your hands on my mother, Mr. Salley. You put your hands on the wrong woman." Razier started stepping toward Mr. Salley, ready to beat his ass.

Mr. Salley looked at Dionne, then back at the young man advancing toward him and realized he was screwed. Of all the affairs he'd had, he had to go and pick the fucking yardman's mother. Christ, what fucking luck. The look on his wife's face made him cringe. She was pissed with a capital P. But he was more worried about the young man coming his way.

"Wait, Razier, there has to be some misunderstanding here. I, I—"

"Don't waste your breath insulting me by trying to lie your way out of this because your wife is here. You're busted, so be a man and fight me like you fought my mom. You hurt her, so I'm going to hurt you."

"That's not true. I was protecting myself. She attacked me." That was it. This man who had hit his mother was now lying about her, trying to assassinate her character, and Razier had heard all he was willing to hear. He rushed Mr. Salley and caught him with a hard right hook squarely on the jaw. Razier instantly followed the powerful blow with a left jab to his nose. That blow caused blood to start pouring from Mr. Salley's nose. He couldn't believe this was happening to him in his own home . . . with his damn wife standing right there watching him being assaulted. "Dionne, get this maniac away from me. Call the police, baby!"

Laughing, Dionne said, "You got to be kidding, you fucking, lying, cheating bastard. Beat his ass some more, Razier."

Oh shit, thought Mr. Salley as Razier swung a wild right hook at him that he ducked. As he tried to run past the angry young man, he paid no attention to Tracy

standing in his path to the front door. He ran directly
into a hard kick to his testicles, dropping him instantly.
Tracy stood over him and kicked him viciously in the
head three times before Razier came and stopped him.

Razier pulled Mr. Salley to his feet and slapped the shit
out of him hard five or six times. "The only reason why I
don't break every bone in your fucking body is that your
wife is here. You're very lucky, Mr. Salley. *Very. Lucky.*
But you're going to own up to the shit you did to my
mother. You're going to apologize to her as well as your
wife for being a piece of shit. You hear me? If you don't,
I swear on my father's grave I'm beating your ass until I
have no strength left." He slapped the defeated man a few
more times for emphasis, then pulled out his phone and
called his mother. "Mama, I'm over here at Mr. Salley's
place, and he has something to tell you."

"Razi, you know I don't need to be talking to that man.
You done did what you did, now come home. Come home,
baby, before you get into trouble, Razier Coleman."

"No. You will listen to this man before I leave here,
Mama." He gave the phone to Mr. Salley and said, "Talk
to my mother."

Mr. Salley accepted to phone and said, "Hello, Rhonda."

"That's *Mrs. Coleman* to your ass."

"Sorry. Mrs. Coleman, please accept my most sincere
apology for the incident that happened at your home. I'm
really sorry about what happened."

"Whatever. Give the phone back to my son." Mr. Salley
gave the phone back to Razier, and Mrs. Coleman heard a
loud slap, followed by Mr. Salley screaming. "Okay, Razi,
you've done what you set out to do. Leave that place and
come home, baby," she pleaded.

"I'll be there in a few, Mama," he said and ended the
call. He turned and faced Dionne who was smiling, but he
could see the pain through the smile on her face, which

made him even angrier. He turned toward Mr. Salley and was about to hit him again, but Dionne stopped him and told him to leave.

"Leave him be, Razier. The jerk has more punishment to receive, but that will be coming from me. Thank you for coming here and exposing this prick. Now his ass belongs to me."

Chapter Twenty-six

Carmi Felton's life had been one giant whirlwind ever since she had been dishonorably discharged from the navy. It seemed that every decision she made was a bad one. The one good thing that happened in her life was the birth of her daughter. Though she was the love of her life, even that decision found ways to haunt her. Every time she looked at her daughter's beautiful face, she was reminded of her child's father. Carmi chose to ignore thinking about Razier, but his handsome features haunted her every time she closed her eyes or looked at their daughter. She hated Razier. That man ruined her life because of his good looks and perfect body. He was her weakness . . . a weakness she had been determined to overcome . . . a weakness she finally accepted she could never overcome.

She tried everything she could think of to get over him but failed greatly. She thought she could get over him by testing the waters in a lesbian relationship that only caused more drama in her life. She admitted that she was somewhat bicurious, but being with another woman in a relationship wasn't the answer. It further showed her how much Razier had screwed up her mind.

After several failed relationships, she finally gave up and focused on her career. After almost three years, she found some solace in her work. Working for a security firm designing the latest security measures for major corporations had been very profitable, as well as rewarding, mentally. Yet, just as soon as she was off of work and back home, all of her thoughts were consumed by the one man she felt she would always love, and those thoughts were driving her insane.

She knew that men like Razier couldn't love any woman because all he loved was sex. He cared for no one but himself, and that infuriated her. Every time she thought back to their time spent on the ship, she cringed and felt so ashamed. But in the blink of an eye, she could get so hot and bothered by the hot, steamy sex they had every chance they could get. Not only did he turn her on then, but also mere thoughts of him turn her on to this very day, and that too drove her to a state of insanity. *How can I care for a man who cared nothing about me? How can I be in love with a man who has never even attempted to get in contact with me? How can I love this man?* These were the questions she repeatedly asked herself. Her life revolved around her daughter and her job, and she was determined to make sure that she gave her daughter the very best of everything, and so far, she'd been able to do that, and that made her proud of herself.

Daisy Carmela Felton was her world . . . the one person in this world she knew would never betray her—the true love of her life. The love she has for her daughter is what made her make the decision she felt needed to be made. It was time for her to go home. It was time to take her daughter to meet her grandmother. It was time to face some demons from her past and let her daughter see that she has family other than just her. In no way could she let anything, no matter how painful, stop her from giving her daughter all that she deserved.

Daisy deserved to meet her grandmother as well as her father. The problem with that was she didn't know where Razier was from. She knew it wouldn't be too hard to find him, but she was terrified that he would deny Daisy, and that would crush her. She didn't want anything from him. She just wanted him to acknowledge his child and have a part in her precious life. Once he set eyes on Daisy, he would see without a doubt that she was his child. She looked exactly like him. She had his eyes, nose, and even his smile. There was no doubt that Razier was Daisy's father because she hadn't been with another man until well after she gave birth to Daisy. She had been so devastated when she found out that she was pregnant that all she did was pack her things and move from her small apartment in San Diego and moved to the San Bernardino area, where she lived off her savings until she gave birth to her daughter.

When Daisy turned 1, she started working for Hollier Security, and then her career took off. Now here she was sitting at home on her bed with her laptop in front of her, debating with herself. *Should I do it? Should I try to locate Razier so that I can put this part of my life to rest? Would I be putting it to rest or opening the door to chaos and confusion? Daisy doesn't deserve that. But she does deserve her father. Don't be selfish and deny her that.* These were the words bouncing around inside of her head as she stared at the screen of her laptop.

She sighed heavily and started tapping the keys on the laptop, logging on to Facebook. She couldn't believe how nervous she was. Her palms were sweating as she put Razier's name in the search box. If he had a Facebook page, she was sure he would be easy to find since his name was so uncommon, and she was right. When she saw his handsome face, her heart began to beat faster. She couldn't believe the effect he still had on her three years later. What made her heart race was when she read his profile and saw that he lived in Oklahoma City. *Oh. My. God. How could Razier live in the same city where I'm from?* she thought as she continued reading his profile, learning all about his, what looked like, thriving businesses. He was a partner in a catering service, lawn service, and a pool cleaning service.

She started looking at his pictures on his page and saw him standing in front of a new Audi with a proud smile on his face. Not realizing she was smiling, she continued to look through his pictures and learn all she could of what he'd been up to. When she came to a picture of him and a woman that had to be his mom, her heart melted because her daughter looked so much like both of them that it caused tears to trickle down her face slowly. She knew for sure now that it was time to go home. Not just to face her demons but to let her child meet both of her grandmothers. Not one of them . . . but both. More important was Daisy could meet the man that helped create her.

She closed the laptop, sat back on the bed, and thought about Razier and how they never took the time to get to know each other. All they did when they were together was have fun and have sex. They would go out to eat and have sex. They would go clubbing and then have sex. They would go shopping and then have sex. Sex. Sex. Sex. If she would've taken the time to ignore his sexy-ass body and talked to him, she would've found out that he was from Oklahoma. She would've been able to remain in contact with him and at least let him know of their child. All of that has changed. Now it was time to correct that mistake. Razier Coleman was the father of her child, and it was way past time for him to find this out.

She stared at the screen of her laptop and wondered if they could be a family. She quickly shook her head violently and said aloud, "No. That's not going to happen. He lives in Oklahoma City and is doing quite well." There would be no way she would even entertain living in that state again. Never. She was now a California girl, and that was that. Other than her mother, she had no one or no reason to go to Oklahoma other than to visit. She was going there to bring her daughter to her family and let them meet each other, and that was that. After that was done, she would let Razier make the next move.

If he even dared to think he could woo me back into having sex with him, he has another think coming, she thought. Suddenly, she started laughing because who in the hell was she fooling? She knew damn well if that man looked at her a certain way, she would get so wet that she would come right then and there. He still had her trapped, and he didn't even know it. She felt foolish because she started making excuses for him. She was just as much at fault at them not talking and learning more about each other as he was. She was just as horny for him as he had been for her. She never gave a damn about trying to talk. All she wanted was his mouth on hers, his touch, and his dick inside of her. All she wanted was him. She didn't realize that lust-driven relationship had love caught right up inside of it all. She didn't realize that she loved that man until years later. And now, she's faced with the most challenging decision she'd ever had to make.

Damn.

When she heard Daisy start to stir in her bedroom, she knew her daughter was waking up from her nap time, so she got off the bed and went and brought her into the kitchen so she could make her a snack. While they sat and ate a peanut butter and jelly sandwich together, she made up her mind. She was going home. She was going home and bringing her daughter to meet her family.

After getting Daisy squared away, she called her boss and explained that she needed a brief leave of absence because she had to go to Oklahoma for a family matter, and she didn't know how long it would be.

"Wow, call this crazy, but this is perfect timing for us, Carmi. We're opening a branch of the firm in Oklahoma. What part of Oklahoma are you going to?" asked Anthony Walker, her boss.

"Oklahoma City."

"That's great. If your family matter isn't too hard on you, we'd gladly pay for your trip as well as room, meals, and transportation so you can spearhead the move we're trying to make out there. This can work out great for both of us. Not only that, but this also comes with a hefty raise, a win-win all the way."

"I don't know, Mr. Walker. I mean, I have no intention of living out there. California is my home. I have some issues I need to address, and just as soon as they're taken care of, I'm returning home."

"That's fine. I respect that. You could do the company a serious service, though, Carmi, and we'll be extremely grateful. The raise will stay whenever you return to California. Your expertise in what we do here at Hollier Security can ensure a smooth transition with the company in Oklahoma. Who knows, you may even want to stay out there and live. The cost of living is drastically lower, and the money you earn will make things nice for you. Give it some thought before you decide and let me know. Either way, you won't have to worry about any leave of absence, young lady. You're employed with Hollier Security, and we always got your back."

"Thank you, Mr. Walker, I appreciate that. I really do. I'll let you know of my decision on Monday when I get to the office."

"That's fine. See you then," he said and ended the call.

Carmi sat back and was trembling. Was God making this happen for a reason? Was it meant for Razier and her to come back into each other's lives? Were they meant to be? She couldn't help but smile. But her smile turned quickly into a scowl when she thought about her stepfather, a man she loathed. The man who was the reason for her leaving Oklahoma in the first place. The man she hated more than she hated any man in the entire world.

Her mind was made up. It was time to face her demons head-on and deal with them once and for all. More importantly, it was time for Daisy to meet her father. "Oklahoma City, here we come."

Chapter Twenty-seven

It had been a few weeks since Carmela returned home to her husband to try to repair their relationship, and so far, everything couldn't have been better as far as she was concerned. Not only were the Wilkins attending marriage counseling, but Mr. Wilkins was also faithfully attending NA meetings. He didn't want to go to a rehabilitation center because he couldn't take time off work, nor did he want his peers or coworkers to learn of his addiction. Carmela respected that and went with him to his weekly NA meetings. She knew it had only been a short time, but so far, so good, and she thanked God for that. She loved the attention her husband was showing her. They went out for walks, and their communication was open and honest. They would share how their day went, come home for a nice meal together, and then end their evening with some intense lovemaking that was really the cherry on top as far as Carmela was concerned. This is what she felt her life should be like.

She had to admit that she missed Razier and the special attention he gave her. He would forever be a special friend. She cared for him deeply, but she cared for her husband and their marriage more. She hoped that he would understand and respect her decision by bringing their special relationship to an end.

She checked the time and saw that it was almost five p.m., and since it was Friday, she knew Razier and Tracy would be arriving any minute. She was apprehensive for some reason and shrugged it off to nerves.

When she heard Razier's truck pull into the driveway, she sighed and straightened out the dress she was wearing, wondering why she did that as she walked to the door and watched as the yardmen began to unload the truck with their equipment. She smiled at Razier's sexy self and knew for sure she would definitely miss that hunk of a man.

He was much more than a yardman to her, and that fact would never change. She stepped outside and asked Razier if he had a moment.

` He smiled at her and said, "Sure, Mrs. Wilkins. You're looking lovely, as usual."

"Thank you, Razi. I won't take up too much of your time. I just wanted to thank you for all that you've done for me."

"Now, you know there's no need for you to be thanking me. I'm the one who's in your debt, for real. I'll never be able to repay you or the others for all that you've done for me. To see you smiling and glowing as you are now only tells me that things have been going well with you and Mr. Wilkins, and if that's the case, I'm very happy for you."

"Thank you, Razi. And, yes, things have been going quite well. I'm proud to say that my husband is finally acting like the man I fell in love with many moons ago."

"That's great. So I guess you and I won't be needing anymore stolen moments?"

"That's correct. We will always remain friends, and if there is anything I can ever do for you, Razi, please don't hesitate to call me, 'K?"

"Okay. You make sure you take that same suggestion. If you ever need me for any reason at all, you be sure to get at me."

"Will do," she said as she stepped close to him and kissed him softly on his lips, then whispered in his ear, "I will never forget your touch, your smell, or how you feel inside of me. You are a special man, Razi; very special." She turned and went back inside her home.

Razier was smiling as he joined Tracy in the front yard and started helping with the work. By the time they finished, Mr. Wilkins had arrived, and Razier could tell he was looking much better than the last time he saw him. He was genuinely happy for both of them. They were some good people and deserved to be happy. A part of him was somewhat saddened because he thought there was something more going on with him and Carmela. *Oh well, at least, I got the other ladies, and that's more than enough.* The more he thought about it, the more relieved he felt because that was one less lady he had to satisfy sexually. The ladies seemed to be more and more demanding lately. *Demanding, my ass. They've turned into some of the coldest freaks,* he thought and started laughing.

Tired from the busiest day of the week, Tracy sat back in his seat and said, "What the hell are you laughing at with that goofy-ass grin on your face, bro? You should be just as tired as I am, bro."

"Oh, I am, but I'm good, bro. Carmela told me that she and her husband were good now, and my services were no longer needed."

"And that makes you happy, bro? You tripping. That's money 'bout your pockets, fool. You should've tried to convince her ass that she still needed you. You're doing good, and all, but you never let go of a cash cow, especially the type of cash cows you got, bro."

"It's not like that. I'm glad she's happy, and it's all good. Trust, if I did call on her, she would be there for me. But I don't need that. I got the others, and that makes me all good all the way around. Our businesses have us in a good place, and it's only going to get better for us, bro."

"I sure hope you're right, bro. Winter is coming, and that means a slow period for us. Have you given that any thought?"

"We need a break anyway. We can check and see if we can snatch another food truck and work some indoor events or cater parties. Olivia's idea about the turkey legs was pure genius, bro. I've been getting several calls, and it looks like we'll be good through the slow times with the yards and pools. The food truck will make up for that, and like I said, we need a break, bro. Please tell me where you got the idea of those Kool-Aid pickles. I admit, I thought you were tripping out, but, bro, that move right there has brought in some loot, for real."

"That props has to go to Mama Briggs. She used to give them to us when we were kids. It's a Briggs's thang, bro."

Laughing, Razier said, "I know that's right because we're getting paid from that Briggs's family recipe. Now, what's up with you and Sunny? Everything all good, bro?"

"Couldn't be better."

"I knew you two would end up back together sooner or later. Way too much history to let go to waste. What shocked me was how gracefully Lavonda bowed out of the picture."

"Shocked you? Bro, that *floored* me. I just knew she was gon' be with the bullshit, acting all crazy and shit. When she didn't, I thanked God for that one, bro. I got at her a few days ago to check and see how she was doing, and she said she was good. In fact, she said she was thinking about quitting her job at the prison and starting her own business."

"What kind of business?"

"She didn't say. Just said she was bored working there, and now that her pockets were cool, she wanted to move from Boley and live in the city."

"You do know that means she will be around more, and there may be some drama headed your way, bro?"

"I doubt that. She knows what it is and respects me. I did her right, and she knows I could have been fucked up with it, for real. There's no bad blood with us, just love, bro. All love."

"Whatever," Razier said as he pulled into his mother's driveway. Ever since the incident with his mother and Dionne's husband, Razier made it a point to stop by and check on his mother at the end of the week. Though he handled the business when it came to Mr. Salley, every time he thought about that man putting his hands on his mother, he got mad all over again.

His mother seemed to have forgotten all about that awful experience. She was even dating a new guy now, some man she met at Walmart and hit it off with. This time, though, before she went out with him, the man had to be properly vetted by Razier. His name was Marcus, and he seemed like a good guy. Razier made sure to let him know if he ever hurt his mother in any way, he would have to answer to him. Marcus respected that, and they got along fine.

Razier got out of his truck and smiled at Mrs. Hopkins, who was sitting on her porch with her regular revealing top and short shorts and some flip-flops on her small feet. She was sporting an extremely long weave that went past her shoulders. Razier shook his head and couldn't help but notice how sexy the older woman was.

"Hey, Mrs. H. How you today?"

Mrs. Hopkins stood and gave him a good look at her tight body and said, "I'm as good as I look, Razier. And you?"

"I'm fine. Tired is all. Have a good day, Mrs. H.," he said as he went inside of the house, leaving Tracy standing outside of his truck while he went to check on his mother.

Tracy was staring at Mrs. Hopkins with hunger in his eyes. He wondered if he could get something popping off with her. He smiled and shook that thought out of his head. Sunny would kill his ass if she found out he was creeping on her. Even if he were getting paid for it, she would have none of that shit.

Mrs. Hopkins caught Tracy staring, smiled sweetly, and said, "You look like you're looking for some education, Tracy. Want me to teach you something brand-new? Give you a few new tricks on sexual satisfaction?"

"I would love to learn some things like that from you, Mrs. Hopkins, but my girl would kill me if I cheated on her."

"What she don't know won't hurt her. I'd never tell a soul," she said and giggled.

Tracy was more than tempted and knew that he'd better hurry up and take his ass in the house before he fell weak to the temptation that was making him picture Mrs. Hopkins's asshole naked, riding his dick. He shook his head and smiled at the older woman and said, "Sorry, Mrs. Hopkins. I gotta be a good boy. See ya later." Tracy hurried and went inside and joined Mrs. Coleman and Razier.

Razier was sitting down at the dining room table eating a sandwich that his mother made him. Mrs. Coleman was standing at the sink when Tracy entered and asked, "Do you want something to eat, Tracy Briggs? Or do you want to go back outside and continue flirting with that old skank neighbor of mine?"

"That's cold, Mrs. Coleman. I wasn't the one flirting. Mrs. Hopkins was flirting with me. And I told her I was a good boy," Tracy said and started laughing as he sat down at the dining room table with Razier. "You already know I'd love something to eat. I'm starving."

"You're always starving." They all laughed as she made another sandwich and gave it to him. "Okay, you two, what you got cracking for the weekend?"

Razier rolled his eyes at his mother's language and said, "Mama, would you stop with that lingo. You know you're too old to be talking about what we got cracking."

"Wish you would stop saying I'm too old. I'm just hip, and you're a hater."

Tracy started laughing.

Before Razier could retort, his phone rang. While looking at the caller ID to see who was calling him, his mother hit him with another jab.

"That's probably one of your old women. Talking about me being old, you're the one dating women who already got one foot in the old folks' home as it is."

"Look who's hating now," he said as he answered the phone. "Hey, Vera, how are you feeling this evening?"

"'I'm good. I was calling to see if we're going to be able to get together. I have an event I must attend with my husband. I should be through by midnight. Will that be too late for you, Razi."

"No, that's fine. That will give me time to get some rest. I'm beat right now. Tomorrow is my late day, so it's all good."

"Okay. I'll be at your place no later than 12:30. Do me a favor and answer the door in your birthday suit for me, 'K? I'm soooo horny, and I need your dick inside of my mouth *bad*." She hung up the phone laughing, and Razier couldn't help but laugh. It was going to be a long night for him. He set the phone down and was about to ask his mother why she was staring at him with that funny look on her face but was stopped by his phone ringing again.

"Look at you, playboy. You do got it cracking," his mother said and then burst into laughter with Tracy joining in.

He ignored both of them and answered his phone without looking at the caller ID this time. "Hello."

There was a brief pause before Carmi said, "Hello, Razier, how are you doing?"

Mrs. Coleman and Tracy could tell that something wasn't right because Razier's face looked as if he could no longer breathe.

"Carmi? Is this Carmi?" he asked after regaining some of his composure.

"Yes, it's me, Razier. I hope you don't have any plans for the evening because we have a lot to talk about and some catching up to do."

"Huh? Are you saying you're out here in Oklahoma City?"

"Yes, I'm staying at the Skirvin."

"What are you doing out here?"

"Several reasons, work being one of them. Listen, I'd like to have dinner with you tonight. Do you think we can do that, Razier?"

Without any hesitation, he answered, "Yes, we can definitely do that, Carmi."

"Good. I'll give you a call in a couple of hours and tell you where we can meet. Someone close to me will be joining us, so be prepared for that, okay?"

Not feeling that at all but totally excited about being able to see Carmi after all this time, he said, "I don't have a problem with that, Carmi. Tell me, how have you been?"

"Later for that, Razier. I have some things I need to take care of before we do dinner. We'll talk then," she said as she ended the call, leaving Razier holding the phone to the side of his face, still in shock from the call he just received.

"Okay, by the look on your face and the name you spoke, I can only assume that the female you were talking to was the one you got busted doing the nasty with when you were in the navy, correct?" asked Mrs. Coleman.

"Yep," was all Razier could say as he thought about how good Carmi sounded on the phone.

"And you thought *I* was the one that would be having drama. Looks like the drama is coming *your* way, bro," Tracy said as he took a big bite of his turkey sandwich.

Chapter Twenty-eight

Razier was a nervous wreck as he sat on his bed, undecided about what he would wear to dinner with Carmi and this person who's "close to her." *Should I wear something casual, or should I dress to impress?* These questions were bouncing around in his head as he still tried to get over the shock of hearing from Carmi after all this time. He had so many questions he wanted to ask her that his head started hurting. He got off the bed, went into the bathroom, and took some aspirin, hoping to remove the headache he had ever since he'd gotten off the phone with her. He not only had questions for her, but he also wanted to share things with her about his feelings and how badly he felt about being responsible for getting them kicked out of the navy. But how could he do that with her bringing someone close to her to join them for dinner? Ugh. His head began to pound harder the more he thought about this issue. His phone suddenly rang, and he saw that it was Carmi. He sighed and answered it.

"Hello."

"Hi, Razier. You ready yet?"

"Yes. I've been anxiously waiting here for your call. Where do you want to meet?" he asked as he stood and stepped to his closet, waiting to hear what she had to say so he could decide what to put on really quick.

"We're at Dave and Buster's."

Okay, that's easy for me, he thought as he grabbed a pair of comfortable jeans and a black tee. He slipped on some Nike running shoes and said, "I'll be there in fifteen minutes."

"That's fine. We'll be in the arcade area playing some games."

"Okay, see you in a little bit," he said and ended the call. After putting on some cologne, he grabbed his keys and wallet, then left his house, feeling even more nervous. No matter what happened at this dinner, he was determined to let Carmi know how he felt about her. What was so crazy to him was that she never left his mind nor his heart. Even with all he had going on in his life, he knew that Carmi was the woman for him, and he prayed that he would have a chance to be with her. He felt somewhat dejected by the fact that she was bringing a man to meet with him. *What does she want? Why does she want to see me if she's involved with someone? Why wait all this time to get in contact with me?* He shook his head and focused on driving to Dave and Buster's out on Northwest Expressway. When he parked his car and got out, he took a few deep breaths and thought back to what Tracy told him when he dropped him off at his place. *Just be cool and don't let her see you sweat. Play it like it's nothing that she's there. Remain cool and let things go from there.*

Yes, just play it cool and calm, Razi, and everything will be all good, he thought as he confidently walked into Dave and Buster's. He went to the arcade area and immediately spotted Carmi looking incredibly sexy in a tiki-inspired floral print bikini top with matching pants. The strappylike sandals on her feet had her pretty, orange-painted toes looking so enticing to him that he was actually moaning as he strolled toward her.

Carmi saw Razier approaching her, and she too moaned. *God, why couldn't you have let that man lose some of his cuteness? Jeez,* she thought as she looked at how strong and confident Razier looked. *Whew, the air in this place needs to be turned down because I'm too damn hot right now,* she said to herself as she smiled just as Razier stopped in front of her.

"Hi, Carmi. You're looking really good."

"Thanks, Razier. You're not looking too shabby yourself."

Before he could respond, a cute little girl who looked no older than 2 or 3 years old dressed in a similar tiki-inspired outfit grabbed Carmi by her pants leg and reached her arms up to her mother so she could be picked up. "I wanna eat, Mommy," the adorable little girl said to Carmi as she wrapped her arms around her mother's neck.

Carmi was staring directly at Razier when she answered her daughter. "No problem, Daisy. The person we came to meet is here now so we can get something to eat, okay?"

"'K, Mommy."

"Say hi to Razier."

"Hi, Razoor."

Laughing at the way Daisy said his name, Razier said, "Hi to you, Daisy. Do you know you are the prettiest little girl in the whole wide world? I am one lucky man to be able to have dinner with two pretty girls."

Daisy giggled.

Carmi sighed.

Razier led them toward the restaurant area of Dave and Buster's and got them a table where they ordered their food. Once they were settled, the conversation was light until their food arrived. Razier watched as Carmi set things right for her daughter to eat and made sure she was situated before she turned and started nibbling on the chicken nacho she ordered.

A daughter? Wow. This is crazy, Razier thought as he took a sip of his soda. *Play it cool,* he reminded himself.

He noticed how nervous Carmi was and that helped him be able to maintain his cool and calm composure. He also noticed no wedding ring on Carmi's wedding finger, which gave him hope. *Time to get to the business,* he thought.

"So, tell me, how have you been since we last saw each other?"

Carmi glanced at Daisy and saw that she was engrossed with her hot dog and french fries and gave him a small smile. "Other than being a single parent for the last three years, my life has been busy. Work and raising this li'l thing here is what my life consists of."

"Hmm. Where do you work?"

"I'm an assistant manager of a security firm based in Los Angeles. Hollier Security."

"I've heard about that company. You guys do all types of security, from homes to big companies."

"Correct."

"I also heard that your company is about to make a move out here in Oklahoma."

"Correct again."

"So, that's what brought you to my birthplace?"

"Yes, among other things. We never took the time to get to know each other. If we had, I would have been able to tell you that I'm from OKC too. I wasn't born here, but I was raised here. I left the city when I joined the navy fresh out of high school."

"No way."

"True story. I graduated from Casady, then joined the navy because I had to get out of Oklahoma pronto. When I left, I had no intention of ever returning to this place."

"That's cold. What? You not feeling the Sooner Land."

She smiled. "I love me some Sooners. I just can't stand the city. That's a conversation for another time, though, Razier. The reason I wanted to see you and talk is about something that we have in common. I've waited far too long to do this, and I sincerely apologize. I've been known to be a heavy procrastinator, and once again, I've found myself in a precarious situation from my procrastinating." She took a deep breath and said, "I hope you won't be angry with me. If you are, I truly understand, and I will accept full responsibility for my actions."

Confused, he said, "What are you talking about, Carmi? You've done nothing wrong. Everything that happened with us was my fault, not yours. I should have had more control, but I couldn't keep my hands off you. I—"

Shaking her head, she stopped him and said, "No, Razier, what happened with us was mutual. I was just as attracted to you as you were to me. You brought out something inside of me that I was surprised was even there. When I left OKC, I swore I'd never get involved with a man. All I wanted to do was focus on my career and see the world on the navy's dime. All of that changed when I saw you that very first time at the Naval Academy. You never knew this, but I called in several favors from a few friends of mine in the navy's higher echelon to have you assigned to the same ship as me. You did something to me that day with your eyes that has me baffled to this very day, Razier. I was more than enraptured. I was captured. You owned my body, mind, and soul from day one."

The only thing he thought to say was, "Wow."

"Yes, wow, it was. The very first time was magical, and every time afterward was even better than the last. Whether it was brief or long, I enjoyed your every touch." Carmi shot another glance toward her daughter before continuing. "When everything went wrong, I was angry. I was angrier at myself than I was at you. I was an enlisted sea woman, and I knew better. I let you take me away from my discipline. It wasn't your fault, though. It was all mine. It took all this time for me to realize that. I blamed you for all the ups and downs in my life. I wanted to hate you, Razier, and in some ways, I still do. But I have to be more mature about things because it's not all about me. It's all about us," she said as she turned and faced her daughter, who spilled ketchup on her top.

After cleaning up Daisy's mess as best as she could, Carmi sighed and said, "Since leaving the navy, I've become more responsible as well as more disciplined. This little thing means the world to me, and there is nothing I wouldn't do for her. It's important to me that I give her the very best of everything and protect her with my life. I never want to cause her any pain in any form or fashion. And that's really the reason why we're having this dinner with you now. Razier, this beautiful 3-year-old child is your daughter."

While Razier stared at Carmi in shock, she continued. "Daisy, this handsome man is your daddy."

Daisy raised her head, smiled, and said, "Hi, Daddy," then went right back to munching her french fries.

Carmi was staring at Razier with her heart racing as fear gripped her chest. It felt as if time were standing still as she waited for his reaction. When she saw him smile, she sighed with relief and asked, "Are you mad at me, Razier?"

His smile quickly turned to a frown when he answered her. "Yes. I'm really mad at you, Carmi Felton. But later for that. I'm more concerned about that gorgeous little girl right here." He stood and went to the other side of the table, where he grabbed Daisy out of her chair and gave her a tight hug and kisses on both cheeks, forehead, and lips. "I want you to know that your daddy loves you so very much. Do you understand that, Daisy?"

Daisy stared at his eyes, nodded innocently, and said, "Yes, Daddy." She then reached toward her food, and he started laughing.

After he set his daughter back down, he sat back and stared at the child. The more he looked at her, the more he saw his features all over her. His heart began to beat faster because staring at Daisy made him feel as if he were staring at his mother when she was a baby. Daisy favored her that much. Tears started welling in his eyes because he had a daughter. He pulled out his phone, aimed it at Daisy, and said, "Smile for Daddy. I want to take a picture of you, Daisy."

Daisy looked up at him and gave him the most beautiful smile he had ever seen in his life. After taking the picture, he sent it to two people. His mother was the first to respond, followed by Tracy. He set his phone down and faced Carmi. "You know we need to do some serious talking."

Feeling as if she were being scolded, Carmi gave him a nod in understanding. Though she was feeling a sense of relief, she felt like maybe there could be some hope for both of them. *Whoa. Don't get ahead of the game. You don't know all that this man has going on in his life. Just because he has single on his relationship status on Facebook doesn't mean anything.* "I know we have a lot to discuss, Razier, and I'm ready for that talk. I should have contacted you long ago, and for that, I sincerely apologize."

Before he could respond, he received a response to the two texts he sent. The first response was,

Well, I be damned. You a daddy!

Razier shook his head and smiled. He read the next text from his mother, which said,

You bring her home right now. And make sure you bring my grandbaby to me! I mean right now, Razier Coleman.

Razier was smiling as he stared at Carmi. "Later for the serious stuff. Right now, we gotta go meet some people."

"Meet whom?" asked Carmi.

"I sent that picture I took of Daisy to my mother and my best friend, and this was their response," he said as he gave Carmi his phone.

Tears slid down her face as she read the texts. She wiped her eyes and said, "You don't have any doubts whether you're the father, Razier?"

He looked at her as if she had lost her mind. "Are you kidding me? Look at me, then look at her. She's damn near my twin. I'm amazed that I didn't figure that out when I first laid eyes on her. My mind was so preoccupied with seeing you that I wasn't paying attention. You read what my mother and best friend said after seeing the picture. There is no doubt whatsoever that I'm Daisy's father. So come on, finish eating. As I said, we got some people you two need to meet. After that, you and I are going to have a very long, and I do mean *very* long, talk."

"Uh-oh."

Nodding his head in agreement to her statement, he said, "Yes. Uh-oh fits perfectly, Carmi Felton."

When she saw him smiling at her after making that statement, she felt good. In fact, she felt more than good—she felt *great*. She had made a giant step toward making things right in her and Daisy's lives. One giant step with one more to go, and that one was critical to everything concerning her and her mother's relationship. But for now, that would be put on the back burner. Daisy was about to meet her grandmother, and this was going to continue to be a good day. A very good day.

Chapter Twenty-nine

When Razier pulled into his mother's driveway, followed by Carmi and Daisy, he was trying his best to come to grips with the fact that he was a father. He couldn't believe it. The smile wouldn't leave his face as he got out of the car and helped Carmi with Daisy, who had fallen asleep on the short ride from Dave and Buster's to his mother's home. He carried the child inside of his mother's house. As soon as he stepped through the door, Mrs. Coleman took Daisy from his arms and held her granddaughter for the very first time. It was love at first sight for both of them. Daisy opened her eyes and focused on the teary lady holding her and smiled as she put her little hand on her grandmother's face and said, "Don't cry, 'K?"

That released a floodgate of tears to flow freely down Mrs. Coleman's face. "Oh my, you sweet little baby, I just love you so much. I'm Grandma, baby, so I can cry happy tears, baby," Mrs. Coleman said as she sat down on the couch, smothering her precious granddaughter with kisses, causing Daisy to giggle from the affection. Razier and Carmi were standing, watching, both feeling about what they were watching.

"Mama, since you've met Daisy, let me introduce you to her mother. Carmi, this is my mother. Mama, this is Carmi."

Mrs. Coleman took her eyes off Daisy for a moment and smiled at Carmi. "It's truly a pleasure to meet you,

Carmi. Now bring me that diaper bag. I think my grand-baby is wet."

Carmi and Razier laughed as Carmi did as she was told. Mrs. Coleman was in grandmother mode, and she was giving the other adults in the room the cold shoulder. Nothing mattered but Daisy. Razier said, "Mama, me and Carmi are about to step outside and talk, okay?"

She waved her hand and said, "Okay, boy. Y'all go talk." Then she looked up at them and said, "Carmi, you and I will talk as well, young lady. Right now, I'm about to make my baby some hot chocolate. She can have that, can't she?"

"Yes, ma'am, she can. I'm looking forward to talking with you when you're ready."

"You better be because it won't be nice at first because you have a lot of explaining to do. Go talk to my son, now. You two figure it out because this precious jewel needs us all to be on the same page. Now, you two go. Come on, Daisy, let's go." Daisy giggled as her grandmother carried her into the kitchen.

Razier led Carmi outside, and they started walking down his mother's street and began talking. Carmi told him everything she been doing since the last time they saw each other. She was amazed at how at ease she felt sharing her life of the last past three years with him. She was even more amazed at how he listened and seemed totally engrossed in the conversation. Razier was listening to her every word. The more she talked, the more he realized how deeply he felt for her. It seemed unreal, but he knew it was real as they strolled around his mother's neighborhood.

When it was his turn, he told Carmi *almost* everything that had transpired in his life since the last time they saw each other. There was no way he could tell her that though he had three successful small businesses, his primary source of income was from eight women he had sex with on a regular. No way . . . Carmi would snatch Daisy from his mother with the quickness if he revealed that. So instead of speaking about that, he turned the conversation to what he felt was most important . . . the future.

"I want you to know that I totally understand why you chose to handle things the way you did. I regret not being in Daisy's life from the time you gave birth. I hate it for real, but I understand simply because of what happened with us. I can honestly say that I've thought about you off and on from the time I left that ship. I prayed that God showed you favor, and I see that He has, and I feel good about that, Carmi. The question now is, where do we go from here? I can't be selfish and ask you to move back here, but on the real, I want to be around my daughter daily, and if it takes me to move to California to be closer to her, so be it."

She wasn't expecting to hear those words from Razier, but she had to admit that she was happy as hell that he said what he said. She loved this man, and there was no denying it. She took his hand in hers and said, "Razier, to hear that you want to be a part of Daisy's life is such a relief because I had so many fears about this. To see the love you and your mom are showing Daisy has me feeling like I'm on a cloud. The decision I made to come to see you was difficult for me, but there was no way I could keep Daisy from you any longer."

"Thank you so much for that. You don't know how happy I am right now. I mean, wow, I got a beautiful daughter."

Carmi smiled and said, "There's so much more that made me make that decision. I have some issues with my parents that I need to handle. I was molested by my stepfather when I was 9 years old until I was 16. See, my mom met my stepfather when we lived in New York. They got married when I was 7 years old, and he moved us here to Oklahoma. We were dirt poor, and my mom had to work two jobs to take care of us. I was too young to understand it then, but everything changed for the better when we moved out here. There were no more hungry nights or eating Ritz crackers and water for dinner. New clothes and a nice, big house with my own bedroom . . . I mean, it was like a dream come true. But that dream turned into a nightmare after I turned 9.

"My stepfather came into my room high or drunk, probably both, but he sat on my bed and told me that he had to talk to me. He told me that he needed me, and if I didn't do as he asked me to, we would have to move back to New York and be poor again because he would take away all of the nice things he'd given us. I was too young to understand it. All I knew was that I never wanted to be poor again and go back to the way we once lived. I would do anything not to let that happen again. That's when it started, and it lasted until I turned 16.

"When I graduated, I left that house that gave me so much, yet took so much away from me. There were times when I wanted to tell my mom, but I just couldn't. Deep down, I felt she knew but chose to ignore me. All I knew was it was time for me to go, and I did just that. I left and never looked back. Now that I'm a grown-ass woman, I'm about to face those demons head-on, so I can continue my life and raise my child. I came back so my mom can meet her granddaughter and to let her see the woman I've become. I want to look her in her eyes and tell her what a monster she married and what he did to me. I need to face this to move on.

"Right now, after seeing how happy Daisy has made you and your mom, it makes me feel like maybe there's a chance I can come live out here again, but I need to talk to my mom before I make that decision. Then there's you."

"Me?"

She smiled at Razier and said, "Yes, handsome. I'm in love with you, Razier. I don't know what you have going on in your life, and honestly, I don't care. I want what I want, and I want you. Before I can address that issue, though, I have to see my mother."

"Wow. I'm trying to grasp all of what you've shared with me, and as I'm processing it, all I want to do is protect you, protect you and our child. I want to go with you and beat the crap outta your stepfather. I want to do everything possible to ensure you and Daisy are safe.

"Now, as for the love, Carmi, I knew I loved you a long time ago. I was so nervous after you called that I could barely think straight. I've missed you so much. I'm never letting you go again, baby. I mean that," he said as he pulled her to him, and they shared a kiss so passionate that they both felt lightheaded when they pulled away from each other.

"It feels so good to hear you say you'll be there for Daisy and me. It feels even better knowing that our feelings are the same for each other. We cannot make the same mistake, though, Razier. Before we take it there, let me deal with what I got to deal with, 'K?"

Though he wanted to snatch her and take her to his home and make love to her all night long, he had to accept and respect her decision because she did have some heavy shit on her plate. Razier smiled and said, "I got you, Carmi. I'll be as patient as you need me to be. I'm proud that you chose to share your demons with me. I can only imagine how hard that was for you. For you to trust that with me confirms how you truly feel for me. I'm here for you however you need me to be, baby."

"Thank you, Razier, thank you so much. Now, come on. Let's get back to your mom's house because I'm sure Daisy is running her around the house. This time change will have her cranky soon. I have to get her to the hotel so I can put her to bed."

"Okay, baby, let's go," he said as he led the way back to his mother's house, smiling at the fact that she didn't know his mother like he did. If she did, she would know that there was no way in hell his mother will let her take Daisy to a hotel for the night. He knew by the time they returned, the guest room would already be made up for Carmi, and his mother had plans to let Daisy sleep with her. *She will see, though,* he thought as they walked inside of his mother's house to see Daisy lying in Mrs. Coleman's lap, sleeping soundly.

Mrs. Coleman put her index finger to her lips, making sure they remained quiet as she stood and took Daisy to her room and laid her gently on the bed. Afterward, she returned to the living room, smiled at them, and said, "That little girl is a ball of energy. I love it. I love her. I already have the guest room ready for you, Carmi, so you can go get your stuff and make yourself comfortable." She turned toward her son and said, "Don't even think about spending the night, boy. You go home and prepare for work tomorrow." She said all of this in a tone that made both of them not trying to hear anything different.

Razier laughed, then went outside so he could help Carmi with her stuff. Once they had all her belongings inside and she was comfortable, Razier kissed Carmi on the cheek and said, "I'll see you tomorrow when I get off, baby."

"That's fine. I have a meeting tomorrow at ten in the morning. Your mom watching Daisy comes right on time because I was worried about what I was going to do with her."

"A meeting? For work?"

"Yes, my firm wants me to check out the new office we have out here. I'm meeting with the top people to see if I would want to come out here."

Razier smiled and asked, "So you're going to take the job and move to the city?"

Shaking her head, she said, "No, so slow down, buddy. There is an offer on the table; a very good offer, I might add. This too depends on the conversation I will have with my mom. Patience, remember, Razier?"

"Patience. I got you," he said as he kissed and hugged her again. He stepped to his mother and kissed and hugged her. "I'm trusting this lady in your care, old woman. Don't you hurt her."

Mrs. Coleman laughed and said, "I won't, but for the rest of the night, you best believe we *will* be getting to know each other."

Laughing, Razier told Carmi, "Don't worry. Her bark is worse than her bite." He left his mother's once again, trying to understand all the emotions that had consumed him. He was a father, and he loved it. His mother loved Daisy and will get along lovely with Carmi. Perfect. Carmi has an offer for an excellent job that may keep her and Daisy in OKC, so cool. Carmi loves him and is in love with him. Wow. He was smiling because he could see nothing that could go wrong.

However, his smile turned to a frown when he thought about the meeting she had to have with her mother. *Man, I'd love to get my hands on her stepfather,* he thought as he pulled into his driveway. When he was inside the house getting ready to shower and rest for the next workday, he remembered that Vera was coming to see him after midnight. *Damn, how could I forget that? How will the ladies feel if I'm no longer available for stolen moments? Damn.* But there would be no way he could keep that going with the ladies if Carmi moved out here. There was no way in hell he was going to risk losing Carmi again. If he had to make that choice, it would be an easy one to make. Carmi was the love of his life. As he showered, he accepted that that choice would not be as easy as he thought it would. *Damn.*

Chapter Thirty

"You gotta be out your fucking mind if you're even considering stopping this monster move you got with them old broads to be faithful and a happy daddy. Bro, you need to get Carmi to go back to Cali. That way, you can still have it your way and keep all that money coming in. You could go see your daughter whenever you wanted to. Don't trick this off, bro, for real," said Tracy as he stared at Razier.

As Razier listened to him, all he saw was Carmi's face, still gorgeous as ever, and he felt himself start to get horny. She still had that effect on him. But it was more than Carmi's looks. He loved her and wanted her more than he ever loved a woman before. What made it better was that she was the mother of his child, and his daughter was his world. He missed three years of her life, and he refused to miss anymore. Daisy was his heart and soul. He shook his head and told Tracy, "I feel you, bro, but it's complicated."

"Look, bro, you know I know you better than anyone, and I know what you're thinking. You want to make sure that you're there for your daughter. That's cool but look at it this way. You can do way more for your daughter from the financial tip if you keep what you got going on with the ole broads popping. Yeah, yeah, you feel you good now with what we got going on, but if you look at it, you really not. Them bills gon' mount as time goes on, and you're going to regret letting that move go, bro. I'm telling you, you are tripping out."

Laughing as he pulled the truck into the driveway, Razier said, "You act as if my decision will get in the way with you or something. Relax, bro. There's a lot of variables in this. Carmi might take the job offer she has here. If she does that, I definitely have to let everything go because there is no way I'd be able to keep that from her. She'd find out sooner or later, and I will not risk that. Now, what you said, if she goes back to Cali, then that's a different story. To be totally honest with you, I'm about ready to end it with the ladies anyway. I got a nice savings, a house paid for, plus a new foreign paid for. I can handle the bills regardless of whether they get heavy with me sending Carmi money for Daisy. It's not like this is about to happen overnight. I have time to make my decision, bro."

"You acting like you all in love with Carmi. I know you said she's a bad female, but damn, bro, look at the money." Tracy was about to continue with his rant until he noticed an odd look on Razier's face, and then he screamed, "Awww, fuck, no. Don't tell me you think you're in love with Carmi."

"I don't think nothing, bro. I know it. I won't go as far as to say in love, but I definitely love her. I knew that as soon as I got back from the navy. She stayed on my mind, and I would dream about her all the time. I used the work to keep my mind off her. The love is real, and that's something I will not fight or risk because she loves me too, bro. I have a family, and I intend on doing right by them."

Hearing the seriousness in Razier's tone, he knew his mind was made up, and there was nothing he could say to change it. "I have to meet this Carmi. I need to see if she's as bad as you make her sound," he said just as his phone started ringing.

Razier could tell something was wrong from the frown on Tracy's face. Tracy said, "Calm down. I'm on my way. I got you." He ended the call and told Razier, "I gotta take the rest of the day off, bro. Lavonda got herself knocked. Dumb-ass broad promised me she would stop the get down in the pen, and now she's in fucking jail, plus outta a fucking job."

"You want me to roll down to Boley with you?"

"Nah, stay on the work. I gotta get to the house, get in the 'Vette, and go snatch this broad before she cracks."

"OK," Razier said as he pulled out of the driveway of the client's yard they were about to cut. After he dropped Tracy off, he decided to call it a day and reschedule the yards they missed today. He grabbed his phone and called Carmi. "Hey, you," he said when she answered the phone.

"Hey. I'm sorry for not calling earlier, but I've been swamped with work here, trying to get these people in line and do things the way we want it done."

"I feel you. So, will I get to see you tonight?"

"Depends on how long I'll be with my mom. We're meeting tonight once I get off work. So can you call your mom and let her know to have Daisy ready?"

"Sure. You make sure you give me a call afterward, OK?"

"I will. Let me go. I need to go over some more things with these slow-minded people. Jeez."

Laughing, Razier said, "It's hard being a boss. Talk to you later, babe."

"OK, bye-bye," Carmi said with a huge smile on her face. *Babe? Mmm, I think I like the sound of that,* she thought as she replayed the last few days in her mind.

Razier had the weekend off, so they spent the weekend shopping for Daisy, and that little girl loved all of the gifts her father and grandmother gave her. The days were for Daisy, and the nights were for Carmi and Razier to get to know each other. They went out to eat and talked. The more they talked, the more she realized she loved this man more than she expected. What surprised her most was not one time did Razier suggest she come to his place at the end of the evening. He stayed over at his mother's house, and they sat in the backyard on the deck and continued to get to know each other. She asked him if he was involved with anyone, and when he told her no, she felt like screaming, *Yes*. Instead, she kept her composure and asked him why. His answer was he was just too busy. His work consumed most of his time. She definitely could relate to that one.

When she was ready to go to bed, he walked her to the guest room in his mom's house and told her how much he enjoyed spending time with her and Daisy. He gave her a soft kiss on her lips, and she wanted to snatch his ass into the guest room so she could fuck him silly. But she restrained herself and let the night end. Now here she was, busy at work but horny as hell.

After I meet with my mother tonight, I'm going to make the first move. I know what he's doing, and that's very honorable and all, but fuck that. It's been three years since I had some of that good dick inside of me. My fine-ass baby daddy is going to give me some to-night, that's for damn sure, she said to herself as she stepped back into the conference room where the others were waiting for her.

Tracy was speeding on the highway toward the city of Boley to get Lavonda's ass out of jail. He still couldn't believe she did that goofy shit and kept on rocking with the cell phones. Damn shame she fucked that up and now has a damn case, plus is jobless. *Stupid, greedy-ass broad,* he thought. He decided to call Sunny and let her know what he was doing. They made a pact . . . no secrets, and he wasn't going to break that solid. When Sunny answered the phone, he told her everything he knew and let her know that he'd call her once he had Lavonda out of jail.

"You do that, and you do everything to make sure she keeps her mouth shut. I'm not trying to lose you to no jail shit again, Tracy Briggs," Sunny said seriously.

"Nah, I'm good. She couldn't tell them nothing about me anyway. I've done nothing with her in over two months."

"Never use absolutes unless you're *totally* positive there's no way. Never say never, baby. Just do what you gotta do to ensure you're safe, honey."

Is Sunny telling me to fuck Lavonda? Tracy smiled at that thought and said, "No worries, baby, I'm good."

"Yeah, OK. Take that damn smile off your face," she said and laughed as she hung up the phone.

Tracy laughed too as he sped on the highway, swearing he had to be the luckiest man on the planet to have a woman like Sunny.

After taking care of Lavonda's bail with a local bail bondsman, Tracy went across the street to get a bite to eat from the Waffle House. He took a seat and waited for the waitress to take his order. He was upset with Lavonda because she broke her promise and let the greed kick in, and now, she had a damn case, plus she would be out of a job. *How stupid can she be?* he thought as he gave the waitress his order. He hoped and prayed that she didn't think he would be taking care of her ass. This was her problem. Hers alone. She should be cool financially because they made a lot of money, so hopefully, she could get another job and be okay. He still couldn't believe this shit.

Even though Sunny gave him the green light to sex Lavonda up to make sure everything was all good, he wasn't in the mood for any of that. He wanted to make sure she was good and had a good plan for the next phase of her life. She wouldn't get any time for this, most likely. Maybe probation and a fine. He would help out with an attorney and her fine. After that, he was outta the way and moving forward with his life with Sunny.

Tracy received a text from the bail bondsman that he was on his way from the jail with Lavonda and to meet him at his office in ten minutes. Tracy quickly finished the last of his food and went across the street to the bail bondsman's office. He didn't have to wait long as he watched the bail bondsman pull into the parking lot. Tracy stood and watched as Lavonda got out of the car. He could tell by the look on her face that she was scared. She entered the office and stepped toward Tracy. He felt sorry for her mainly because he thought it was his fault partly, but none of this would have happened if she had kept her word. He opened his arms, and she gave him a tight hug and began to cry softly. He held her for a few more seconds, then pulled from their embrace.

"It's all good, baby. Everything will be all right. Calm down, you know I got you."

Wiping her eyes, she asked him, "You're not mad at me, Tracy?"

"We'll deal with that later, baby. Right now, I need you to sign the necessary papers with the bondsman so we can get you to the house." She nodded and went and did as he told her. Thirty minutes later, they were sitting in Lavonda's living room. After she finished explaining what had happened at the prison, Tracy was shaking his head in disgust.

"I know I messed up, baby, but it was going to be my last time. I mean, they wanted four phones, and I thought it would go smooth like every time I brought them. I'm so damn scared, baby. I don't want to go to jail."

"You don't have to worry about any jail time, Lavonda. Trust me, all you will get is a fine and probation and maybe some community service. The worst you will face is losing your job. I'm salty at you, for real, for real, but I understand. What has me really heated is that you had to have been set up for you to get caught up like that. Who made the order for the phones?"

"Miller. It wasn't like he hadn't made an order for phones like that before, so I was comfortable with it."

"That weak-ass nigga got caught with his phone and made a deal with the captain to set you up. You did what you felt was a good move. You never could see that coming. But you still broke your promise. If you would've kept your word, none of this would have popped off. That's neither here nor there, though. What's done is done. Now we have to get an attorney and pay court costs and go through all of that weak shit."

With her head bowed in shame, Lavonda said, "I know. I'm sorry for not keeping my word to you. I let greed get the best of me, and now I'm in this mess."

"That part. The good thing is we can afford to get you a good attorney, so this can be taken care of in the right way. Once everything is said and done, you can go on with your life. Get that nail shop you was talking about and keep it pushing."

"I sure hope it works out that way."

"It will. All right, I'm about to head back to the city. I'll get at a few attorneys I know and see which will be best suited to handle your case. Until then, lie low and relax. All will be well."

"Thank you for being there for me, Tracy. I thought you would be so mad that you wouldn't mess with me at all."

"You should've known better than that. No matter how it went down, I'm still the one that got you doing the phone thing. Even though you did the goofy shit, it's still partly on me. I got you, though, baby," he said as he stood. Still sitting down on the couch, Lavonda looked up, and Tracy sighed. *OK, here she goes with her play,* he said to himself. And he was absolutely correct.

"You don't think you can stay the night with me and go back to the city in the morning, Tracy? I really need to be held tonight. We don't have to do anything if you don't want to, but I need you."

Shaking his head, Tracy said, "Now you know damn well if I spent the night with you, it wouldn't be me just holding you. On the real, baby, I'm staying true to Sunny, so that would not be a good look. She knows I'm down here, and she knows I got your back, so let's let that go. Now walk me to the door, so I can bounce before I fall for temptation and get us both in trouble," he said as he reached for her hand and gently pulled her to her feet.

She stood and gave him a tight hug as she whispered in his ear, "Damn, I miss you inside of me. Please stay, please?"

He pulled from their embrace and frowned when he spoke. "I'm good. Stop with that. If you don't, I'm going to look out for you from afar. Respect my relationship, and we will be good. If not, I'm falling back from you, Lavonda."

"OK, but you can't blame me. You are the one man I've been with in my life who truly treated me right. I apologize, and I do respect what you have with your girl. It won't happen again, Tracy."

"Cool," he said and kissed her on her forehead and walked out of the house. Once he was safely back inside of his car, he started laughing. "Well, I'll be damned. I'm truly in love. I got to be. Here it is that I had a pass from Sunny to get my fuck on, and I went the other way. Wow." He grabbed his cell and sent Sunny a text.

I'm on my way home, baby. Should be there in an hour or so. Everything is everything.

Sunny responded right back.

OK, love you, baby. And for being such a good man, I'm going to do something special for you when you get here, so hurry.

He moaned at the thought of her in his arms naked and texted her.

What do you mean 'for being such a good man'?

She responded with:

I know my man. So hurry up before I change my mind and take off this sexy outfit.

He laughed and asked, The red one?

She gave him a one-word answer to his question.

Yep.

That was all he needed as he pressed his foot down harder on the powerful Corvette and sped home to his woman.

Chapter Thirty-one

Carmi looked calm and cool as she sat in her seat at The Olive Garden, but she was angry—angrier than she thought she should be. This day had been a long time coming, and she couldn't help being so mad at her mother. What kept her calm was her beautiful baby girl. Daisy sat in her booster seat, making a mess of the butter roll she was chewing on without a care in the world. Her baby girl was her world, and there was no way in hell she'd never protect her with all she had. Those thoughts were making her angrier, so she took a deep breath and continued to wait for her mother to arrive.

Her mother finally arrived at the restaurant with knots in her stomach. She couldn't believe that she was about to see her daughter after all this time. When she received the call from Carmi asking to meet her, she almost fainted. She truly felt she would never see her daughter again. She had so many nightmares over the years that she would receive a phone call, and someone would tell her that her daughter was dead. God had kept His hands on her daughter and brought her home to her. Thank you, God, she said to herself as she got out of her car and headed toward the restaurant entrance.

She stood in the waiting area and let her eyes roam over the restaurant until she spotted her daughter. She thought that the young lady was her daughter, but she had a little child sitting with her, so she continued to let her eyes roam. When her eyes made it back to the young lady with the young child, she gasped as her eyes locked with the young woman, and sure enough, it was her daughter, Carmi. She rushed to the table and smiled at the gorgeous little girl seated in the booster seat with bread crumbs all over her beautiful face. She looked back and forth to Carmi and the baby with a question in her eyes.

Carmi didn't want to do this. This was a bad decision, she thought as she stood and hugged her mother. Her mother squeezed her, and the anger, the pain, all the hurt seemed to melt away.

Carmi pulled from their embrace and said, "Hi, Mommy. You've aged well."

Wiping tears from her face, her mother said, "Hi, baby. You're just as beautiful as can be." There was a brief awkward moment. Then Carmi's mother smiled at the child and asked, "And what's this pretty little baby's name?"

Daisy looked up from her bread, smiled, and said, "My name Daisy."

"Hi, Daisy."

"Hi," Daisy said and put her focus on another piece of the bread she was enjoying.

Carmi sat back down next to Daisy, and her mother sat on the other side of the table.

After another awkward silence, Carmi said, "So tell me, how have things been, Mommy?"

She shrugged and said, "Living and trying to enjoy life. How about you?"

Carmi told her about the navy, skipping the dishonorable discharge part, and her current job. She intentionally didn't speak about Daisy's birth.

"So, how old is your daughter?"

Daisy looked up, held up three small fingers, and said, "I'm 3. Right, Mommy?"

"That's right, baby. You're 3."

"Ooh, and just as pretty as can be."

"I had some business to take care of with my company, and since we would be here for a few weeks, I thought it would be nice for you to meet your granddaughter. It has taken a lot of praying to make this happen."

With a puzzled look on her face, Carmi's mother asked, "Why would it take a lot of praying for you to let me meet Daisy? You left home without saying goodbye. I mean, no reason at all. You chose to leave us, Carmi. You're a mother now, so try to imagine if Daisy left home without telling you where she was going or why. We did everything we could to find you, from calling the police and even hiring a private investigator. I'm glad you chose to let me meet Daisy, but you have some explaining to do," she said in a stern voice to her daughter.

A little too damn stern for Carmi.

"You can't be serious. Are you *really* sitting there telling me you—not your husband, I'm talking about you—you didn't have a clue about why I left as soon as I graduated? You can't be serious, Mother. You just can't be."

"Carmi, I am telling you both your father and I have been clueless about why you left us."

"That man is *not* my father, and if you refer to him as such, this small family reunion will be over and done with," Carmi said in a tone that caught Daisy's attention. The toddler looked up from her bread and stared at her mother. Carmi reached over and squeezed her baby's hand, letting her know that all was well. She stared at her mother and processed the innocent look on her face, and realized that she really didn't know. *Oh. My. God*, she said to herself. Suddenly, all the anger she held in her heart for her mother slowly dissipated. A tear slid from her eye. She quickly wiped it away. She didn't want her daughter getting upset.

She quickly regained her composure and told her mother, "Every day, I've blamed you for not protecting me. I hated you more than I did him. I just *knew* you knew what was going on. And now, after all these years, I find out that you truly didn't know. Wow, I can't believe this."

While Carmi was talking, her mother's facial expression went from blank to confusion. Then as if her face had been slapped, it turned beet red from the uncontrollable anger that consumed her as she realized exactly what her only child had just told her. In a low tone, her mother looked directly at her daughter and asked, "Are you telling me what I *think* you're telling me, Carmi?"

The anger displayed on her mother's beautiful face made Carmi want to rejoice because what she thought when she left that home was wrong, and she had never been happier to be wrong in her life. "Yes, Mommy, your husband molested me. He hurt me, Mommy. He would always tell me if I told you, he would put us out, and we would go back to being poor like we were before you met him. That worked until I was 16. That was the last time because I told him if he ever touched me again, I would have him arrested. I hated you so much because I *knew* you knew. You had to. To know that you didn't know helps me so much because I hated you, Mommy. I couldn't believe you would choose him over me."

Carmi's mother couldn't control the anger as she asked, "Why, Carmi? Why didn't you come to me? You have my word. There is no way I wouldn't protect my child. I didn't have a clue, but as I listened to you tell me what happened to you, what he did to you, I can actually see back to those times when you would always try to go with me when I would be leaving the house. My God, I didn't know. I swear to you, Carmi, I didn't know he was touching you. That bastard. He will pay for what he's done to you, baby," she said with venom in her voice.

She then told her daughter everything that had happened since she left. They held hands and talked for more than three hours. The only time they would pause was when they ordered and ate their meals. They finally had to end their conversation because Daisy had fallen asleep in her booster seat.

"So, what do we do now, Mommy?"

"We keep this close to our chest for now. But we will get him for what he did to both of us. I can't believe I could ever love that man. It's okay because we will be just fine."

"I can't bear to lose you again, Mommy, so don't do anything we'll regret."

Carmi's mother smiled at her daughter and said, "Don't you worry, baby. You won't lose me again. I'm back in your life, and I'm not going anywhere. Now, take my grandbaby and put her to bed. Speaking of bed, where are you two staying?"

"At Daisy's other grandmother's house."

"What? Daisy's father lives in OKC?"

"Yes, and his mother adores us."

"And her father?"

"The same. He loves Daisy, and I think he kinda loves me too."

Confused by her daughter's words, Carmi's mother said, "You lost me."

"Don't worry. We'll talk about Daisy's father later." They paid the tab for their meals, scooped Daisy out of her seat, and left the restaurant. Once Carmi had Daisy secure in her baby seat, she turned to her mother and hugged her with guilty tears sliding down her face. When they pulled from their embrace, Carmi's mother wiped the tears from her daughter's face and said, "No more tears. Mommy's going to make sure of that. Now, take my grandbaby home and put her to bed. No worries, Carmi. Mommy is going to make everything all right. That, I promise you," Carmela Wilkins told her daughter as she turned and walked to her car, barely able to control the rage she was feeling.

Chapter Thirty-two

Razier laughed at his best friend as he listened to Tracy tell how he found the willpower to resist Lavonda's sexual advances. "You laughing, bro, but that shit was crazy hard for me. Especially knowing I had the green light to fuck her."

Razier pulled the truck into the Wilkinses' driveway, killed the engine, and said, "That's why I'm laughing, bro. I can't believe you would turn her down, knowing you had a pass to get yours on. That was some realness right there. Sunny is the one for real, bro."

Nodding his head in agreement, Tracy said, "That's why I didn't do it, for real. I'm loving the fuck out of Sunny. For her to green light that shit showed me what I already knew. Sunny is a real one, and there is nothing I'm going to do to fuck us up."

"Well, bro, I'm proud of you. Come on. Let's knock out this last yard for the day," Razier said as they got out of the truck and went to work.

Carmela Wilkins watched as Razier was trimming the bushes in her front yard and smiled. Razier had been the only real reason why she smiled. The smiles her disgusting husband gave her were nothing, meant nothing, and will always be nothing. Thinking about what he put her child through made her so angry that she wanted to grab his gun and blow his balls off. But she knew that would be too easy for him. She was going to make him pay dearly. *How* was the problem, she thought as she continued to watch her lover as he worked.

Razier saw Carmela watching him as he watched her using his peripheral vision and tried to hide his smile as he continued to work. Everything was perfect in his life, but he knew that a change was coming and coming fast. He hoped and prayed that nothing would backfire in his face because the mere thought of losing Carmi scared him to death. They haven't taken that step yet, but it was coming, which made him excited in ways he could never explain. After he finished trimming the bushes, he headed back to the truck when Carmela called him from the front porch of her home. He turned and faced her and saw she was telling him to come to her with her forefinger.

Once Razier was in front of her, she asked him, "Do you miss me, Razi? I've been missing you, baby."

Whoa, he thought as he stared at her for a moment. He quickly regained his composure and said, "You know I've been missing you as well. I'm actually kinda jealous, but at the same time, happy that you and your husband have made it through that rough patch."

She frowned, grabbed his hand, and said, "Things change quickly and trust me, things have changed, and I'm badly in need of a stolen moment. I need your touch, Razi—bad. So bad that I want to feel you right now." She grabbed his right hand and put it inside of her slacks, and when his hand touched her pussy, it was soaking wet.

He moaned, pulled his hand from her slacks, and she pulled him into her house. She closed the door and quickly pulled down her slacks, never taking her eyes off Razier, who stood there looking dumbfounded. Though he was caught off guard, his manhood rose to attention, and he didn't hesitate to pull him out of his pants and watched Carmela as she dropped to her knees and began to give him some bomb head. So bomb that he came so fast that his head was spinning.

Carmela was in rare form as she took all his seed in her mouth and swallowed every drop. She stood and turned around and bent over, silently inviting Razier to give her what she wanted, needed, and craved. Knowing that he was breaking one of the rules that Olivia gave him from the start, he didn't give a damn. All he was thinking about was being balls deep inside of that hot pussy. And he did just that. He pounded and pounded that pussy so hard that Carmela's screams could be heard in the backyard.

Tracy was in the middle of putting some gas into the lawn mower he was using when he heard Carmela's screams. He shook his head, finished gassing up the lawn mower, and then went back to work, thinking once again how lucky Razier was.

When Razier came, he tried to pull out, but Carmela refused to let him get away from her. She held on tightly to his thighs and moaned loudly as she felt his seed burst deep inside of her. When she was sure he was finished, she stood on wobbly legs, grabbed her slacks, and led him deeper inside the house.

She pointed down the hallway and said, "You can go clean yourself in the bathroom there. I'll go freshen up too and meet you in the doorway, baby."

Razier did as she told him, entered the bathroom, and cleaned himself, not believing what he had just done. *But damn, it was hot,* he thought as he finished. When he stepped out of the bathroom, he saw Carmela standing at the end of the hallway, smiling at him. He returned her smile, but all he was thinking about was getting the hell out of that house.

As he walked past the living room, he saw a framed picture on the mantle that stopped him in his tracks. It was a high school graduation picture of a young Carmi. He was so absorbed by the picture that he didn't hear Carmela call his name. She grabbed him lightly but firmly and led him to the front door. He snapped back and said, "Sorry, Carmela, I must still be dizzy from that quickie you just put down on me."

She laughed and said, "I just wanted to get you out of the house before the jerk came home. Honestly, though, I wouldn't have given a fuck if he caught us."

"Whoa, what's up with that? I thought everything was cool with you two."

"Fuck him."

"Yikes. OK, then tell me, what's the young lady's name in the graduation cap and gown picture on your mantle?"

"Oh, that's my lovely daughter, Carmi. She left for the navy right after she graduated from high school. We had dinner last night, and I had a great time. I even met my granddaughter. Her name is Daisy. She is so sweet. I can't wait until we can get back together."

Razier felt as if he had just been sucker punched. Carmi was Carmela's daughter? *Just my fucking luck. I knew my luck was going to run out. Fuck.* He was trying to think of what to tell Carmela but couldn't summon the nerve to say to her that he was the father of her granddaughter. He left the house and quickly told Tracy.

"Well, I'll be a mothafucka. What the fuck are you going to do, bro?"

"One thing for damn sure, I'm telling Carmela everything so she can be on point. That way, she'll have my back. She'll understand."

"Understand? Are you sure the dick is that good, bro? I mean, this is heavy—*real* fucking heavy."

"Who you telling?" Razier said somberly. He wasn't going to lose Carmi again. And that's some real talk.

Chapter Thirty-three

Razier was still in a daze as Tracy drove. He was trying to figure out the best course of action with this dilemma he now faced. Should he tell Carmi? Should he be honest with them both and let the chips fall as they may? He shook his head slowly. No way was he telling Carmi. That would be the end of reconciliation for them. He may not know her all that well, but he knew for sure that would irk the fuck out of her. She would look at him like she did her perverted stepfather.

Oh shit. Her stepfather was that same cokehead bastard married to Carmela, he said to himself and felt a rage like no other build inside of him. He cared for Carmela, but he loved Carmi, and that alone made him want to tell Tracy to turn around and take him back to the Wilkinses' home and beat the fuck out of Mr. Wilkins for all the pain and torment he caused Carmela and Carmi. But he knew he couldn't because that would expose what he was doing with Carmela. He had to talk to Carmela and let her know about Carmi.

When Tracy pulled the truck into Razier's mother's driveway, he made his mind up, telling Carmela now would be the best way to go. He jumped out of the truck and told Tracy he would see him in the morning. Instead of going inside his mother's home, he got into his car and pulled out his phone to call Carmela.

When Carmela answered, he wasted no time. "Carmela, can you talk? I have something extremely important to tell you."

Noticing the urgency in his voice, she said, "Sure, Razi, I'm on my way to Walmart to get a few things. What's wrong?"

He got right to it and told Carmela everything from how he met Carmi in the navy and how they both got kicked out because they were caught with each other. When he finished, he sat back in his seat of the car and waited silently for Carmela's response. The silence was killing him.

Suddenly, Carmela started laughing and said, "Well well well, look what we have here. I can't believe this, but then again, such is life."

"How are we going to deal with this? I don't want to hide anything from Carmi, but this is something I don't think she should know."

"Exactly. I haven't seen my daughter in years, and there's no way I want to go through that again, even though she really shouldn't be mad at us because we never planned for this to happen. Yet, she would still be mad at the fact that her child's father had slept with her mother. Silence is golden in this case, Razi."

Razier sighed and said, "Yes, that was the same thing I thought. I had to run it by you and see how you felt. There was no way I was keeping this from you."

"I'm glad you're an honest man. It's going to be nice having you as a son-in-law. It's going to suck that I'll never be able to make love to you again, though."

"This is so wild. I couldn't dream something like this would happen to me."

"You do know that you will have to end it with the ladies, right?"

"Definitely. I intend on being a one-woman man. I want to take care of my family and be happy. Thanks to you and the ladies, I'm in a good position, financially, to do that. Everything else is on Carmi."

"I thought you said she was in love with you?"

"She is. She told me to be patient because she wanted to see how things went after meeting her mother. After that, she would make her decision on whether she would move back here in the city."

"Well, that's good to know because we had a great visit, and that gives us something solid to build on." Carmela paused for a few seconds and then asked Razier in a hushed voice, "Carmi told you about her stepfather and—"

Razier cut her off and said, "Yes, she told me everything."

"You two really are close."

"Yes, we are," he said with a hint of sarcasm in his voice.

"That's good. Real good. She will tell you everything about our visit. I knew nothing about what that monster did to my baby. I would have protected her with all I had, Razier."

Hearing the sincerity in her voice made him feel good about Carmela because when Carmi told him how she felt her mom knew what had been happening to her, it made him sick to his stomach. Now that he found out Carmela was Carmi's mom, and she hadn't done what Carmi thought she had, it was a major relief because he felt he knew Carmela intimately, so he knew her words were true.

"I knew you would. The thing is, what's the next step in this craziness?"

"That's exactly what I've been thinking about. I want to get a gun and blow that no-good bastard to hell."

"Nope. That's no good. If you do that, Carmi loses her mom, Daisy loses one of her grandmothers, and I lose a dear friend. We have all the time we want to figure this out, so you must remain cool at home. Don't blow your cool. You do that, and we lose the advantage."

"I understand. To know what he did to my child makes me want to hurt him. I mean, hurt him *bad*."

Seeing Carmi pulling into the driveway behind him, he told Carmela that they would talk later and ended the call. He got out of the car, stepped to Carmi, wrapped his arms around her, and gave her a tight hug.

"Mmm, you smell so good, baby," he said as he kept his arms tightly around her.

"I'm sorry, booboo, but you don't. You smell like grass and gas," she said as she pushed him away and started laughing.

When they entered the house, their nostrils were hit by the aroma of some good food being cooked. "Thank you for coming to Oklahoma City, Carmi."

Carmi turned and faced him with a grin and asked, "Where did that come from, Razier?"

He smiled as his mother came into the living room, followed closely by Daisy. He pointed at his mother and said, "If you and Daisy weren't here, there would be no way we would have a meal like this being prepared for us. This is Thanksgiving stuff only."

Ms. Coleman threw a dish towel at her son and said, "This meal isn't for you, anyway, jerk."

"If Daisy and I can get these kinds of meals made for us, we're *definitely* moving to Oklahoma," Carmi said as she picked up her daughter and gave her kisses all over the little girl's face, which made Daisy squeal with laughter.

"Both of you slick-talking fools need to go and wash your hands so we can eat," Ms. Coleman said as she took Daisy from Carmi's arms. Carmi and Razier were laughing as they went and did as they were told.

When they finished eating, Carmi put Daisy in her stroller, and Razier led the way outside so they could take a walk around the neighborhood. As they were walking, Razier felt a peace that he'd never experienced, and he loved this feeling with his family. *Wow,* he thought as he took over pushing Daisy.

"I really can get used to this, Razier," Carmi said as she grabbed his hand and entwined her hand with his.

"Me too. I fell in love with our daughter right after you told me I was her father. I don't think I can ever feel right if I couldn't see her every single day. I know you're faced with the decision of whether y'all will move out here, and in no way will I try to force you. I totally understand how big of a life change this will be for you. I want you out here with me just as badly as I want Daisy. So, how did the visit go with your mom?"

Carmi stopped walking and faced him with a huge smile. "It went well. Actually, it went great. We touched on a lot of things, and I honestly think we will be all right. I won't lie to you, Razier. I'm nervous about making the change. Yet, I'm excited about it as well. I need to know if what I want is real. I don't want to move out here and move into a bunch of drama. If I do this, I need to know we are together as a family. You don't have to put a ring on it. At least not yet," she smiled and continued. "I love you, sir, but I'd never try to force you to be my husband, Razier, so take that look off your face."

Laughing, he said, "No funny looks, baby. I know we still need some time to get to know each other and strengthen our bond. I love you, Carmi, and I want us to be together forever. I want this, what we have now . . . always." He pulled her into his arms, and they shared a long, passionate kiss.

She sighed as they ended the kiss and asked, "Can I spend the night at your place tonight?"

"Are you sure?"

She smiled as she thought about how wet her pant-ies became and said, "I've been ready, baby. I just had to wait to make sure we were on the same page. I want you,

I need you, and now that I have you, I'm never letting you go, Razier. So whatever you got going on with any women, please let them know that Carmi is in the building, and she's not going anywhere. Do you understand me, Mr. Coleman?"

With a smile on his face, he gave her a thumbs-up and said, "Yes, baby, I understand, and please don't worry about any woman because . . ." then he finished with . . . "Carmi is in the building."

They both laughed as they hurried back to Mrs. Coleman's house to put Daisy in his mother's hands. They were craving each other something terrible, and the excitement of knowing they were about to make love for the first time in a long time had them horny as fuck.

Chapter Thirty-four

Razier and Carmi made love off and on until the sun came up. They couldn't keep their hands off each other. Each orgasm they shared was more powerful than the last. They finally passed out in each other's arms and fell into a peaceful sleep. Razier woke first and went to take a shower while Carmi was still sound asleep, snoring softly. While he was showering, thoughts of the ladies were heavy on his mind. He didn't think it would be an issue once he told them the ride was over . . . no more stolen moments. He was about to be loyal to his woman. Though he figured it wouldn't be an issue, he was still somewhat worried in the back of his mind. What if they tried to take back all the gifts they blessed him with? He didn't think they were petty like that, but with women, you never knew. He finished his shower and returned to the bedroom to see Carmi sitting up on the bed, wiping her eyes.

"Hey, sleepyhead," Razier said as he smiled at his lover's body. He felt himself stir and started to get hard as he stared at Carmi's firm breasts. He quickly shook his head because he didn't think he could perform like he had the night before so quickly. He needed time to regain his strength.

"Hey, to you, you handsome stud. You wore my tail out. If this is what I have to look forward to when I move out here, it's a done deal, sir." She laughed as she got off the bed and walked past him to the bathroom.

Razier slapped her firm ass cheeks as she passed and said, "All that and some sexy."

He was dressed when Carmi came out of the bathroom. "I'm about to go to the grocery store to get some breakfast food. I don't normally eat breakfast, so I need to get us something to eat. Do you have any requests?"

"Nope. Whatever you get is fine."

"Cool. I'll be back in a little bit," he said as he grabbed his keys and left. Once he was inside his car, he checked his phone and saw that he had a few texts from Olivia and Carmela. He saw a missed call from Tracy and called him back. After filling him in on what happened with him and Carmi and how it looked as if Carmi would move to Oklahoma and live with him, Tracy's reaction was not what he expected.

"I'm happy for you, bro. This must be meant. I know you two will be happy, raising that adorable baby."

Razier pulled the phone from his face and stared at the name on his phone, baffled because this couldn't be his main bro. "Are you feeling OK, bro? You not sounding like your normal self."

"I'm good, bro. I came to realize that we have very few chances at real love in life, so when you have it, you must hold on to it as tightly as you can. After dealing with that situation with Lavonda, I'm happy as fuck to have Sunny still by my side."

"That's real."

"So when are you going to break it down to the ladies?"

"It depends on how my day goes. If I get some time away from Carmi, I'll take care of it today."

"Right. You do know you can ask them if they'd like for me to be your replacement. I'm all for it," Tracy said and started laughing.

"Ahh, there's my *real* bro. For a minute there, I thought you were someone else."

"You know me. I'm the type that cares for people's needs, especially those ole birds you got. It would be a pleasure to fill in for you, bro."

"You stupid. Anyway, what's good with you?"

"Nothing much. I plan on enjoying this day off with Sunny. You wanna do a doubles thing later and grab some grub?"

"I'll see if Carmi's with it and let you know."

"OK, bro, hit me," Tracy said as they ended the call.

By the time Razier returned to the house, Carmi was dressed in a pair of his basketball shorts and one of his T-shirts, looking sexy as can be. Razier smiled and said, "Only you can look good in my clothes, baby." He set the bags on the counter, grabbed her, and gave her a long kiss. "Yes, I can really get used to having you around, lady."

"Mmmmm, you better move and let me cook this breakfast, or we'll be right back in that bedroom, mister."

He stepped back from her and said, "The bedroom isn't the only place where we can get down, baby." He grabbed her, turned her around, and pulled his shorts down to her knees, then quickly pulled out his manhood and eased into her piping hot pussy. She moaned loudly and pushed her ass back, and they had a hot quickie that ended with them exploding simultaneously.

They spent the day lying in bed, binge-watching shows on Netflix, both completely comfortable in each other's arms. Tracy called Razier and asked him again if he and Carmi wanted to join him and Sunny for dinner. Razier asked Carmi, and she thought it would be fun. Carmi took Razier's car and went to his mother's house to get dressed, which was perfect. It gave Razier time to call Olivia first to let her know that he was bringing the stolen moments to an end.

"Everything comes to an end. I hoped it would have lasted longer, and I'm sure the other ladies will agree. Oh well, do you want me to let the ladies know, or would you prefer to tell them yourself?"

Razier gave her question some thought for a few seconds, then said, "I'd feel better telling the ladies myself."

"I agree. That shows that you're a class act through and through. "You know what else would top things off smoothly?"

"What?"

"If you gave us all a farewell stolen moment. I know you're with your girl and all, but you can bring our thing to an end in a very special way. Just a suggestion. Either that or I want you to know that I've enjoyed every time we were together, and you will forever have a place in my heart."

"Thank you, Olivia. That means a lot to me. I can't promise that I'll give a farewell stolen moment, but I can promise that you'll always have a friend in me."

"I know, honey. Well, if you do decide to bless us, please, let me go first." They both laughed as they ended the call.

After speaking with Olivia, Razier proceeded to call the rest of the ladies and was pleased that he received no anger from them. They expressed their disappointment, but each gave him their blessing and wished him well. He knew he shouldn't have been surprised, but every one of them had the same request as Olivia. They all requested one last stolen moment. He didn't give them an answer, only that he would see and that he couldn't promise them. When he finished speaking with the ladies, he called Carmela and brought her up to speed, and she was very proud of him.

"You must really be in love with my daughter. I'm so happy for you, Razier. I know you will treat her and my granddaughter with the utmost respect and take excellent care of them. Now we need to figure out a way to let Carmi know that we know each other," said Carmela.

"If you don't have any plans tonight, I think I know the perfect way we can let Carmi know about our acquaintance."

"How?"

"We're about to meet Tracy and his girlfriend to go out to dinner. Once I know where we're going, I'll text you the name of the restaurant, and you can get there before or after us, and when we see you, we'll speak, and Carmi will know that Tracy and I do your yard."

"Splendid idea. That will also give me a chance to see for myself how that bastard will react when he sees Carmi."

"So you're going to bring Mr. Wilkins?"

"Yep, I sure am. Okay, let me get showered. I'll be waiting for your text, Razi."

"Okay, see you in a little bit," Razier said as he ended the call. He didn't know if he liked what Carmela planned. He didn't want to see Carmi in any kind of pain. Carmela is her mom, so he would just have to roll with it and see how it went down. He hoped and prayed that Mr. Wilkins didn't try to show his ass because if he did, Razier knew that he could easily hurt that man.

Chapter Thirty-five

As Razier pulled into his mother's driveway behind Tracy's Corvette, he got out of his car and entered his mother's house to see Sunny holding his daughter in her arms, and he smiled.

"Looks like you got baby fever, Sunny. You can't have her, so you better make your own."

Tracy laughed and said, "Bro, don't be giving her no damn ideas like that. I like being the godfather to Daisy, not no damn full-time father."

Everyone laughed as Razier hugged his mother and asked, "Where's my woman?" "Your woman, huh? Not you, big playa. So you giving up your current lifestyle to be a one-woman man?" his mother asked with a smirk on her face.

He gave his mother a look to be quiet, then said, "Where's Carmi? In the guest room getting dressed?"

Razier turned toward Tracy and Sunny and asked, "Have you picked a place for us to eat?"

"Yep. Let's hit Louie's out on Lake Hefner," Tracy said as he grabbed Daisy from Sunny and kissed her, making Daisy start laughing, loving all of the attention she was getting.

"That's cool," Razier said as he pulled out his phone and sent a text to Carmela letting her know where they were going. She responded with thumbs-up emoji. Carmi came into the living dressed casually in some jeans, a red T-shirt with some red, low-top Converse tennis shoes. Razier shook his head as he stared at her, thinking, *Damn, this woman is fine as fuck. I'm never letting her get away from me again.* "Baby, you're sure looking good in them jeans. We better hurry up and get to the restaurant before I change my mind about dinner and eat you instead of food."

Carmi laughed and said, "Be quiet, silly. I'm ready if you guys are."

They all gave their goodbye kisses to Daisy and left in good spirits. Fifteen minutes later, they pulled into the parking lot of Louie's at Lake Hefner. Razier saw Carmela and Mr. Wilkins pulling in right behind them and thought that was perfect timing. Once they were out of their cars, Razier turned toward Tracy and said, "Look, bro, there goes Mr. and Mrs. Wilkins."

They all turned and looked in the direction of where the Wilkinses were. With her heart rate starting to race, Carmi said, "You guys know that couple?"

"Yep, we do their yard every other week," said Tracy as he grabbed Sunny's hand.

Carmi stopped suddenly and stammered, "I, I, I don't want to eat here. Can we go somewhere else, please?"

Razier saw the fear on her face, and he wanted to run up on Mr. Wilkins and beat the crap out of him again. He hated himself for what he was putting Carmi through, but he had to stick to the script.

Right on cue, Mrs. Wilkins said, "Razier, is that you? Hey, Tracy. How are you guys doing?"

Carmi was now squeezing Razier's hand so hard he winced with pain. "What's wrong, baby?"

Before Carmi could answer him, Carmela said, "Oh my God! Carmi? You know Razier and Tracy? Small world. Come here, Carmi, and give me a hug, girl."

Carmi's eyes never left her stepfather as she stepped toward them. The closer she got to them, the more her fear turned to anger as she stopped and hugged her mother.

Her mother hugged her tightly and whispered in her daughter's ear, "Relax, baby. Everything is going to be all right." Mrs. Wilkins then turned toward her husband and said, "You're not going to speak to your daughter?"

Mr. Wilkins stared at Carmi and saw the rage in her eyes. "Hey, Carmi, how have you been? It's been a real long time," he said coolly.

Too damn cool for Carmi's taste as she went ballistic. She got right in her stepfather's face, spit in it, and screamed, "Fuck you, you fucking pervert!" She then began clawing at his face, trying to hurt him—trying to make him feel as much pain as she could. Razier and Carmela tried to get ahold of her, but the rage inside of her body gave her the strength to shake them both off her, and she continued her assault on the man who had molested her repeatedly over the years. Every strike felt like pain relief to her. Tracy ran up and pulled her off Mr. Wilkins and held her tightly.

"Come on, Carmi. You gotta calm down," Tracy said as he continued holding her as he stared at Razier with a look that asked, "*What the fuck?*"

Razier was about to lose it, and Carmela knew it was time to intervene before someone really got hurt. She stepped to her daughter and told Tracy to let her go. "Carmi, you have to calm down. What's wrong with you, baby? Talk to me."

"That monster you're married to molested me from the age 9 until I was 16," she screamed.

"That's fucked up," Tracy said to himself as he stepped toward Razier because he knew his best friend better than anyone, and he could tell that Razier was about to explode.

"He did *what?*" Carmela screamed.

Mr. Wilkins's white face turned beet red as he stammered, "Th-th-that's a lie."

Hearing him deny what she accused him of infuriated Carmi, and the rage inside of her gave her another burst of energy to break away from Tracy and lunged toward her stepfather, but this time, Razier grabbed her and carried her toward his car.

"Let me go! Let me hurt that molester. Let me kill his bitch ass," she screamed, her face contorted with pain and anger.

Once Razier had her inside of his car, he tried his best to calm her down, but she wasn't trying to hear any of that. "Baby, listen, that coward will get his. You can't let him win by losing your cool."

She was crying so hard that she couldn't speak. She lay her head on his shoulder and cried uncontrollably.

Carmela stared at her husband with rage on her face. "Let's go," she said as she went to their car, followed by her husband with a defeated look on his face. Once they were inside of the car, she turned toward her husband, and in a menacing tone, she said, "You hurt my baby—my one and only child. You put your disgusting hands on her and violated her. Not only violated, but you also tortured my baby, and I swear to God, you're going to pay for what you did. As soon as we get back to your house, I'm packing my things and leaving your disgusting ass."

"You need to calm down, Carmela. I didn't do none of what your daughter said I did. I'm not like that. I don't know why she's lying on me like this."

"No woman would lie about something like that. You did it—I *know* you did. I just can't believe how I missed the signs from my baby, how she hated to be alone with your trifling ass. You white piece of shit! You hurt my baby," she screamed as she pulled into the driveway. She ran into the house and began packing her things. She wanted to hurt him physically but knew she had no win doing that, so she would hurt him where it would do the most damage. His reputation at his job meant everything to him. A messy divorce would do the trick . . .

Mr. Wilkins came into the house and went straight to his office, where he quickly pulled out a small plastic bag that held the cocaine he had truly wanted to get rid of, but he knew one day he would need it—and today was *definitely* that day. After he snorted a few lines, he felt good . . . so good he was ready to deal with his wife and the bullshit she was talking. He left his office and went into the bedroom to see Carmela packing her things. He couldn't believe that little bitch had come back to ruin his marriage. No. That was *not* going to happen.

"You need to stop that packing, darling, and calm down. You must believe me, dear. I'd never do what Carmi said I did. Never."

Carmela stopped packing her bags, stepped to him, and repeated what her daughter had done to him. She spat in his face, then slapped him as hard as she could. She felt so good after that, that she slapped him again . . . and again . . . until Mr. Wilkins lost it.

"You bitch!" he screamed as he grabbed Carmela and began punching her hard on her face and body. When the cocaine fog cleared, he saw his wife and could barely recognize her.

Carmela stood on wobbly legs and staggered into the bathroom. When she saw her face, she couldn't believe what he had done to her. She left the bathroom and saw the look on her husband's face and instantly knew that he was high. She shook her head as she grabbed her phone and called Razier. She knew she should have called the police, but she called Razier because she knew he would hurt her husband, and that's *exactly* what she wanted to happen. When Razier answered the phone, she said, "Please come get me, Razi. He hurt me. Please come get me."

"I'm on my way," Razier said as he ended the call and quickly made a U-turn, headed toward Edmond to the Wilkinses' home. He called Tracy and told him to meet him there.

"What's going on, Razier?" Carmi asked.

"Your stepfather is about to get the shit knocked out of him."

"Did he put his hands on my mother?"

Razier saw the pained look on her face and couldn't find his voice to answer her question. He nodded and pressed down on the accelerator. When he pulled into the Wilkinses' driveway, he shot out of his car with Carmi right behind him. Razier began banging on the door, and when Carmela opened the door, he couldn't believe what he saw. Her right eye was closed shut, and her lips were swollen. She wrapped her arms around Razier and said, "Please get me out of here before he kills me. He's high off cocaine. Please help me leave."

Razier led her to the couch and let Carmi tend to her mother. "Where is he?"

"In his office, probably snorting more dope," Carmela said.

Razier stepped to the door of Mr. Wilkinses' office, took a deep breath, and opened the door to see Mr. Wilkins sitting at his desk, head down, snorting cocaine like Carmela said he would. Mr. Wilkins looked up with a cocaine haze and saw his yardman. "What the fuck are you doing in my house? Get the fuck out."

"I want you to hit me like you did your wife, you coward, weak piece of shit."

Just as Razier made it to his desk, Mr. Wilkins stood, and Razier saw that he had a gun in his hand. "Come on, yardman, show me how tough your young ass is. I don't play to lose, you fuck."

"Yeah, you a coward through and through. You can molest a child that you were to protect. Now, on top of that, you beat on your wife. Don't you think you've hurt those ladies enough?"

"Fuck you, kid. You don't know what the fuck you talking about. Now get the fuck out of my house before I blow your fucking brains out."

Razier was standing opposite of the desk and was trying to control a rage that was building rapidly. Before Mr. Wilkins could say another word, he reached across the desk, grabbed him by his shirt, and with a mighty yank, he snatched the stunned man off his feet and slammed him on the floor, falling on top of Mr. Wilkins. He was trying to wrench the gun from his hands. They tumbled and wrestled around the floor. Suddenly, the gun went off, and everything was silent.

Carmi, Carmela, Tracy, and Sunny came running into the office to see Razier sitting on the floor next to Mr. Wilkins, who was lying there gasping for breath. He was reaching out toward his wife and begged for her to help him.

"Hel-help, Carmela," he begged.

Razier was sitting there stunned at what he had done, so stunned that it didn't register what happened next. Carmela stepped slowly toward her husband. Once she was in front of him, she knelt as if she were going to try to help him. She reached out toward her husband's out-stretched hands. Instead of grabbing his hand, however, she picked up the gun by the side of her husband's leg and shocked everyone in the room as she unloaded the weapon into his body. She was still pulling the trigger, even though there were no more bullets in the chamber. Carmi ran to her mother's side, took the gun from her, and tossed it aside. Then she held her mother tightly in her arms.

"I got him, baby. He'll never hurt us again, baby."

Crying, Carmi said, "Yes, Mommy, he won't ever hurt us again."

Tracy was by Razier's side, trying to make sure his best friend was okay. "Come on, bro, shake it off."

Razier stood and took a deep breath. "Damn, I messed up, bro."

Tracy stared at Mr. Wilkins's dead body and said, "Yep."

Sunny spoke to everyone inside of the office. "I need for everyone to snap out of it and listen to me. I got a way to fix this shit. Now, listen up."

Chapter Thirty-six

The homicide detectives told everyone that this was a justifiable homicide. Obviously, Mrs. Wilkins had been beaten by her husband, and in self-defense, she shot him nine times. They still had everyone involved come down to the police station so they could get everyone's statement. Two hours later, everyone was sitting in Razier's living room with a stiff drink in their hands. Tracy downed his drink, gave everyone a refill, then took a healthy gulp straight from the vodka bottle.

"I know this may seem fucked up, but it is what it is. Sunny came up with the plan, and we followed the script to a tee. The bad man got what he deserved, and so did y'all."

"I know what I did, and I was willing to spend the rest of my life in prison for it," Carmela said and took another sip of her drink. "Thank you, Sunny. Your quick thinking saved me."

"Saved *us*," Razier said as he too took a sip of the vodka.

Carmi hugged her mother tightly and said, "Everything is as it should be, Mommy. I'm moving back here so that I can take care of you." She looked at Razier and said, "I'm coming home to be with my family."

Razier smiled and mouthed the words "I love you" to his baby mama.

Tracy held the bottle of vodka in the air and said, "To family. We all we got."

Everyone raised their glasses in the air and yelled, "*Family!*"

Epilogue

Razier was under the gun in a major way. The ladies were all in his living room, trying to decide his fate. Olivia, Lia, Dionne, Louise, Erica, Marie, and Vera all had their poker faces on, and it really was making Razier uncomfortable. He was baffled because all the ladies agreed and understood when he gave each a call explaining that he was about to be with Carmi. Suddenly, someone knocked at the front door, and he was happy to break the tension he was feeling from the ladies' dark stares.

When he opened the door and saw Carmela, he cringed because she was wearing a look on her face that didn't give him any confidence that she was here to save him.

"Hello, Carmela."

"Razi," she said as she stepped past him and sat down next to Olivia.

"Okay, now that we're all together, I say we take a vote."

"Fuck a vote. I want more dick," said Lia.

Shit, Razier said to himself.

"So do I," said Erica.

"Me too," said Marie.

One more against me, and I'm screwed, Razier thought.

"I say we set him free with our blessings," said Olivia.

"I agree," Dionne said with a smile.

Come on. I need two more on my side, he prayed.

"I say we let our lover go," said Louise.

Oh my God, they're killing me.

"I don't want to, but I have to vote for Razi. Let's let him be," said Vera.

Thank you, God. Either it's going to be a tie, or I'm free. I know I got Carmela's vote, so there won't be no tie. Yessss.

"Well, it's only fitting that Carmela has the deciding vote," said Olivia.

Carmela looked at Razier lovingly and smiled at him, wearing that confident smile. He was optimistic that she would vote in his favor. She took a deep breath and said, "I feel selfish. Even though it's my daughter Razi is going to be with, my vote should be for Razi to be free, but it isn't. My vote is we keep our lover."

Razier's face dropped, and he felt sick to his stomach. *How could Carmela do this to him?* he thought.

"Well, ladies, we have ourselves a tie. What do we do to fix this?" asked Olivia.

All the ladies were back staring at Razier, making him feel uncomfortable as hell again.

In unison, the ladies burst into laughter. Razier's face showed how confused he was.

"We would never do anything to cause you any ill will, Razi. We love you too much for that," Olivia said, with the others nodding in agreement.

"That was so cold. Y'all had me really worried."

"The look on your face when Carmela went against you was priceless," said Erica.

"We were just having a little fun with you, Razi. We wish you all the happiness you deserve. You're a good man," said Marie.

"Thank you all so very much for all that you've done for me," he said sincerely.

"I have something to say, and I'm dead serious," Lia said as she looked around the room. "I gotta have one last stolen moment. That dick is too good not to get one last shot of it."

It was quiet for a few seconds. Then everyone started laughing. Razier stepped to Lia and gave her a deep tongue kiss. When he finished the kiss, he whispered something in her ear that made her smile.

"Okay, I give up," said Lia.

"What did Razi whisper to you, girl?" asked Erica

Lia stared at Razier and said, "That's for me to hold dear to my heart." Everyone laughed, and now Razier could focus on the two women he loved with all of his heart . . . Carmi and Daisy.

Family.

The End

Author's Note

This was somewhat different than any other books I've penned. I wanted to push myself to do something out of the box. I know the saying, if it ain't broke, don't fix it, but this time, I had to do it, and I feel kind of good about *Stolen Moments*. I hope my supporters like it. I'm back in the lab now, getting ready to get *Gangsta Twist 4* out. Hot Shot meets Taz. What do you think about that? No worries, I'm back at it strong, and best believe, my pen is still sick with it.

-*Spud*